W9-BIF-725

Date: 4/9/19

LP MYS ROWSON
Rowson, Pauline,
Lethal waves

LETHAL WAVES

*Recent Titles by Pauline Rowson from
Severn House*

The DI Andy Horton Mysteries

DEADLY WATERS
THE SUFFOCATING SEA
DEAD MAN'S WHARF
BLOOD ON THE SAND
FOOTSTEPS ON THE SHORE
A KILLING COAST
DEATH LIES BENEATH
UNDERCURRENT
DEATH SURGE
SHROUD OF EVIL
FATAL CATCH
LETHAL WAVES

The Art Marvik Mysteries

SILENT RUNNING
DANGEROUS CARGO

LETHAL WAVES

Pauline Rowson

Severn House Large Print

London & New York

This first large print edition published 2018
in Great Britain and the USA by
SEVERN HOUSE PUBLISHERS LTD of
Eardley House, 4 Uxbridge Street, London W8 7SY.
First world regular print edition published 2017 by
Severn House Publishers Ltd.

British Library Cataloguing in Publication Data
A CIP catalogue record for this title is available from the British Library.

ISBN-13: 9780727829399

Severn House Publishers support the Forest Stewardship Council™
[FSC™], the leading international forest certification organisation. All
our titles that are printed on FSC certified paper carry the FSC logo.

Typeset by Palimpsest Book Production Ltd.,
Falkirk, Stirlingshire, Scotland.
Printed and bound in Great Britain by
T J International, Padstow, Cornwall.

Acknowledgements

With grateful thanks to Portsmouth International Port, Condor Ferries and the captain and crew of the Condor Commodore Clipper Ferry.

One

Andy Horton took Violet Ducale's delicate hand with its paper-thin skin in his large, strong one, taking care not to crush it, but found her grip surprisingly firm. He returned the pressure with a smile as she nodded him into the high-backed chair across a round, waist-high table in the conservatory which they had to themselves. It overlooked impressive landscape gardens complete with a working fountain. She was fragile and attractive, even at eighty-nine, with clear skin, and he saw at once that nothing but honesty would be acceptable. She reminded him so much of his foster mother, Eileen, Violet's niece, that he felt a great sadness tinged with guilt. He regretted bitterly not telling Eileen how much she and Bernard had meant to him – a difficult and rebellious teenager with a chip on his shoulder and a great deal of pain and anger inside him.

'They'll bring coffee and cake shortly,' Violet said. She spoke without any accent or tremor.

She was dressed smartly in a soft-pink cashmere jumper and black trousers and wore a pearl necklace, earrings and some expensive rings on her bony fingers, although not on the third finger of her left hand. Her lipstick gave a hint of pink

1

and her spectacles were fashionable and suited the shape of her lean face. Violet Ducale, like the Guernsey nursing home, just off St Georges Esplanade, exuded good taste, exclusivity and expense – none of the neglect and smells of sickness, urine and death he was familiar with as a police officer in some of the nursing homes in his home city of Portsmouth, seventy miles to the north across the English Channel. Guernsey, a small island just nine miles by six, situated in the bay of St Malo, was geographically closer to France than it was to England, being only twenty-seven miles from the Normandy coast. But it, and its neighbouring islands, were British Crown dependencies, although with their own legislatures.

She said, 'We won't be disturbed. We're far enough away from the other old cronies not to be overheard. And if they do shuffle along here, I'll soon get rid of them even though I doubt they'd be able to hear what we say, let alone understand. Deaf and batty, most of them.' She smiled as his expression must have betrayed his surprise at her turn of phrase.

'Do you like it here?' he asked, curious and interested.

'I'd rather be out there.'

'In the garden?'

'No. On the sea.'

'You sail?' he asked, warming to her even more. It was something he was passionate about.

'I did, once, a long time ago.' She looked reflective and sad for a moment and Horton was filled with a desire to take her to the sea and maybe even out on it.

Their coffee and cake duly arrived and the assistant retreated. Violet slowly pressed down the plunger in the cafetière with her lined and liver-spotted, slender hand, but it was steady as she poured him a coffee. She studied him with keen, intelligent blue eyes. After a moment, she said, 'I wondered what you looked like.'

His heart skipped a beat. 'You and Eileen talked about me?'

'No, she wrote to me, not long after you went to live with her and her husband.'

'What did she say?' He took a swallow of coffee to disguise his eagerness.

'That you'd had it tough.'

'So do a lot of people,' he answered lightly but felt the slight tightening in his stomach at the memory of his bewilderment and desperate hopelessness following those dark days after his mother had abandoned him at the age of ten. The scars never really healed. For years he'd tried to push them away. He thought he'd succeeded until an investigation thirteen months ago had re-opened them and revealed that Jennifer's disappearance was not down to her desire to be rid of a kid in order to run off with a lover, as he'd always been told, but was instead a tangled web of lies, treachery and murder, the trail of which he was still following to get to the truth. His visit here was just another leg in his tortuous journey and one he didn't think for a moment would give him all the answers. In fact, he'd wondered as he had flown here from Southampton that morning if it would give him any at all.

He said, 'Did Eileen say how I came to be

fostered by her and Bernard?' It was a question he was very keen to find the answer to because he'd discovered that there was no official record of it. His social services' file had been lost, or destroyed, or perhaps even taken by someone, but the fact that he was able to spend his teenage years from the age of fourteen with the Litchfields without being disturbed meant someone had enough clout with the authorities to make that happen. Violet Ducale said that Eileen had never mentioned it. Maybe she hadn't. Horton watched her take a sip of coffee.

'How did Eileen die?' she asked after carefully replacing the cup in its saucer.

'Cancer. I was with her at the end.'

'I'm glad of that. I wish I could have seen her but . . .'

'I didn't know you existed. Eileen never told me about you and there was nothing in her personal belongings to indicate she had any relations. I only found out about you a month ago, from a neighbour of hers. Or rather, I discovered that she had made a comment to a neighbour about how much she loved Guernsey. From there I learned she had a twin brother, Andrew, and an aunt, you.'

'And you sent Inspector Guilbert to check me out and obtain those photographs of the twins in their teens.'

'Yes.' Horton had met John Guilbert of the States of Guernsey Police some years ago on a joint drugs operation that had involved a run from Portsmouth to the Channel Islands. They'd immediately hit it off and remained good friends.

Horton didn't find friendship easy. His childhood had taught him never to trust, but both Guilbert and Horton's Portsmouth CID sergeant, Barney Cantelli, were the exceptions. However, neither man knew of the depths of his research into the truth behind his mother's disappearance. And neither man would pry. Horton knew he could trust both implicitly but he found it hard to confide.

He said, 'Why didn't Eileen tell me about you? Did you row?'

'Of course not.' Her surprise at his question was genuine. 'We simply lost touch over the years. Eileen left Guernsey in 1961 for London and the Civil Service and Andrew went to Cambridge. There was nothing for them to come back here for.'

'Except you.'

She smiled. 'There was no need for either of them to do that. I had a busy life. I was personal assistant to Vincent Zuber, the financier. He was founder and president of Zuber Bank, now Manleys.'

Horton hadn't heard of them.

'They were world-renowned in the sixties, seventies and eighties,' she explained. 'Vincent left me a very generous legacy and I have an excellent pension not to mention investments. It's how I can afford to spend my declining days here. I had my own life to lead and Eileen and Andrew had theirs.'

But Eileen hadn't stayed working for the Civil Service in London. According to the neighbour Horton had spoken to in December, she had ended up as a typist at the Inland Revenue in Belfast,

5

Northern Ireland, in 1978, where she had met Bernard, who had been serving in the RAF Police during the Troubles. Bernard had been shot in the shoulder while patrolling the airfield at RAF Aldergrove in 1978 and had returned to Portsmouth, or rather Gosport, and the then Royal Navy Hospital at Haslar, now closed, a location Horton believed his mother, Jennifer, had been making for on the day she had disappeared in November 1978. He had no proof of that except for a set of numbers inscribed on the reverse of a manila envelope bequeathed to him by a dying man, Dr Quentin Amos, who had known Jennifer when she had been a typist at the London School of Economics and Amos had been a lecturer there. The numbers tallied with the grid location of Haslar Marina, which hadn't existed in 1978 but was a stone's throw from the hospital and situated very close to the heavily secured Fort Monckton, allegedly a communications training centre for MI5.

'Did you keep the letter Eileen sent you?' Horton asked, already guessing the answer, and he was correct.

'No, and I have nothing personal belonging to either of the twins. When you move into this sort of place,' she waved an elegant arm around the surroundings, 'you have to get rid of a lot of things, and besides, when I go, who would want them? They'd all end up on the fire or the waste tip.' She smiled as though to show she didn't care. Horton returned it but he wasn't certain she was telling the truth. Was it coincidence he was named after her nephew? Was Andrew Ducale his father? Did she know that? Perhaps that was why he'd been placed with Eileen, who'd had no children of her own. Perhaps that was what Eileen had told her aunt in that letter and in subsequent conversations despite Violet's denial they'd not kept in touch. Or had Andrew told his aunt that?

'When did you last see them?'

'At their father's funeral – my brother – in 1967.'

Horton's ears pricked up at that. It was a year he was particularly interested in. He reached across to his sailing jacket which he'd discarded on entering the nursing home and retrieved a piece of paper from the pocket, saying, 'I believe I saw Andrew last June. He came into the marina where I live on board my small yacht. He was on a motor boat.'

Horton recalled the well-built, athletic man, about mid-sixties with an air of command and intelligence. He was almost certain it was the same man he'd seen years ago when he'd come home from school early, talking to his foster father, Bernard. There was something about his bearing and Horton had remembered him because he'd admired the motorbike he'd ridden away on. Bernard had said nothing about the visitor and Horton had never asked about him.

He continued, 'He claimed to have been assaulted but I didn't believe him. I think he used that as an excuse to make contact with me.' Horton didn't tell her that Andrew Ducale had also used an alias – Edward Ballard. But on seeing the pictures of Ducale in his teens, Horton had been convinced he had been looking at the same man over forty years later on his boat. There was the same shape of face, the same bone structure and the same penetrating eyes.

Unfurling the piece of paper and handing it across to Violet, Horton said, 'After he left my boat and the marina, I found a photograph he had pushed behind one of the cushions. That's an enlarged copy of it.' She took it with a puzzled expression as he continued, 'As you can see, it is of six men. It was taken during the student sit-in protest at the London School of Economics in 1967, the same year you last saw Andrew. My mother worked there as a typist. Do you remember Andrew talking about any of the men?' He began to point them out. 'The man on the far right is Zachary Benham, the one next to him is Antony Dormand and the man with the beard who has his arm around Dormand is Rory Mortimer.'

'No, the names mean nothing to me, Mr Horton.'

'Andy, please.'

She gave a brief smile. 'I'm sorry, I have no recollection of Andrew talking of the men you mention.' But her eyes were still fixed on the picture and he saw a frown of puzzlement cross her face.

'The one next to Mortimer with the Beatle haircut is James Royston and the one on the far left is Timothy Wilson. Sadly, all those men are dead.' He didn't tell her how they had died. She didn't need to know. 'The fair man between Wilson and Royston is Richard Eames.'

Her head shot up. His heart skipped a beat. Clearly, she recognized that name. He felt a small stab of victory. Maybe this wasn't a waste of time after all. 'You know him?' he asked, curbing his excitement.

'Well, yes, and his brother, Gordon. Are you sure that's Richard?' She studied the picture again then looked at him as he nodded before adding, 'But, yes, I can see it is now.'

'Andrew's spoken about him?' he asked eagerly.

'He and Richard were friends years ago. In fact, we all were. Richard and his brother, Gordon, their father, Lord William Eames, Eileen and I, we all used to go sailing here in Guernsey.'

So now he had a connection between Andrew Ducale, his foster mother, Eileen, and Lord Richard Eames, the man he believed knew a great deal about Jennifer's disappearance but wasn't going to say. Where that took him, though, he had no idea.

'When was the last time you were in contact with Richard Eames?'

She looked vexed at the question for a second before she answered, 'Years ago. I don't remember when.' She picked up her coffee cup. 'His brother, Gordon, died very young. Drugs, I believe.' She sipped her coffee. Horton thought she seemed distracted.

He'd read that Gordon Eames's life had spiralled out of control somewhere between the mid-1960s and early 1970s and he'd died in Australia in 1973, leaving Richard Eames, the only surviving son, heir to his father's vast estate and fortune and successor to the peerage.

'Did Andrew speak of either man?'

'No. As I said, I haven't seen Andrew since 1967.'

The truth or a lie? She replaced her coffee cup and held his eyes boldly, almost defiantly, and there was a sharpness in her tone that hadn't been there before.

'Aren't you curious or worried about him?' he asked.

'Sometimes.'

'He could be dead.' But Horton knew he wasn't. He'd checked with the General Register Office database.

'I would have been informed if that were the case. I'm his only living relative,' she answered somewhat crisply.

'He could have married and had children.' But not according to the General Register.

'If that were so then one of them would have told me. I'm sorry I can't help you find him, if that's what you want.' Her voice was brisk and she looked troubled.

It was. But he hadn't finished yet. After a moment, he said lightly, 'What was Andrew doing in 1967?'

'I don't understand what you mean?' She glanced away, into the garden.

Oh, but she did. 'Where was he working? He must have finished his degree by then.'

'Oh, I see. Yes, he was working at the Foreign Office.'

Which was what Horton had half expected and in Andrew Ducale's case he believed it to be a euphemism for British Intelligence. He also believed that Richard Eames had been employed by them and probably still worked for them, likewise Ducale. He had nothing to back that up

10

except for the fact that all his attempts to find an employment record or further details for Ducale, or his alias, Edward Ballard, had drawn a blank. All he'd managed to discover was that Ducale had got a first-class honours degree from Cambridge in oriental studies. After that, nothing.

When his silence continued, she said, 'Why are you interested in that picture, aside from the fact that you believe Andrew left it for you?'

'Because it has something to do with my mother's disappearance. I'm not sure how. But I believe Andrew knows what happened to her after she walked out of our flat and vanished but couldn't tell me directly.' And Horton sincerely wished he had instead of leaving him to stumble about trying to fit together the pieces of what had turned out to be a very complex puzzle. He was still far short of completing it.

'I'm sorry, Mr Horton, but I can't help you.'

The continued use of his surname might have been from habit or it might have been her way of putting the conversation firmly on a business footing. She consulted her jewelled watch. The gesture and her manner made it clear to him that the interview was over. Should he press her? He'd like to but from the set of her mouth he knew from experience he'd get nothing more. Perhaps she was tired. Perhaps he'd stirred up too many painful memories. But something about their conversation had unsettled her.

He took a card from his wallet and handed it to her, asking her to call him at any time if she remembered anything that could help him or if she heard from Andrew, but he knew she wouldn't.

He left knowing that even if he returned tomorrow to press her she'd stick to the same story. He had enough experience of suspects to gauge that. But Violet Ducale was not a suspect in one of his cases.

He took his farewell, silently acknowledging that she did look more tired than when he had arrived, and struck out towards the sea in the damp, chilly drizzle. He had two hours to kill before his dinner with Guilbert. It would be good to catch up. His thoughts veered back to the photograph he'd shown Violet Ducale and what he had discovered about the men in it: James Royston had died of a drugs overdose in 1970; Timothy Wilson had been killed in a motorbike accident while returning to Southampton from Lord Eames' Wiltshire estate in 1969; Zachary Benham had died in a fire along with twenty-three other men in a psychiatric hospital near Woking in 1968 and Rory Mortimer had been murdered by one of the other men, Antony Dormand, who Horton had traced to Northwood Abbey on the Isle of Wight in October.

He halted and leaned on the railings, staring out to sea in the gathering twilight, recalling Dormand's confession. He claimed to have killed Mortimer because Mortimer had been spying for the Russians in the days of the Cold War, and that Zachary Benham had been sent to that psychiatric hospital to unearth a spy and had died in the attempt. He'd also said that Jennifer had been involved in intelligence gathering in 1967, informing on the Radical Student Alliance who had been engaged in violent protests and demonstrations in London. But Dormand had gone further. He'd said that Jennifer had also been involved in providing intelligence on, or possibly for, the IRA in 1978 at the time of her disappearance, which coincided with bloody carnage on the streets of Britain with bombs going off in Bristol, Coventry, Liverpool, Manchester and Southampton. There had also been the horrific bombing before then at Aldershot Barracks in 1972 and in Manchester City, Victoria Station, King's Cross and Oxford Street in 1973. And in 1973 Jennifer had left London with him for Portsmouth.

His mobile rang. It was Guilbert. Perhaps he was just checking that they were still on for their meal tonight but as Horton answered it he thought it more than likely that work had intruded and Guilbert might have to delay or cancel. He hoped the former rather than the latter.

'I've got a death, Andy,' Guilbert said apologetically. 'A woman's been found dead on the Condor Commodore Clipper ferry which sailed from Portsmouth this morning.'

Horton often saw the vessel in Portsmouth Harbour but he'd never travelled on it and he'd never had cause to board it in the line of his work, thankfully.

'On the surface it looks like natural causes but the officer who attended called us in. My sergeant's on board now. The dead woman was a foot passenger. She was found in her cabin, which was locked. We don't have a name for her yet because she wasn't travelling on to France so she didn't need to show her passport at the

Portsmouth terminal, and she paid cash for both her single ticket and her cabin. No visible signs of violence but it's best to be certain. Don't want it rebounding on us later. DS Martell's called in the police doctor. He and the scene of crime officers are already on board.'

Guilbert was cautious, as he was right to be. He was a painstaking, thorough cop but with an intuitive feel for cases and an instinctive understanding of people including the criminal class.

'I know you're not here officially, Andy, but as Portsmouth is your patch I thought it might be helpful if you could join me.'

Horton didn't hesitate. He said he would be with Guilbert within ten minutes. Briskly he struck out towards the lights of St Peter Port, the marina and the Condor ferry terminal, sorry for the death but glad to put his personal machinations behind him for a while.

Two

'All right if I turn her over?' Dr Carston looked up from where he was crouched over the body in the cabin. It was lying face down in the confined space between the twin beds.

Guilbert nodded and waved in one of the two crime-scene officers who were standing beside Horton in the narrow, thickly carpeted corridor. Carefully but with some difficulty they manoeuvred the body and Horton found himself studying

14

the blank eyes and purple flesh of a woman he thought to be in her fifties. There were some expensive rings on her fingers, and her clothes – black trousers and a jade jacket – looked to be of good quality. Her hair was cut short and highlighted blonde. Above the smell of death he caught the scent of her spicy perfume.

Guilbert gave a shake of his head. 'She's not known to me.'

Horton didn't recognize her either but then there was no reason why he should. Although she had travelled from Portsmouth it didn't mean she had originated or lived there. And even if she did the Portsmouth population of over two hundred thousand meant he might never come across her.

Carston addressed them from his crouched position. 'Rigor is well established, as is lividity in what we can see of the body. It doesn't disappear when I press it.' He demonstrated this on the neck. 'Therefore I estimate she's been dead between seven to ten hours.'

Horton rapidly made some mental calculations. That put the time of death somewhere between nine and eleven that morning, not long after the ferry had sailed from Portsmouth. Had she come straight to her cabin and stayed here, he wondered, or had she gone on deck and watched the ancient fortifications of Old Portsmouth slip past her on her left and the shores of Gosport on her right as the ferry sailed out of the narrow entrance of Portsmouth Harbour into the Solent? If so, had anyone seen or spoken to her?

'No obvious signs of cause of death,' Carston

15

continued, straightening up. 'I can't detect any smell on the breath. It looks like natural causes or possibly suicide to me.'

Horton originally thought she would have been lying on the bed if she had committed suicide. But perhaps she had decided at the last moment to try to summon help. She'd risen but the drugs she'd swallowed had begun to work, she'd staggered as she made for the cabin door, had fallen and died. He had already noted that there was no sign of any luggage in the cabin, only a red handbag on one of the beds beside a short black raincoat. That, and the fact she'd bought a single ticket, seemed to back up the doctor's theory of this being a possible suicide. There was also a silver and black thermal cup flask on the little table between the beds, which he thought might have contained a drug, self-administered, and which she might have drank in the privacy of the cabin.

Guilbert thanked the doctor and waved in the two SOCOs. He stepped back into the corridor with Horton where a fair-haired woman in a red waterproof jacket who Guilbert introduced as Detective Sergeant Trisha Martell was waiting. 'None of the crew remembers seeing her on the deck or in the restaurant or lounges,' Martell crisply reported. 'And there were no passengers booked in any of the cabins in this corridor. There are only fifteen passengers left on board for the onward sailing to Jersey.'

Which was now delayed, thought Horton.

'We haven't spoken to them yet. The Guernsey passengers had already disembarked before her

16

body was found. I'm getting a list of them, and of the crew.'

Horton wasn't certain that Guilbert would need to question them but it was Guilbert's call, not his.

Guilbert turned as one of the SOCOs approached them. 'No suicide note in the pockets of her coat, trousers or her handbag, sir,' she said.

Horton knew that suicides didn't always leave notes – in fact, few of them did.

She handed over two plastic evidence bags. In one Horton could see the dead woman's handbag; in the other the contents of that bag. There was a small bottle of antiseptic hand gel, some tissues, a bottle of perfume – which he recognized from his time spent married to Catherine to be a very expensive brand – a small cosmetics bag and a pair of sunglasses, hardly needed in January. In another small evidence bag was a set of keys, of which there were five on a silver key ring with a ruby-coloured stone in the middle, a purse and a mobile phone.

With latex-covered fingers, Guilbert opened the purse. 'No address, no driver's licence. No ticket either. She must have thrown that away after boarding. Some coins and three twenty-pound notes. Credit and debit card in the name of Mrs Evelyn Lyster.' He addressed Martell. 'Run her name through the Police National Computer and check if she has a driver's licence.' As Martell headed down the corridor to the stairwell with her mobile phone pressed to her ear, Guilbert retrieved Evelyn Lyster's mobile phone from the evidence bag.

'Last call was made Saturday at eleven fifty-three a.m. to a mobile number. No name but it might be in her address book.'

Horton knew that Guilbert wouldn't call it. It could be a husband, son or daughter and relaying the tragic news over the phone wasn't the most sensitive way of doing things. If her address was Portsmouth then Horton would call it in and get an officer round.

He said, 'Any numbers in her address book with a Guernsey telephone code?'

Guilbert quickly scrawled through them and shook his head. 'No. There are hardly any numbers listed. Just a handful.'

'Any with a Portsmouth telephone code?'

'Yes.' He handed the phone to Horton, who had put on the pair of protective gloves Guilbert had given him. The numbers were for the doctor, dentist, a hairdresser and a beauty salon. It was clear that she had lived in Portsmouth. There were also mobile phone numbers for someone called Rowan and a Gina – no surnames. Other than that, nothing, which surprised him. He was even more surprised when he flicked to her log of calls and texts, both those sent and received, and found there weren't any.

'She was either very disciplined in clearing her phone or she cleared it before deciding to take her own life,' he said.

'If she did,' Guilbert reiterated.

Horton scrolled to her photographs and received another shock. There weren't any.

'Perhaps she didn't like taking pictures.' Guilbert took the phone from Horton.

18

'Or perhaps she was determined to strip her phone of anything personal before doing the deed. Anything in the flask?' Horton addressed the other crime-scene officer who was placing it in an evidence bag.

'No sir, empty. There are no pills anywhere or empty pill bottles or sachets, and no toiletries in the shower room.'

Which meant the drug, if she had taken one, must have been in the flask. But she could have suffered a heart attack, aneurism or a massive stroke.

'If she did kill herself I wonder why she chose to do so on the way to Guernsey?' Guilbert mused.

'Maybe the island held a special memory for her.'

Guilbert shrugged. Then added, 'Sorry to have dragged you into this, Andy.'

'You didn't. I agreed to come.'

'About dinner tonight—'

'We'll do it another time.' It would have to be on his next visit, whenever that might be.

There was little more for SOCO to do but prints and swabs would be taken. There didn't seem any need to seal off the cabin or question the remaining passengers.

Martell was heading back towards them. 'Evelyn Lyster has a clean driving licence but she's not listed as currently owning a vehicle. She has no previous criminal convictions. Aged fifty-five, lives at Penthouse One, Governors Green, Old Portsmouth.' She flashed a look at Horton.

'Expensive. It's situated in the oldest part of the city overlooking the Solent.' He wondered

19

if Evelyn Lyster lived alone. Reaching for his phone, he said, 'I'll get an officer around to the address.' It was too late to call Cantelli. He and DC Walters would probably already have left the station for the night. And there was no need to drag out whichever one of them was duty CID. There was also no need to notify DCI Lorraine Bliss, his boss, as this looked in all probability to be suicide or death by natural causes. Horton relayed the details to Sergeant Warren and gave him Inspector Guilbert's number. Warren would send round two uniformed officers to break the bad news to any relatives and then call Guilbert back.

Guilbert gave instructions to Martell to super-vise the removal of the body while he updated the captain. Horton took his leave, saying that he'd call Guilbert in the morning. He was driven back to the terminal where he walked into St Peter Port and found a bistro. There he ordered a Coke and something to eat but when the food arrived he found he had little appetite. Several things troubled him. There was the thought of Evelyn Lyster dying alone and possibly afraid and in despair. There were also his memories of sailing here with Catherine and his daughter, Emma. The last time had been just over two and a half years ago before his world had imploded following that false allegation of rape while working undercover. He'd subsequently been cleared but an eight-month suspension and his drinking bouts during it had sealed what he now knew had been a marriage destined to fail. And he had so badly wanted it not to. His divorce had put paid to sailing trips with his ten-year-old daughter and so much more. Catherine's stubborn refusal to let him share in Emma's life was frustrating and needless.

Leaving half of his meal untouched, he stepped outside and made for the esplanade, also disturbed by thoughts connected with his meeting that afternoon with Violet Ducale and his ongoing search for the truth behind his mother's disappearance. He was certain that Violet Ducale had spoken to and possibly seen her nephew, Andrew, since 1967, but if so why not tell him? Was it because she knew that he had worked for and was possibly still working for British Intelligence? And there had been more troubling her as their conversation had progressed.

He stared across the inky black expanse of sea, lit occasionally by a fleeting moon and the blinking lights of the buoys. The sound of the waves washing on to the sandy beach in the still, cold night were softer, more calming than he was used to in his home town where the sea would crash on to the pebbles and suck the stones under as it rolled back. The light, drizzling rain had ceased.

The trilling of his mobile phone pierced his thoughts. It was Sergeant Warren.

'Thought you'd like to know, Andy, that there was no response at Evelyn Lyster's flat but I got the details of her next of kin from her doctor.' Horton had relayed the number on Evelyn Lyster's phone earlier. 'The GP said that she suffered from low blood pressure but otherwise was a very healthy woman. He's never treated her for depression. She leaves a son, Rowan Lyster.'

The name on her mobile phone. Horton wondered how he'd take the news. 'Divorced?'

'Widowed. I've sent PCs Somerfield and Johnson round to the son's and I've informed Inspector Guilbert. Do you want me to ring you back and let you know how they get on?'

'I'm on leave?'

'Sounds like it.'

Horton rang off, turned away from the sea and began to walk back through the quiet, narrow cobbled streets towards the guest house where he was staying. It was very different here in the height of summer when tourists thronged the little town with its distinctive French feel. He wondered again about Evelyn Lyster, alone, locked in her cabin. Had the fact she suffered from low blood pressure caused her death or had she taken a drug in order to end it?

He recalled his own dark days of despair during his suspension and marital break-up. He'd gone out to sea on his small yacht in a brewing storm and had pitted himself against the elements, daring them to take his life. But his instinct and desire for survival had been too strong. He'd learned his lesson well during the hellish days in the children's home.

Warren called him just as he stepped out of the shower. 'Rowan Lyster has no idea why his mother was on the ferry to Guernsey. She'd said nothing to him or his wife, Gina, about going there. The last they saw of her was on Saturday evening at her flat when they had dinner with her. She was in good spirits and there was no sign that she was depressed. The family has no relatives on Guernsey or on any of the other Channel Islands.'

The autopsy would give them some of the answers for her death but if it was suicide then although they might discover the how they might never know the why.

He spent a restless, dream-filled night but on waking couldn't remember the exact fabric of the dreams. It left him feeling slightly hungover and with a nagging sensation that somewhere buried deep in them was a tiny fragment of information that would help him unlock the past. He'd have liked a run but hadn't brought his running gear. Instead he set out for a brisk walk, hoping the chilly sea breeze would blow away his muggy head.

He called Guilbert before he set out to see if anything new had come in. It hadn't. But Guilbert said he had put out an appeal for information about Evelyn Lyster. Maybe someone would come forward to say she had intended staying with them or she'd booked into a hotel on the island. Except she'd had no luggage. Perhaps she'd owned or rented a property on the island which her son and daughter-in-law had known nothing about. Or perhaps she had a lover and her clothes and belongings were at a property they shared. Guilbert said her son was arranging to fly over tomorrow and that the autopsy result would be through by midday.

It was just after two o'clock, though, as Horton was on his way to the airport, that Guilbert called him.

'Evelyn Lyster died of severe hypovolemic shock.

23

It occurs when low blood volume causes a sudden drop in blood pressure and a reduction in the amount of oxygen reaching the tissues. In effect, her blood pressure dropped so low she died.'

'Wasn't she on any medication for it?'

'Her doctor says not. He'd advised just simple lifestyle changes such as increasing her salt intake, eating small portions several times a day, limiting high-carbohydrate foods and drinking plenty of fluids. There was no underlying cause for the low blood pressure – it was genetic, apparently – and the autopsy findings bear that out because Evelyn Lyster was generally in very good health. There's still the results of the toxicology tests to come, though, which could reveal she took something to end her life.'

But if she did why do it on the ferry to Guernsey? Maybe Guilbert would get the answer. He'd continue with his enquiries. And Horton with his. Not into the whereabouts of Andrew Ducale, though, because there was nowhere to go with that – unless Violet Ducale had a change of heart – but as the lights of Southampton came through briefly in a break in the clouds beneath him four hours later, he wondered if Richard Eames knew he'd been to Guernsey and that he'd spoken to Violet. Perhaps she was still in touch with him despite her denial and would tell him. Or tell her nephew, who would relay it to Eames. He hadn't been followed but it would be easy for someone with Eames' resources to check his movements and discover he had booked a flight to Guernsey. Would Eames be worried that Violet might reveal something of his past? She hadn't but Horton had come away with the sense that she knew a great deal more than she was prepared to say, not about Jennifer but about Eileen and Andrew's relationship with Richard Eames.

The aeroplane hit the concrete with a thud and began to sharply decelerate. Horton let out a sigh of relief. He hated flying. It was being confined that he despised, a legacy of having once been locked in a dark, dank basement in the first hellhole of a children's home as a form of punishment. The home had long since closed. If it hadn't he'd have burnt the bloody place down himself.

Thirty minutes later he was on his Harley heading east along the motorway to Portsmouth. It was dark and raining heavily. The wind was growing stronger by the minute and by the time he reached the marina just before seven thirty it was howling through the masts and rattling the halyards.

He showered and made himself something to eat. His thoughts turned to Emma and the Christmas she had just spent on the Riviera on her mother's new boyfriend's luxury motor yacht. No gale-force winds and freezing nights for her, he thought with bitterness. He'd tried to sound pleased when Emma had excitedly told him over the phone about her presents but all he could hear was how cheap his meagre offerings seemed compared to those of Catherine, her parents and lover boy. Emma had chatted on innocently about the Côte d'Azur and the big boats all around them, not realizing how dismal and inadequate it had made him feel. God, how Catherine must have loved it. How she must have sat there sipping her bloody champagne, gloating.

He took a coffee up on deck, despite the weather. Sheltering under the canvas awning watching the rain bounce off the deck, he felt Emma's words stab at his heart. She was back at her expensive school now, where she was a weekly boarder. He felt he was being driven further and further away from her by Catherine, who refused to let Emma sleep on board his own yacht. It was too small, too cold and Emma was too young to tolerate such primitive conditions, Catherine had said. Any family law court would agree. But he couldn't rent a flat. He'd feel too hemmed in and, even if he did rent one, he was convinced that Catherine would find another reason to deprive him of his daughter's company. As it was, he only got access two days a month and that was far too few. But come the spring and summer he'd make certain that Emma stayed with him and he was determined to take her on several sailing trips, maybe even to Guernsey again, just the two of them, if he could persuade Catherine to let Emma stay for longer.

His phone rang. With surprise he saw it was the station. He wasn't duty CID. In fact, he wasn't even due back at work until the morning. He considered ignoring it but he didn't have anything else to do except drink coffee and get maudlin.

'Thought you might like this, Andy, it's right up your street,' Sergeant Warren said cheerfully.

'You mean Guernsey.'

'Heard you were flying back today.'

'News travels fast.'

'We've got a body, male, Caucasian, and as

you're on the spot, so to speak, I thought you'd like to take a look.'

Guilbert had said almost the same yesterday evening.

Warren added, 'If it's a suspicious death then you can get the Big Man out of his nice warm house instead of me.'

Warren meant Detective Superintendent Uckfield, head of the Major Crime Team. Horton was already heading below to fetch his jacket and keys. 'Where?'

'By one of the houseboats at the end of Ferry Road.'

'Tell the officers I'm on my way.'

'Already have.'

Horton gave a grim smile and rang off. He grabbed his powerful torch, shrugged into his waterproof sailing jacket and locked up. There was no need to take the Harley – the handful of houseboats were barely half a mile at the end of the road which culminated in Langstone Harbour. They had been there for as long as he could remember.

He turned left out of the marina and broke into a run. The wind was singing through the masts of the boats on both sides of the spit that extended into Langstone Harbour. There were no houses here, just the marine institute building belonging to the University of Portsmouth on his left and the sailing and diving club on his right facing out on to the Solent. To its left was a narrow strip of beach, then the lifeboat station and opposite that the houseboats and the turning circle for the bus which had stopped running this late. Parked in its space was the police car and, inside it, sheltering from the wind and slanting rain, was PC Johnson. In the back PC Seaton sat with a man Horton didn't recognize, so he had to be the person who had reported the gruesome find. Seaton climbed out. The wind whipped around them and the stinging rain drove into Horton's face.

'The body is partly wedged under the houseboat,' Seaton said solemnly, leading Horton towards a black-and-white painted wooden structure. It was propped up on stout wooden stilts resting on square concrete blocks which in turn were bedded in the shingle. 'By his appearance, I'd say he was a vagrant.'

Horton played his torch over the body, swiftly registering the sturdy walking boots, the old and worn trousers that were soaked through, threadbare, patched and dirty, the camel-coloured overcoat tied around the waist with a thin leather belt and the bloody mess around the chest. If he wasn't mistaken it looked very much like a gunshot wound. There was no question of this death being suicide or natural causes like Evelyn Lyster's. This clearly was homicide. A brief sweep of the ground around the body with his torch revealed no weapon.

His beam travelled up to the face. It was deeply etched with lines but clean-shaven. The hair was light brown with grey flecks and reached the collar. The eyes were open and looked slightly startled but perhaps that was his imagination.

He turned away and, reaching for his phone, called SOCO. Then he rang through to Warren and requested more officers to seal off the area. Not that they needed to worry about nosy parkers at this time of night and in this weather, but the scene would need to be preserved as best it could. The rain would have destroyed a great deal of evidence if the victim had been killed here but he could have been dumped by car or by boat.

Finally Horton punched in a number on his mobile phone and called Uckfield. It was going to be a long night and he wasn't the only one who was going to get wet, cold and very little sleep.

Three

'He's been dead about two or three hours but that's only an estimate. Rigor's present in the jaw and the neck.' Dr Sharman straightened up and pulled off his latex gloves. Arc lights illuminated the gruesome scene. The wind buffeted the canvas tent which had been erected to protect them and the body. It howled in through the gaps as the rain lashed against it.

Horton turned to Uckfield. 'That puts it sometime between eight and ten. It was reported just after ten by Lionel Packman.'

'Are we sure he's not the killer?' Uckfield grunted nasally under the scene-suit mask. His cold sounded to be in full force. That, the weather and being called out in it were all causing him to be grouchier than usual.

29

'He seems to be on the level and he wasn't covered in blood. I take it there would have been blood on the killer.' Horton addressed the doctor.

'Probably,' Sharman answered cautiously.

Was he afraid of committing himself, wondered Horton, but then Sharman was only a GP and only there to confirm officially that the victim was dead. He wasn't a forensic pathologist like Gaye Clayton. Uckfield hadn't suggested they call her. Maybe he would after Sharman had left but there wasn't a great deal she could do here in these conditions and Uckfield probably wanted to get back to his nice warm home as soon as he could.

Grumpily Uckfield said, 'Packman could have stashed his blood-stained clothes somewhere or threw them out there.' He waved vaguely in the direction of the sea. 'And why the hell was he here in this godawful weather when any sane person would be at home sipping whisky and watching the box?'

Which was probably what Uckfield had been doing when Horton had called him – the drinking whisky bit, anyway – because he could smell it on Uckfield's breath. He'd had the sense, though, to summon a car to bring him here.

Horton relayed what Seaton had told him about Packman. 'He was worried about his houseboat in this storm. He inherited it from his mother in September and he's been painstakingly restoring it since. He's a retired carpenter. We've got his details and we've asked him to come into the station tomorrow to make a statement.'

'Which houseboat is his?'

30

'The one to our left.'

'Convenient, it being next door.'

Horton didn't think Packman was the killer because from what he'd seen of the man he'd been genuinely shocked. Still, Horton wouldn't rule him out yet, not until they had more information about the dead man. For all Horton knew Packman could be the best actor since Sir John Gielgud. He said, 'He says there were no cars parked here when he arrived and he didn't see or hear anyone leave.'

Uckfield grunted and addressed the doctor. 'How did he die?'

'No idea.'

'You did go to medical school, I take it?'

'They didn't teach us second sight,' snapped Sharman, a long, thin man in his forties. 'For all I know he could have died of heart failure and someone came along and threw a bucket of blood over him.' He picked up his case, nodded at Horton and left.

In a voice that carried, Uckfield said, 'Think I preferred Dr Price even if he stank of booze and turned up pissed. Smell any alcohol on him? The dead man, that is, not Dr Sharman. I can't smell a damn thing with this ruddy cold.'

Horton said he couldn't. 'And there are no beer cans or spirit bottles lying around. There aren't any carrier bags of personal belongings either, which is unusual for a tramp. He would have had some even if it was just a few sorry items.'

'Perhaps the killer stole them.'

Horton raised his eyebrows, causing Uckfield to add, 'Yeah, I know, a vagrant would hardly have

31

anything of value on him. But someone thought it worth shooting the poor sod because although I might have a bunged-up nose and I didn't go to medical school I've got eyes enough to see that's a bullet wound in his chest. If it's not I'll kiss the assistant chief constable's arse and, talking of the devil . . .' He shot a glance at his watch under the scene suit, '. . . it's about time I called Wonder Boy. Get the team in, Inspector.'

Horton knew the Super would take great pleasure in spoiling ACC Dean's night. It was almost eleven twenty, so the chances were he had retired to bed. Uckfield was probably hoping Dean had already sunk into a very deep sleep.

Climbing clumsily out of his scene suit, Uckfield handed it to Beth Tremaine, a scene of crime officer, before dashing out into the sheeting rain to the police vehicle that had brought him here. Horton remained where he was and nodded Phil Taylor, the head of the crime-scene team, into the tent. He gave instructions to Jim Clarke, the forensic photographer, to take pictures of the shore behind the houseboats and the pontoons down by the Hayling Island ferry when he'd finished photographing the body. Clarke would use specialist night equipment. He'd also return in daylight to take further shots. It wouldn't be light until eight and the first commuters would be on the little ferry from Hayling to Portsmouth at seven a.m.

Could robbery have been the motive? Horton wondered. Had there been something of value on the victim that the killer had wanted? Something he'd kept all the time he'd been on the road, or

32

something he'd found or which someone had given him? Horton would have suspected a fellow vagrant of killing the man except for the fact he'd been shot and he couldn't see a vagrant owning a gun. It wasn't impossible, though. And neither was it impossible for the victim to have been forced to hand over something at gunpoint.

Horton squinted through the rain at the black expanse of Eastney Lake stretching across to the lights of the houses on the Milton shore opposite. It had been high tide half an hour ago. He could hear the waves washing on to the shingle shore. Behind him on the opposite shore, which faced the Solent, the waves would be crashing on to the beach, but here the harbour afforded some shelter from the worst of the storm. Not much, though. To the north of the houses he could see the dark space that was Milton Common, a nature reserve that bordered Langstone Harbour on its western side. This was a strange place for a vagrant to come. There were no pubs, no super-markets, no off-licences to sell alcohol and very few places to shelter except under one of the houseboats or upturned dinghies. By the position of the body, he hadn't crawled under there to sleep. He wasn't curled up and he hadn't been shot in his sleep, not unless he slept lying on his back and didn't mind the lower part of his torso and legs getting wet. But he couldn't have been shot standing up and fallen back because he'd have hit his head on the houseboat and either fallen forwards or slid down to land outside the houseboat, not partially under it.

Dr Clayton would be able to enlighten them on that score.

He turned to PC Johnson who, along with Seaton, was huddled just inside the awning beside the blue-and-white police tape that was flapping alarmingly in the gale-force wind which showed no signs of easing.

'Did Mr Packman mention hearing a boat?' Horton raised his voice above the wind.

'He didn't say.'

Which meant Johnson hadn't asked him. Horton didn't blame him for that. In this weather, who would have been mad enough to arrive by boat? A killer, could be the answer. But why should he just so that he could kill a tramp?

Clarke's lanky figure unfurled itself from the tent. He discarded his scene suit and threw the hood of his waterproof jacket over his head before heading for the shore. Horton stepped back inside. Dr Sharman had gone through the pockets of the victim's coat but not his trousers. Horton didn't relish the job but he did it nonetheless. Both were empty. There might be something in the back pockets or in the pocket of his shirt but he'd leave that to the mortuary attendant.

'Anything?' he asked Taylor.

'Some blood spatters. We'll bag up the stones around the body and underneath. There's no sign of any weapon.'

In the morning Sergeant Trueman would mobilize the major incident suite, organize a fingertip search of the area and find out who owned the houseboat. Perhaps it was the victim's or belonged to a relative. Lionel Packman said he didn't know

34

who the owner was and he'd never seen anyone in it.

Horton rang through to Warren and asked him to call the undertakers.

Uckfield returned with a grin on his craggy face, which meant he *had* woken the assistant chief constable.

'I've told Dean I'll call a press conference for nine. By then the news will probably be all over the Internet and Leanne Payne from the local rag will be badgering me for a press statement.'

News travelled rapidly in the Internet age and Horton, like Uckfield, knew this would be big if the media got hold of the fact the victim had been shot. Gun crimes were still thankfully rare in the UK and Uckfield would keep that nugget of information from them. How long for, though, was another matter. Horton wouldn't like to bet on it being very long. Someone was bound to leak it.

'Found any ID?' asked Uckfield, taking a large white handkerchief from the pocket of his sailing jacket and blowing his nose loudly.

'No. Do you want me to call Dr Clayton?'

'First thing in the morning will do. No point in disturbing her beauty sleep. There's sod all we can do tonight and it doesn't look as if there will be a grieving relative for this poor soul.'

Not like Rowan Lyster who, Guilbert had said, was due to formerly identify his mother, Evelyn, tomorrow on his arrival in Guernsey.

If there was no ID in the rest of the victim's clothes then tomorrow, with the aid of one of Clarke's photographs, officers would do the

35

rounds of the hostels, which wouldn't take long, there only being one in the city, but they'd circulate his photograph to other hostels in the outlying towns and start asking on the streets if anyone had known the dead man.

'I'll give a briefing at eight,' Uckfield said, sniffing strenuously and pushing the handkerchief back in his pocket. 'Make sure you and your team are there.'

'Shall I inform DCI Bliss or will you?'

'You can. I'm going home.'

Horton was tempted to call her now and disturb her beauty sleep as Uckfield had done his boss's but decided against it, not because he thought Bliss needed all the beauty sleep she could get but he didn't fancy having to listen to her firing questions at him so late in the day. And it had been a long one.

He stayed until the body had been removed to the mortuary and SOCO had finished. There had been nothing under the dead man except stones, shells and some seaweed, the latter of which Taylor had bagged up. 'Just in case,' he'd said. Horton had taken another look at the victim. Under the sodden and blood-soaked coat he'd seen a frayed checked shirt collar and a V-neck green woollen jumper. The victim displayed no body piercings in his nose or ears. Horton hadn't and wasn't going to check the tongue and other parts of his anatomy. Gaye and her mortuary assistant could have that dubious pleasure. There was no jewellery on his fingers, which were stubby but clean. The nails hadn't been bitten down either and they were also remarkably clean.

No tattoos were visible. The fact that the victim's hair wasn't overlong or matted and he was clean-shaven, plus the condition of his hands meant he couldn't have been on the road for very long. Horton tried to guess the victim's age but it was impossible given the death mask and his lined face.

The tent was dismantled, the arc lights switched off and packed away. Only the police tape remained in place in a wide circle around the houseboat and two uniformed officers arrived to take over from Seaton and Johnson, who would need to return to the station and dry out. Their replacements would spend the stormy night in their police vehicle, making sure nobody came stumbling along to disturb the area.

It was just after one a.m. when Horton finally climbed into his bunk. His eyes were scratching his eyelids with weariness but his head was still spinning. He knew it would take some time to get to sleep. It had been a very long and frag-mented day. So much seemed to have happened. He tried to let his mind go blank but it refused to cooperate, shifting as it did to the death of the tramp and then to Evelyn Lyster, back to his interview with Violet Ducale and then to thoughts of his mother. Eventually when he drifted into sleep Evelyn Lyster became the vagrant who turned into Andrew Ducale and then to Jennifer, and he woke with a start, shivering but feeling the sweat on his brow. Something in the dream had alarmed him, more so than last night. But just as he had that morning, he couldn't recall what it was.

He felt stiff. His muscles ached as though he'd run a marathon. He hoped he wasn't going down with Uckfield's wretched cold. His head felt heavy through a combination of lack of sleep and an overactive brain throughout the night. It felt as though he'd only slept for twenty minutes so he was surprised to see he'd managed five hours. He didn't have time for a run, which annoyed him. He made some breakfast, showered, shaved and rang Dr Clayton's mobile phone just after seven, preparing to leave a message, but she answered.

'You've got a corpse,' she said, her voice muffled. 'You never ring me at this hour unless it's connected with a body.'

He never rang her at all, he thought, unless it was work. Was she hinting that she'd like to take him up on that long-postponed dinner engagement he'd promised her? He apologized for waking her.

'You didn't. I'm eating toast.'

Swiftly he relayed what had happened, adding that Trueman would email over the photographs.

She said she'd examine the body as soon as she arrived at work, which would be within the next hour. Horton then called Cantelli. He could hear Cantelli's children laughing and chattering in the background. He brought Barney up to speed.

'You think the victim was shot?' Cantelli said thoughtfully.

'Yes, why?' Horton asked, picking up a hint of anxiety in Cantelli's question.

'I sent Walters to a burglary yesterday, a house just off the seafront behind the nine-hole golf course, a Mr and Mrs Clements. Antique pistols were stolen.'

'Working pistols?'

'Mr Clements claims not. He doesn't have a firearms licence because they were classified as antiques. I've checked with the firearms licensing officer who says that's correct but there's no record of Clements consulting him about them, which he should have done.'

The illegal possession of pistols and revolvers under the Firearms Act 1968 carried a minimum custodial sentence of five years. All handguns had been banned in the UK in 1996 after the Dunblane school massacre when a gunman had entered a primary school and killed sixteen children and one adult before turning the gun on himself.

'Walters has organized a house-to-house. The neighbours might have seen or heard something. Bliss thinks the pistols could have been stolen by a criminal gang who have connections with underground armourers who can manufacture ammunition to make them fire, so she's notified the National Crime Agency and asked me to circulate details of the weapons to other forces. I've also been liaising with the National Ballistics Intelligence Service. They're checking out the MO of known villains and seeing if the stolen pistols match any others taken in robberies around the country. It doesn't match any in Hampshire. There have been no gun thefts antique or otherwise that we're aware of.'

'And no shootings,' added Horton, except for one a year ago, and that had been on the Isle of Wight and a rare occurrence. The killer had been apprehended but had drowned before being detained.

Cantelli said, 'I take it no weapon was found at the scene of the crime?'

'None. It could have been taken away or tossed in the sea. The pattern of death doesn't match the method of a gang though, Barney. Call Walters and tell him to be at the briefing. I'll call Bliss.'

He did so on his way up the pontoon to the car park. She answered promptly and listened without comment as he relayed the facts of the incident, finishing with the news that Cantelli was calling Walters and both they and he would be at the briefing. She rapidly made the connection between the theft of the antique pistols and the method of murder as Horton knew she would, asking him if he believed one of the stolen guns could have been used. He refrained from saying that he wasn't medically qualified to comment but instead reminded her that he hadn't been on duty so didn't have all the details concerning the gun theft, to which she curtly replied, 'Then you'd better get up to speed on it, Inspector.'

He rang off, not bothering to reply. There was no point. He had time to take another look at the crime scene. The storm had blown itself out but the morning threatened to be overcast and the wind was still blustery and damp. There was little to see in the early morning gloom, only the bleary-eyed commuters alighting from the small passenger ferry at Portsmouth. It was essentially one-way human traffic, there being very little employment on Hayling Island and certainly not enough to attract a horde of commuters. Some of them seemed cheered to have their routine disturbed by the sight of the police car and flapping crime-scene tape. Horton saw a couple of people taking photographs on their mobile phones. It would be all over the Internet in seconds; it probably was already.

PC Allen in the police vehicle had nothing to report. They'd remain there until relieved. Horton crossed to the houseboat. It was in a sorry state of repair, or rather disrepair. It stood in sharp contrast to its neighbour, Lionel Packman's houseboat, which was in pristine condition. The external structure hadn't been touched for years. The wood was rotten and a few strong pulls might cause sections of it to collapse. He was amazed it had withstood last night's storm and those of previous years. At some stage someone had patched up parts of it by nailing planks of wood across the more rotten sections and the boarded-up windows. God alone knew what it must look like inside. It was probably one of the original houseboats that had been here since the 1930s when there had been many more of them intermingling with fishermen's huts and railway carriages. They'd spread out all around Eastney Lake and across the other side to the Milton shore opposite. During heavy bombing in the Second World War, many people had flocked here from all over the city to take cover in whatever temporary structures they could find. There had been no plumbing or electricity and no insulation. It must have been bloody freezing in winter, he thought. Many had stayed after the war, having lost their homes in the bombing, until the council had finally re-housed them in 1960 – some in the high-rise tower block where he had lived briefly with his mother.

41

Horton stared across the tidal lake. It was just over two hours to high water. The huts and houseboats had been cleared on all sides now except this one, and here only this handful survived. How had the victim got here? Had he walked? Probably. But again, Horton considered the possibility that he could have been brought by car or van, possibly already dead and his body dumped. Or perhaps he'd been brought by boat, although given the weather of the previous night Horton thought it highly unlikely. Despite that he rang Sergeant Dai Elkins of the marine unit and asked if he'd heard about the body found by the houseboats. Elkins had.

'Get the details from Trueman and circulate them to the sailing and diving club. Ask if any of their members were in Ferry Road last night between eight and ten and if they saw anyone. Contact the Langstone Harbour master. Find out if he or any boat owners heard or saw anything unusual in the harbour last night during that time.'

'In that weather! I doubt anyone was on or near their boat. And I wouldn't have thought anyone, even a killer, would be suicidal or crazy enough to attempt to land on the shore or the pontoon,' Elkins rather predictably replied.

'Someone could have come across Eastney Lake from Milton. It would have been calmer that side of the harbour.'

'I suppose it's possible,' Elkins grudgingly admitted, 'but it would still have been a nightmare journey. I'll have a word with Chris Howgate, though. He's one of the helmsman on the lifeboats.

They didn't have a shout last night but someone might have been at the station.'

Horton knew Howgate. He ran the sailmakers adjacent to the marina.

Horton climbed on his Harley and headed along Ferry Road towards the seafront. If the victim had walked to the houseboat then someone in the houses on Horton's right might have seen him, although the weather would have kept many people indoors with their curtains drawn and blinds firmly pulled down against the elements. He certainly hadn't seen or heard anything when he'd arrived at the marina. The wind and the clamour of the rigging had masked the sound of any cars approaching.

At the junction, he considered what Cantelli had told him. Was the vagrant's death linked to the Clements' robbery? Their house was about two miles to the west, set back off the seafront. It sounded unlikely, because why steal a gun to shoot a tramp? It didn't fit the usual pattern. A knifing or a beating, yes. But someone *had* shot him and, as Horton indicated right and headed for the station, that wasn't the only thing disturbing him about the vagrant's death.

Four

'He looks familiar but I can't think why,' Cantelli said, frowning at the photographs of the victim which Trueman was pinning up on the crime board. The incident suite was packed with people and humming with activity as computers and phones were being set up. In Uckfield's office beyond the crime board, Horton could see the bulky, squat, shaven-headed DI Dennings and beside him the lean figure of DCI Bliss with her scraped back high ponytail. They were seated at Uckfield's conference table.

'Perhaps you arrested him,' Trueman answered.

'Maybe.' But Cantelli sounded dubious and his dark eyebrows furrowed in thought.

Horton studied the pictures. Did he know the victim? Had he seen him somewhere before? Was it that which was troubling him? Maybe, but there was more. He asked Trueman if he'd come across him. Trueman, like Cantelli, had an excellent memory for faces, especially criminal ones.

'He's a new one on me,' Trueman answered, which meant neither man could have arrested him and Horton didn't think he had either. Clarke's pictures of the area were also on the board. There were those taken last night under the arc lights and some from this morning which he'd emailed over and Trueman had printed out. Again, Horton wondered why the victim had been there when there was little, if not anything, to attract him to that area. He guessed he could have been looking for somewhere to shelter from the storm but it was a long way off the beaten track. He said as much to Cantelli.

'Perhaps the place held special memories for him.'

Horton had said almost the same to Guilbert about Evelyn Lyster heading for Guernsey but

44

that had been when he thought she might have committed suicide.

Cantelli added, 'Maybe he played at the house-boats as a kid or knew the owner.'

'He didn't pick a very nice night for a trip down memory lane.' Horton saw Uckfield rise. 'Looks as though we're about to be briefed. Where's Walters?' His car had been in the car park but there had been no sign of him in CID when Horton had walked through it to dump his leathers in his office.

'Where do you think? He said he had better fill up in case it got so hectic that he didn't get the chance to eat again for the rest of the day.'

'And knowing how lithe he is we wouldn't want him to fade away. Talking of which, he's made it by the skin of his teeth.' Horton nodded to where Walters' sixteen stone, flabby frame squeezed into the incident suite just as Uckfield's door flew open and he strutted in like a senior medic with his entourage behind him.

Bliss caught Horton's eyes but he made sure to keep his expression neutral and hide his surprise because, for the first time in the thirteen months since she'd taken up her promotion and become the Head of CID, she was wearing something other than her customary knee-length black skirt and black suit jacket. The white shirt was still there but the black suit skirt had been replaced with a grey trouser suit. He wondered what momentous event had occurred to make her discard her habitual wardrobe.

The room fell instantly silent. A red-eyed, cold-filled Uckfield scowled at everyone and asked

45

Dennings to brief them, which he did, giving the bare bones of the case, most of which Trueman had inscribed on the board. Horton hadn't yet written up his report, a fact that Bliss would probably reprimand him for despite the fact he hadn't officially been on duty and it had been very late when he'd left the crime scene.

'Does anyone recognize him?' Uckfield demanded nasally when Dennings had finished. 'If he's been a vagrant in this city then one of us must have moved him on or arrested him for being drunk and disorderly at some stage.'

Everyone looked blank.

Horton now expressed the thoughts that had disturbed him last night at the scene and again a moment ago. 'He's not what you'd expect a vagrant to look like. OK, there's the clothes and his face is heavily lined, especially around the eyes and mouth, as though he's had it tough, but his skin isn't dirty, he's clean-shaven and there was no smell of alcohol on his breath or on his clothes. And I couldn't see any dirt under his fingernails, either.'

Bliss piped up. 'Perhaps he hasn't been on the road long enough to get the grime in his pores.'

'Then his clothes would be in a better condition.'

'Maybe they're not his clothes,' she rejoined. 'He could have pawned them and got those he's wearing in exchange. Or his original clothes could have been stolen by another tramp and he was left those to wear in their place.'

That was possible. But it didn't explain why they hadn't found anything belonging to the dead man

46

beside his body, no matter how meagre, except that he supposed the killer could have stolen them. But what would the vagrant have had that would have been worth stealing?

Uckfield blew his nose. Several officers shifted a little further away from him. He addressed Trueman. 'Do we know who owns the boathouse?'

'Not yet. We've got to wait until the council offices open at nine.'

'OK, so what have we got?'

Trueman rose and addressed the room. 'The last bus leaves there at eight forty-nine p.m., which puts it close to the possible time of death. The driver, or one of the passengers, could have seen the victim walking to the rendezvous. The bus company has given me the driver's name and contact details. She's not on shift until one o'clock.'

'Get someone over to her home,' Uckfield ordered, pushing his handkerchief back in his pocket.

Trueman continued, 'The last ferry in winter is at seven p.m. from Portsmouth to Hayling and seven ten from Hayling to Portsmouth, so that probably rules out anyone seeing the victim or the killer, unless they met earlier or had met up there on a previous occasion. We're checking with the ferry company and I'll get officers down there tonight at the time of the last two crossings. They'll show passengers pictures of the victim in case anyone saw him loitering. I'll also get an officer to ask the owner of the mobile café by the lifeboat station if he's seen the victim around.'

Horton said that he'd detailed Sergeant Elkins to check with the sailing and diving club, the lifeboat crew and the harbour master. He added, 'We should also check with the staff and students at the marine institute – they often work late and they've got CCTV, although the camera only points over the entrance to the building and not the road.'

Trueman nodded. 'We'll have a team doing a house-to-house along the upper part of Ferry Road today in case anyone saw the victim walking towards the ferry.'

Uckfield addressed DC Marsden. 'Is the hostel missing one of its residents?'

'No, all present and accounted for, sir. I could only give them a vague description of the ead man over the phone but the manager of Millane House doesn't recognize him.'

Millane House was a forty-five minute walk from where the victim had been found. Horton couldn't see him having the money to take a bus, and even if he had he wouldn't have squandered it on public transport. What little he'd had would have been needed to pay for food and drink and maybe alcohol. Equally, if the vagrant had been given a bed for the night at the hostel, Horton wouldn't have thought he'd sacrifice it, not unless he'd been contacted after being allocated the bed, and even then it would have needed a very powerful motive to make him abandon it.

'What time do they kick them out in the morning?' Uckfield asked.

'Nine o'clock.'

'Get over there and show the dead man's photograph around. Take Somerfield with you. She's been seconded to the Major Crime Team for this investigation.'

PC Kate Somerfield was trying hard not to show how pleased she was. Horton had noted earlier that she was out of uniform and in civvies. He wondered how Bliss viewed that. Although Somerfield was a much lower rank, Bliss tended to view every female as the competition, especially an ambitious one, which Kate Somerfield was. Horton tried not to let his suspicious mind go into overdrive as his gaze swivelled between Kate Somerfield and Uckfield. She was his type: fair, attractive, shapely, under forty and female. But Horton had thought Uckfield's latest conquest was Alison from the canteen. Maybe he'd already tired of her or was getting greedy and had two on the go, not counting his wife, also called Alison, the former chief constable's daughter. One day Uckfield would get his fingers burned and ACC Dean would be only too pleased to pin his balls to the wall and cut his libido – and his career – down to size.

Horton suggested they should also check with the Salvation Army. Uckfield added that to Marsden's and Somerfield's list. He sniffed loudly, sneezed and glanced at his watch. The press call was due in forty minutes.

'It looks very much to me as though this poor bugger was shot but until we have confirmation of that from Dr Clayton we say nothing to no one about how he died. Right?' he barked as loudly as his croaky throat would allow him. Everyone

49

quickly agreed. He swivelled his gaze on to Horton. 'I want you looking into this reported theft of antique firearms.' His office phone was ringing. Quickly, he continued, 'And get over to the mortuary, find out if Dr Clayton's found the poor sod's ID sewn in his underpants. DCI Bliss and DI Dennings will work the investigation from here.' And that, thought Horton, would suit the two of them perfectly – no going out on the streets and getting their hands grubby and an ear bashing from the less salubrious members of the public. Uckfield disappeared into his office, where he snatched up his phone.

Bliss turned to Horton and Cantelli and flapped a scrawny hand at Walters to join them. Addressing Horton, she said sharply, 'We need to know every-thing there is to know about those weapons and the likelihood of them becoming active. We've already lost a valuable day's investigation, and a day in which a man has been murdered.'

She made it sound as though it was their fault the guns had been stolen and the victim killed. Her words also implied that he shouldn't have taken a few days' holiday and that Cantelli and Walters had done nothing but sit around and wait for his return. Walters didn't appear upset at the insult because he rarely recognized one when it was given and Cantelli was too used to Bliss's ways to take umbrage. Horton was tempted to remind her that she had been the officer-in-charge and whatever blame anyone wanted to lay was at her door. But it would have been a waste of his breath because Bliss, like Uckfield, was very good at ditching the dirt on someone else if necessary.

50

She continued, 'I want those guns found.'

As if they didn't. He turned, and with Cantelli and Walters, headed down the stairs and back to CID. He asked Walters to brief him.

Taking a packet of salt and vinegar crisps from the pocket of his jacket, Walters said, 'The Clements returned from a cruise early on Monday morning and found the property had been entered through a sash window that gives on to a flat garage roof at the front of the house. No prints from the window or from anywhere else, except those of Mr and Mrs Clements.'

'How did the Clements know the thieves had come in that way?'

'They said it was the only window that wasn't double-glazed and it was open when they returned – only a fraction, though.'

Horton considered this. 'How did the thieves leave?'

'Through the same window, I guess.'

'Which they forgot to close after them?' Horton said dubiously.

'Maybe they panicked, thought they might be seen and wanted a quick getaway.' Walters crammed some crisps into his mouth before continuing. 'They live in Darrin Road, just behind the nine-hole golf course on the seafront. The pistols were kept in a basement room. Loads of old stuff in it, all arty-fartily displayed. Clements claims some of it is worth a fortune. Can't see why the thieves left it behind unless they were disturbed or thought it a load of old junk, which is my opinion, because most of it looks like the stuff my nan had in her living room on the sideboard, or the crap you can pick up at a car boot sale or junk shop.'

'What kind of stuff?'

'Ornaments and the like,' Walters dismissed vaguely.

'So it was the pistols they were after?'

'Guess so. Nothing else was stolen. Vivian Clements claims he set the alarm when he left the house on the nineteenth of December and it didn't sound when they arrived home on Monday morning at eight fifteen.' Walters belatedly offered some crisps to Horton and Cantelli, who both declined. With his mouth full, he continued, 'There are sensors in every room but if anyone heard the alarm they didn't report it. It's not linked to the security company who supply and service it – Treadware's.'

Horton knew them. They had an excellent reputation. 'Did you contact them?'

Walters nodded. 'They serviced the alarm in October.'

'And the engineer is trustworthy?'

'So Howard Treadware says. Chap called Trevor Lukein. Been at Treadwares for eight years.'

'But he'd know the code.'

'Howard Treadware says all his engineers are instructed to tell the owners to re-set the code after the alarm has been serviced. Whether they do or not . . .' Walters shrugged. 'Do you want me to interview Trevor Lukein?'

'He's probably out on a job.' Which could be anywhere in Hampshire or along the coast in the neighbouring counties of Dorset or West Sussex. 'Call Howard Treadware, find out when Lukein will be in the office or where he's working today. If it's local go and speak to him; if not wait until he gets back in the office.'

They turned into the CID operations room where a phone was ringing. Cantelli answered it while Walters, after tipping the dregs of the crisp packet into his mouth, said, 'Mr Clements sent over the details of the pistols – the serial numbers, full descriptions and photographs. I'll get them listed on the arts and antiques database and circulate them to all officers to ask around the antiques and junk shops to see if anyone has been trying to pass them off. I'll also check online to see if anyone is trying to flog them on the Internet.'

And that sort of job was right up Walters' street because it didn't involve expending any energy. This sounded as though it was a specialist theft and not your average housebreakers. These thieves had known exactly what was there and were stealing to order, otherwise why leave the ornaments, unless, like Walters said, they were of little value. They probably already had a client or clients lined up for the guns. They might even have already shifted them. It certainly didn't sound as though one of the guns could have been the weapon used on their victim.

'What are the Clements like?' he asked.

'He's a pompous little windbag and his wife is timid and nervy.'

Horton couldn't always go by what Walters said. He would see for himself soon enough. He and Cantelli would interview the Clements after visiting the mortuary.

He entered his office and gave his desk a surprised

53

glance. There wasn't a single piece of paper or a note on it. Maybe Bliss had cleared it in readiness for a new inspector to arrive. He plucked his sailing jacket from the coat stand and gathered up Cantelli.

'Why the change in wardrobe?' he asked Cantelli as they made for the car park.

'I didn't think you'd noticed,' Cantelli said camply, fluttering his dark eyes.

Horton smiled.

Cantelli continued, 'She was wearing that yesterday, probably in honour of Her Majesty's Inspector of Constabulary's visit.'

'I'd forgotten about that.'

'Wish I could have done.'

'Is that why my desk is so tidy? I thought she might have found a way to get rid of me and cleared it. Or that you and Walters had solved all the crimes in the city in my absence and the scumbag criminals had seen the errors of their ways and turned over new leaves.'

'Chance would be a fine thing. I just shoved your papers in the drawers.'

'Thanks! Did it go all right?'

'Must have done because she didn't bollock us. She told Walters to stay hidden if HMIC deemed to enter CID while he was there.'

'Given Walters' appearance I can't say I blame her. In that suit he's enough to frighten anyone, unless he bought himself a new one especially for yesterday.'

'You're kidding. It's not a solar eclipse year.'

Horton smiled and stretched the seat belt around him.

Cantelli started the car and pulled out of the station. 'If the report of that robbery hadn't come in I think she would have invented or committed a crime to get him out of the way. I was also out when HMIC did his rounds so she had a nice, empty CID room to show him. Not sure that pleased her or HMIC but we'll no doubt find out in due course. If it hadn't been for this homicide we'd have known by now. I was about to compliment her yesterday morning on how nice she looked but she gave me her beady-eyed stare so I kept my mouth shut, knowing I was on a hiding to nothing.'

'She would probably have accused you of being sexist.'

'Then I'll tell you how nice you look, sir.'

Again, Horton smiled.

Cantelli indicated on to the motorway into the heavy rush-hour morning traffic making north for the mortuary. 'How did you get on in Guernsey? And I don't mean getting called in by John Guilbert to look at a body.'

'You heard?'

'Warren told me.'

Horton glanced across at the international port where Evelyn Lyster had caught the ferry to Guernsey. He could see the Condor Commodore Clipper in its dock but the Brittany ferry had already sailed to France. He wouldn't tell Cantelli that the Ducales had known the Eames family, especially Lord Richard Eames, because he didn't want to draw Barney too deeply into his personal investigations even though he trusted him not to tell anyone. If Eames was working for the intelligence services, and had been involved in Jennifer's disappearance and the ongoing cover-up, then Horton wasn't about to reveal anything that would put Barney at risk.

'Dead end,' he said.

'So where do you go next?'

Where indeed? Maybe that would be down to Eames. He left a short pause before answering, 'To the mortuary.'

Five

'I've still no idea why he looks familiar to me,' Cantelli said as they stared at the naked body on the mortuary slab. 'Perhaps I've just seen too many like him,' he added a little wearily.

There was that, thought Horton, trying to blot out the stench of the mortuary, which he always found difficult. He ran his practised eye over the corpse. He was lean and tall, about six foot one. He was also remarkably clean for a tramp and Horton knew that Tom, Gaye's auburn-haired, burly mortuary attendant, hadn't washed the body. Horton could see the wound on the right-hand side of the chest. It struck him, not for the first time, how something so remarkably small could have such devastating consequences.

Cantelli said, 'It was just that first sight of him on the crime board . . . Something jarred with me for a second, then it was gone. Must be getting senile.'

'Surely not,' Gaye said brightly, marching in. Decked out in her green mortuary garb, Horton thought it made her look younger than her thirty-four years. 'You're only a few years older than Inspector Horton and he looks far from senile to me.'

'Glad to see all that running and working out at the gym is paying off,' Horton joked.

She held his stare and in her green eyes he wondered if there was an invitation to put his claims to the test.

Briskly, she continued, 'I don't think the victim's clothes are going to help you much either. There was nothing in the pockets to provide an ID. They're the usual chain-store ones, except for his coat, which is from Gieves and Hawkes, and of excellent quality, as one would expect from the Savile Row tailor patronized by royalty.'

'Don't tell me Prince Charles is a suspect,' Horton teased.

'Who knows? Maybe your victim moved in elevated circles.' She nodded at Tom, who handed Horton the large evidence bag containing the grubby camel-coloured coat. 'It's a little on the large side but your victim could have purchased it before he lost weight, although, as it's also too short for him it was probably given to him by the Salvation Army or another charitable organization. From my examination of his clothes I can tell you that he was shot while fully clothed rather than being shot naked and then dressed.'

'It's definite then that he was shot?' asked Cantelli, chewing his gum.

'One hundred per cent. Why? Do you have a suspect or someone in mind for it?'

'No, but we have some stolen pistols,' Cantelli answered. 'Antique ones that we've been told can't fire and for which there is no ammunition.'

Gaye raised her eyebrows as though to say a likely story. But she said, 'I'll know more about the type of weapon used once I've done the autopsy. For now, Tom's recorded a detailed study of the bullet's position in relation to the collar, seams and pockets of the coat and taken photographic evidence of all the clothes. They've also been examined radiographically for bullet fragments. There doesn't appear to be any but I've sent the images over to the ballistics expert in case he can pick up anything from them. The forensic lab will obviously examine the clothes very carefully for evidence of soot or stippling which will help in determining the range at which he was shot but I should be able to give you more on that once I open him up and delve inside.'

Cantelli shuddered and chewed his gum a little faster.

Gaye continued, 'But this is what we have so far.'

Horton listened eagerly.

'The victim was dressed in heavy walking boots which have seen considerable wear. Size eleven. But the boots are not misshapen and his feet are in good condition, no bunions or callouses, his toenails clipped.' She glanced at Horton to see if he was following her. He was, avidly. 'His socks are grey wool, no holes and not darned, and fairly new. Trousers, cotton, waist forty-two

58

inches, inside leg thirty inches, which again is too short for him and the waist too large. Dirty and worn around the seat and knees.'

'Why the knees?' Cantelli interjected.

'Maybe he inherited them from someone who liked gardening. There was no belt in the waistband, possibly because it was being used to keep his overcoat fastened around his torso. The belt is leather, again well worn. His check shirt was frayed around the collar and cuffs, extra-large size, and the woollen jumper, also extra-large, was worn and faded.' She paused. Horton could see there was more to come and his interest quickened. 'But this is where it gets very interesting. Firstly, the outer garments were old, worn, patched and frayed but, with the exception of the coat and trousers, all clean.'

Horton exchanged a knowing look with Cantelli.

Gaye interpreted it. 'Unusual, yes, if he was homeless and had been for some time. Of course, there is the possibility that he'd just been given the clothes.'

As Bliss had suggested.

'His boxer shorts are from John Lewis. They are also clean, of good quality and are the correct fit. And if you take a close look at his hands,' she lifted the left hand, 'especially his nails, what do you see?'

Horton knew. He'd already pointed it out. 'They're clean.'

'Yes, and what's more, they've been manicured. Now, I don't know about you but I've never met a vagrant who takes the trouble to keep his nails clean and manicured.'

Neither had Horton.

'In addition, his teeth, although containing a lot of fillings, have been cosmetically enhanced and fairly recently, certainly within the last few years. There's also no hint of stubble on his face. He seems to have been a very fastidious vagrant.'

Cantelli voiced what Horton was thinking. 'He was dressed as a tramp but he wasn't one.'

Gaye answered, 'That's what it looks like.'

Horton said, 'It would explain why there weren't any carrier bags of belongings with him, but not what he was doing in that location, although the obvious answer was to meet someone.'

Gaye continued, 'From my initial examination I'd put his age as being mid-fifties. He's been dead for between twelve to fourteen hours, so he was killed sometime between seven and nine last night.'

'That early?'

'Yes, why? Don't tell me the police doctor said it was later. Who was it – Dr Sharman?'

Horton nodded.

'I wish you'd called me last night.'

He held her eyes. He wished he had too but not to view a body.

'And he told you the poor soul was dead. Anything else? No,' she said pointedly.

Horton wondered what had occurred between them to cause the icy temperature but now was not the time to ask. If Dr Clayton was right, and she usually was, then it was possible that the victim or his killer, or both, could have travelled on the last Hayling Ferry to Portsmouth or someone on the ferry might have seen them.

She said, 'Lividity is now well established and from its pattern the victim hasn't been moved. There are no marks or scratches on his hands or forearms, which indicates he didn't defend himself.'

'Would he have had time?' asked Cantelli.

'Probably not. But it's always worth checking in case he'd been in a fight before being shot. He hadn't been. Or rather, there is no external evidence of that but I'll obviously examine him for internal bruising. There are no tattoos, birthmarks or any other distinguishing marks, and no scars indicating assault or surgery. That's it for now. I hope to have more in about four hours, maybe less, unless you're staying for the floor show?'

'Other things to do,' Horton said hastily.

Outside in the corridor, he was about to discuss Dr Clayton's findings with Cantelli when the sergeant's phone rang.

'It's Charlotte. Mind if I take it, Andy?'

'No need to ask.'

Horton walked on, leaving Cantelli to take his wife's phone call. Outside the mortuary, Horton took a deep breath of the damp, cold January air and stared down at the city spread out before him in a dull grey haze which merged with the sea beyond to make the Isle of Wight almost invisible. He reached for his mobile phone and called Uckfield.

'Great,' was Uckfield's predictably grumpy response after Horton had relayed what Gaye had told them. 'So now we've got a vagrant who sounds more like a male model. I'll get Marsden to contact

61

the tailors. They might know who they sold that coat to and when.'

Horton doubted it unless the label contained some kind of code or the make had been discontinued at a certain time. Even then he doubted that it would lead them to the vagrant. The forensic analysis of it might tell them more. But he didn't say. Uckfield wouldn't thank him for it. And besides, Uckfield would know that.

Uckfield continued, 'Trueman's still trying to find someone in the rates office who can give us the houseboat owner's details. You'd think he was asking for a catalogue of where every stone on that beach came from judging by the difficulty he's having.'

'Surely it's easy enough to look up on a computer.'

'It would be if he could find someone to do it. Marsden says the warden at the hostel doesn't recognize the dead man, which isn't surprising given what you've just said, so he and Somerfield are doing the rounds of the other places he might have hung out, but as he wasn't homeless – just dressed up to appear homeless – that'll be a waste of time.'

Horton said he'd give Elkins the earlier time of death and ask him to interview the Hayling ferry staff.

Uckfield said, 'Could our victim have been an actor, getting into costume to get the feel of the part or some such crap? You know what these poncy actors are like.'

'Not really. But if he was then why go out on such a dreadful night? And who would want to kill him?' Uckfield's suggestion had sparked another thought, though. 'He could have been working undercover.'

'Christ, you don't mean he's one of us!'

'If he is then sooner or later someone will start shouting.'

'Not if they don't know he's missing or dead.' By Uckfield's tone of voice Horton could tell he was worried.

'Dr Clayton estimates the victim is in his mid-fifties. He might be too old for one of our lot to be undercover but he could be a private investigator or an insurance, benefit or tax fraud investigator. That would give someone a motive for killing him if whoever he was investigating wanted him silenced. Perhaps someone objected to his benefit being taken away.'

Uckfield sniffed loudly. Horton held the phone a short distance away.

'It would help if we knew what kind of gun he was shot with,' Uckfield grumbled. 'Trueman's pulling off a list of the usual scumbags who have had guns in the past and those caught bringing them in illegally and selling them but most of the villains are banged up, thank God. It could be a new kid on the block, though, or some nutter from outside, or someone who's been watching too much of the *Antiques Roadshow* on the telly and thinks he's found a niche market. See what these Clements have to say for themselves, and if they can't explain why they had an arsenal in their house, bring them in.'

The line went dead. Cantelli joined him. 'Sorry about that. Mum's not been feeling well and

63

Charlotte's managed to persuade her to come and stay with us for a few days. It took some doing – she's fiercely independent, even more so now dad's gone. She doesn't want to be a burden and all that sort of thing, not that she ever can be or will be to us.'

'It's nothing serious, I hope.'

'I don't think so. She's got a heavy cold and is tired. She hasn't been eating or drinking properly. Could lead to pneumonia if she's not careful.'

And Charlotte would know about that, being a former nurse. Cantelli's father, Toni, had died thirteen months ago and his death had left a big hole in the Cantelli family. Horton had admired and liked Toni Cantelli, who had been an Italian prisoner of war during the Second World War, had met and fallen in love with a land girl on the farm he'd been detailed to work on, married her and built up a successful business which had diversified from ice-cream selling to owning cafés, one of which was on the seafront run by Cantelli's sister, Isabella.

'Charlotte can keep an eye on mum and get the doctor out to check her over. You know what some people are like, especially mum's generation – they don't want to trouble the doctor.' Cantelli zapped open the car. 'What do you make of Dr Clayton's information? Not sure this makes it easier or harder to identify our victim,' he added, removing his chewing gum and pushing it into a piece of silver paper and in his pocket before starting the engine.

Horton agreed. 'I've just broken the news to Uckfield. He's going to see if we can trace the ownership of the coat but our victim could have picked it up anywhere.'

'Like the rest of his outer garments. He might even have taken them from a charity bag left outside someone's house ready to be collected. The best we can do is circulate the pictures to the media, put them on the Internet and hope someone recognizes him.'

Horton's phone rang. It was Guilbert.

'Rowan Lyster's confirmed the body is that of his mother,' Guilbert said.

There hadn't really been any doubt. But the formalities had to be observed and it was always best to make sure. 'How did he take it?'

'Much calmer than I expected. He didn't cry or express regret but he was clearly very agitated. When I explained about the inquest being held tomorrow he looked annoyed rather than distressed. He couldn't understand why there had to be one but I told him that given the circumstances of his mother's death it was standard procedure. No one's come forward yet to say they recognize or know her, or to say that she was booked into a hotel. And we can't trace her owning a property on the island. Her son is adamant she didn't and certain that she didn't have any connections here, and that bothers me. If her death is due to natural causes as the pathologist found then why travel without any luggage?'

Horton's concerns exactly.

'Rowan Lyster has given us permission to look over his mother's apartment – rather reluctantly, I might add. He couldn't see why it was necessary but I told him the coroner would ask and we didn't want to delay matters. There might be something in there to tell us why she came to Guernsey. Could you send someone to meet Rowan's wife, Gina, at the apartment? She has a key.'

'I'll go myself.' He didn't think Bliss or Uckfield would like that very much given that they were in the middle of a murder investigation but he had seen the body and was curious about Evelyn Lyster.

'I was hoping you'd say that.' Guilbert relayed Gina Lyster's mobile number. Horton rang her, introduced himself and made arrangements to meet her outside the apartment at twelve thirty. That gave them enough time to interview the Clements. Next he rang Elkins and gave him the revised time of the vagrant's death, explaining that he didn't appear to be a vagrant, and asked him to interview the skipper of the Hayling ferry and get some details of their last passengers from both Portsmouth and Hayling. Not that the ferry company would be able to give them names and addresses – they simply issued a ticket to cross the small stretch of water – but they would be able to tell them how many people had been on that ferry and the skipper would be able to identify his regulars. They could probably be ruled out of the investigation but someone might have seen either the dead man or the killer hanging around. Elkins reported that the harbour master hadn't noted any movement in the harbour last night, which wasn't surprising given the weather, and Chris Howgate had said there had been no one at the lifeboat station and they hadn't had any shouts.

Cantelli turned on to the seafront and headed east. There were a few people walking along the promenade and a French warship was making its way out of the harbour. There were a couple of yachts on the Solent but it was too chilly and too dull for all but the hardiest of sailors and strollers.

Just past the nine-hole golf course Cantelli indicated left and almost immediately left again. After a few hundred yards he turned right into a wide road of substantial detached Edwardian houses. The Clements' was the second on the left.

'Surely someone must have heard the alarm before it was disabled by the burglars,' Horton said, studying the large three-storey house behind double wrought-iron gates and a brick paved driveway where a top-of-the-range Mercedes was parked.

'Uniform have called on the neighbouring houses and put leaflets through the doors but so far no one claims to have heard or seen anything suspicious. It's the kind of street where people keep themselves to themselves.'

And the kind of house that would set you back a small fortune, Horton thought, climbing out of the car and viewing the large double bay windows on the first and second floors, rooms in the eaves on the top floor that in the days when the house was built would have been for the servants, and a basement that would have harboured a kitchen where a cook would have slaved over a hot stove.

'It's a large house for only two people,' he said, approaching the front door. He noted there was a grill on the basement window on his right.

67

According to Walters, that was where the guns had been kept.

'I could lose my five in it,' Cantelli said winsomely, pressing his finger on a shiny brass bell. Horton heard it chiming through the house. 'Walters says that Vivian and Constance Clements don't have any children or lodgers.'

They also seemed reluctant to answer. Cantelli rang again, keeping his finger pressed on the bell and this time, after several seconds, the door was flung open and a grey-skinned, grey-haired, squat man in his early sixties glared at them. 'How many times do I have to tell you people this is a no cold calling zone so—'

'Police, Mr Clements,' Cantelli hastily broke in, flashing his warrant card.

Clements didn't look appeased or impressed. He squinted at it with bloodshot eyes, sniffed and said grudgingly, 'I suppose you'd better come in.'

Six

'Can't you just do the job you're paid to do and catch these thieves instead of pestering us every five minutes?' Vivian Clements rounded on them as they followed him into a modern, white, black and chrome kitchen that looked to Horton like something out of mission control. It opened up into an expansive conservatory. Beyond was a small garden laid with decking and surrounded by well-tended evergreen shrubs cut in a variety of shapes. Hovering nervously in the centre of the kitchen was an elegantly dressed, slender woman with short, highlighted blonde hair, blue eyes and an expression akin to embarrassment on her oval-shaped, lined face. Horton thought Walters' description of the Clements had been spot on.

Vivian Clements' reaction wasn't a total surprise. It wasn't unknown for the victims of crime to vent their anger at the police but it wasn't every burglary victim who got a detective inspector and sergeant working on their case. Then again, it wasn't every householder who was robbed of firearms, antique or otherwise. And Clements' anger could be masking his fear that he knew one or more of those guns were quite capable of being fired.

'Vivian is very upset and angry,' Constance Clements hastily and unnecessarily explained, turning to her husband with a pleading look in her faded blue eyes which seemed to make him even angrier. His small mouth tightened.

'They know that,' he snapped, his eyes flashing contempt.

Horton saw her flinch.

Sternly, but making sure to show nothing of the dislike he felt towards the pompous little man, Horton said, 'This is a gun theft, Mr Clements, and as such is a very serious matter.'

'They were *antique* pistols. How many more times do I have to say it? They aren't capable of being fired.'

'Are you certain of that?' Horton held his eye contact.

'Of course I am.'

'When did you inform the police that you had guns on the premises?'

'I didn't because being *antiques* I didn't need to tell the police,' he said loftily and in a superior tone as though speaking to an idiot.

Time to wipe that sneer from his face. With a steely glare and an icy tone Horton said, 'Section 58 of the 1968 Firearms Act does not define "antique". It is for the police and the courts to consider each case on its merits. You should have contacted us with a full description of the weapons. Possession of a firearm without a licence, and one which does not fall under the heading of antique or historic, carries a mandatory prison sentence of five years. Not just for you but also for your wife.'

Constance Clements' eyes widened with alarm, her skin paled and her slender hand flew to her neck where it played with a bold, turquoise stone necklace matching the colour of her top. Her husband's skin blanched. Good, but Horton could see he wasn't beaten into submission yet.

'This is ridiculous. I've broken no law; it's the bastards who stole them who should be imprisoned.'

'And they will be *when* we catch them.' Or at least Horton hoped so but, given the way some of the magistrates and the slippery solicitors the crooks engaged operated that was doubtful. 'That still doesn't alter the fact that the weapons were in your possession and that you did not notify the police. Now I'd appreciate some cooperation.' He didn't mention they had a man

70

who had been killed by a firearm. Uckfield wanted that kept quiet for now.

Clements opened his mouth to retort but the trilling of his mobile phone intervened. Glancing at it, he snatched it to his ear and marched off into the conservatory, bellowing down the line at the poor soul who had chosen the wrong time to ring. Horton caught the sigh of relief from Constance Clements.

'I'm sorry, Inspector. This has really shaken Vivian.' Fearfully, she added in a low voice, 'Is it true he should have told you about the guns being on the premises?'

'Yes.'

'He couldn't have known that. It must have been an oversight.'

'That's no defence in law,' Horton sternly retorted.

She shifted nervously.

'Perhaps you could show us where the alarm is.'

'Of course.'

She threw a glance over her shoulder to her husband, who was raging down the line to what sounded like the insurance company. It was, Horton thought, as though she was seeking permission to leave the room. But Clements was intent on pursuing his irate phone conversation and Horton was already moving towards the door. She gave him a nervous smile and eased passed him. Horton caught Cantelli's raised eyebrows.

They followed her into the ornately decorated hall with its flamboyant wallpaper of birds and flowers in pale blue and mauve stretching up to the high ceiling from which an elaborate

71

candelabra was suspended. The cream ceramic floor was spotlessly clean. The staircase on their left was covered with an immaculate cream cord carpet and brass stair rods which gleamed. The staircase also led down to the basement where the pistols had been displayed.

She waved a slender arm at the alarm panel to the right of the front door.

'Was it set before you left for the cruise?' Horton asked. Walters had already told him it had been but there was no harm in going over it again in case the Clements remembered something they'd omitted first time around, either deliberately or accidentally.

Cantelli took out his notebook and removed his stubby pencil from behind his ear.

'Yes. Vivian had re-set it with a new code after it was serviced by the engineer.'

'Have you or your husband set it in view of anyone, perhaps before leaving the house with a friend, neighbour or relative?'

'No. There hasn't been anyone inside the house.'

'Not since October when it was serviced?' he asked, sounding slightly incredulous.

She blushed. 'No.'

'No friends or neighbours?'

She shook her head.

'Family?' asked Cantelli.

'We don't have any. Both our parents are dead. We don't have children. We haven't been married very long and neither of us has been married before.'

Again, she blushed. Horton wondered why. He asked to see where the thieves had entered.

72

'They came in through the side window in the drawing room.'

She turned and they followed her up the stairs to the first floor and a door on the left. Horton caught Cantelli's look. He knew what Barney was thinking: there was no such thing as a drawing room in his three-bedroom semi-detached house with a loft conversion. But as Horton stepped inside the sumptuously decorated, high ceiling, spacious, ornately furnished room he thought the term drawing room was an apt description. It certainly wasn't the sort of place you'd sprawl out on a sofa watching a plasma television screen fixed on the wall; it was more Jane Austen like, somewhere you'd sip afternoon tea in china cups and make polite conversation. In fact, there wasn't a television in sight. Catherine would have despised it, though. There were too many paintings on the walls and too much gilt, including the mirror over the Adams-style fireplace, and she'd never have stomached the cream-coloured wallpaper with grey swirls. There was also too much furniture of the material kind. Catherine preferred cream leather and bleached wood.

He turned his attention to where the burglars had entered. The long sash window had a wooden frame rather than a PVC one. As though reading his mind, Constance Clements said, 'It's the only window apart from those in the eaves that we haven't renewed. We've applied for planning permission to turn the garage roof into a terrace. I'd like French doors here in keeping with the style and design of the house and railings around the terrace. You get a nice view of the sea across the golf course. It would be tastefully screened with plants.'

Horton climbed out of the window on to the flat garage roof and saw immediately what she meant. The neighbouring house on the right on the corner was set back behind this house and if he turned to face into the chilly, damp, southerly wind he had a clear view of the small golf course, the seafront road, promenade, shingle beach and the grey, choppy Solent beyond. He could even make out the Bembridge peninsula on the Isle of Wight and the lifeboat station at the end of its long pier. Facing east, though, he merely looked out at the similar properties on the opposite side of the road. To the north, there were others spaced out along the road which culminated in a T-junction, giving on to more large Edwardian detached and semi-detached houses. Several cars were parked in the street even though the houses had garages.

He looked down. The thieves must have brought a short ladder with them to scale the side of the garage because there was no drain pipe or any other climbing structure. He wondered what time the house had been burgled. He assumed probably sometime between nine and midnight because an alarm sounding briefly would have been disguised behind the sound of televisions. And even though there were street lights, given the time of year, the occupants of the nearby houses would have been tucked up inside their homes, much as they had been last night when the vagrant who hadn't been a vagrant had been killed.

Horton climbed back inside and glanced at the sensors above the window.

Constance Clements said, 'There are infra-sensors in every corner of the room.'

Horton could see them. 'And you found this window open when you came in here on your return?'

'Yes. When the alarm didn't sound Vivian at first thought we must have a power cut. He tried the light switch and everything was fine. He then thought the circuit must have fused. It was only when I came in here after I'd been in the kitchen and put the coffee on that I noticed the window was open. I was horrified, thinking that I must have left it open by mistake, but I knew I hadn't when I heard Vivian shouting. I rushed down to the basement and found him so upset he could barely tell me what had happened. He phoned the police while I checked over the rest of the house.' She frowned, puzzled. 'Nothing else has been taken and there are some rather valuable pieces in this room and elsewhere in the house. Why didn't the thieves take them? We were away – they could have emptied the place.'

Why indeed? Perhaps something had happened to disturb them. But his earlier belief that the pistols had been stolen to order and that this was a professional job was being confirmed except for the fact that the sash window had been left open. But even professionals made mistakes, thank goodness. He'd get Clarke out here to photograph the point of entry and the basement, which he'd view in due course, but first he said, 'I'd like to talk to your husband.'

75

She nodded and gave him a timid smile. They followed her back to the kitchen where she offered them refreshments but Clements, who was now off the phone and sitting in front of a laptop computer at a table in the conservatory, snapped, 'They haven't got time for that.'

'Coffee would be nice, Mrs Clements,' Horton said firmly, especially as he saw it was the fresh variety concocted in a sophisticated machine.

Cantelli plumped for tea.

Clements glowered at them. 'There's nothing more I can tell you. I've already been over it twice, once with the first uniformed officers who arrived on Monday and again on Tuesday with that detective.'

Clearly, by his tone, he didn't think much of Walters.

Cantelli politely answered, 'It sometimes helps us if you can go over it again, sir. There might be something you missed the first couple of times, or something that has only just occurred to you.'

'There isn't.'

With a hint of concern in her voice, Constance Clements threw her husband a pleading look. 'Darling, please.' Then her eyes swivelled between Horton and Cantelli. 'Vivian's tired, he's been working very hard and coming home to this has been an appalling shock.'

'Working?' Horton picked up. 'I thought you'd just returned from a cruise?'

Clements glanced at his wife, then heaved a heavy sigh and sat back in his chair. 'It was a working cruise, Inspector. I was a guest lecturer on the *Savana*, the cruise ship that sails from

Portsmouth. It's part of the cultural lectures fleet. They're smaller than the huge liners that sail from Southampton and, shall we say, have a more discerning clientele.'

As well as prices to match, thought Horton. He'd seen the ships when he'd been out sailing in the Solent and he'd also seen them docked at the international port.

Constance Clements took up the conversation. 'They're discovery cruises. Vivian gives lectures about the places the ship is visiting.'

Clements broke in. 'It sounds glamorous, and of course my wife and I get the cruise for free, but it's bloody hard work. I have to give a different lecture every day and attend some of the tours with the local guide. We also have to mingle with the guests at cocktails and dinner and, quite frankly, it's difficult being pleasant and looking and sounding as though you're interested in the person who is boring the pants off you or insists on telling you all the things you already know because you've just told him that. When I come home I've had enough of my fellow creatures. I just want to be alone and quiet for a while. I certainly didn't need all this.'

His wife put the tray of drinks on the table and waved them into seats. She took the one next to her husband and handed him his coffee. Horton had already noted the expensive rings on her well-manicured fingers and his thoughts flicked to the rings on the fingers of Evelyn Lyster – diamond clusters and coloured stones, much like the missing brooch his mother had once owned.

He heard Cantelli say, 'How did you get to be a cruise lecturer, sir?'

Horton wondered if Clements would retort, 'What's that got to do with the robbery?' but his wife's presence and the coffee seemed to be having a soothing effect. His anger had subsided and he now appeared to Horton to be a very disturbed man with a hint of despair in his haunted eyes.

'I won't bore you with the full CV, Sergeant, so to summarize, I have a degree in oriental studies and the history of art.'

Horton recalled what he'd learned about Andrew Ducale. He too had a degree in oriental studies from Cambridge where Lord Eames had also graduated, but they hadn't been there at the same time. He'd checked. Eames had left there in 1967, three years after Ducale, with a first-class honours degree in economics, politics and philosophy, after which he'd joined the Foreign Office – another thing he and Ducale had in common.

Clements was saying, 'I've worked for auction-eers, art galleries and universities. Six years ago I met Constance and began helping her to source items for her clients. Constance is an interior designer.'

That explained the décor in the house, thought Horton.

'Three years ago we got married, sold our apartments in London and moved back here. Or rather, Constance did. She used to live here. She was reluctant at first but it's been OK.' He dashed her a glance as though seeking her to confirm this. She gave a weak smile. She wasn't going to contradict her husband but Horton thought she looked as though she'd like to. He wondered why she had been reluctant to move back. Maybe she disliked the city or perhaps she would have preferred to stay in London with her clients.

Vivian Clements was steaming on. 'I felt at a bit of a loss giving up my consultancy and lecturing and Constance suggested that I would make a very good cruise lecturer so I wrote to the shipping companies – the select ones,' he quickly added as though he was fearful of being accused of having bad taste, 'and I was immediately accepted. I've cruised with Constance to Japan, China and Asia. But this last one took it out of me. I'd already decided it would be the final one then to come home to this.' His voice was dejected now rather than angry.

'And you left on the nineteenth of December, returning on Monday morning?' Cantelli asked, his pencil poised.

'Yes.' His shoulders drooped. Constance Clements gazed anxiously at her husband and fiddled with an expensive-looking silver or possibly white gold bracelet on her right wrist.

Horton said, 'I know you've already given a list of what was stolen to DC Walters but perhaps you'd tell us about the pistols taken.'

Vivian Clements sighed heavily before beginning in almost a monotone: 'One was a Webley Fosbery self-cocking, or semi-automatic revolver, invented by Lieutenant Colonel George Vincent Fosbery, holder of the Victoria Cross, in 1894, manufactured in Birmingham from 1901 to 1915. I have, or rather had, one of the very first that was manufactured there. It's worth approximately six thousand pounds.'

Horton was surprised at the value but made no comment.

Clements continued, 'The others are a Volcanic Repeating Arms Company lever-action navy pistol dated about the same time and in good condition. It would probably fetch about three thousand pounds – maybe more – at auction. There was a US Model 1842 navy rifled percussion pistol by Deringer, again worth about three thousand pounds; a French 25 Bore Double Barrelled Percussion Travelling Pistol, valued at six thousand pounds; and a Joseph Egg rare 70 Bore Over and Under Double Barrelled Percussion Overcoat Pistol circa 1840, valued at five thousand pounds.'

Horton was quickly totting this up. The value came to at least twenty-three thousand pounds.

'How much are they valued for insurance purposes?'

'My total collection is insured for one hundred thousand pounds but the thieves only took the pistols, so I will be making a claim for those amounts I've just relayed to you, Inspector. I'd rather have my pistols returned, though.'

Horton rose, saying, 'Could I see where they were kept?' He dashed a glance at Cantelli, who would correctly interpret it. Cantelli made no attempt to move, a fact that Vivian Clements didn't seem too keen on. He scowled at Cantelli, who simply sipped his tea and, as Horton was already at the door, it left Clements no option but to join him.

Horton followed Vivian Clements down the stairs leading to the basement.

'My study is next to my collection room and there's also a utility and a shower room on this floor at the rear,' Clements explained. Horton could see steps from the passageway leading up into the garden.

Clements turned to his right and a door facing the front of the house.

'Do you keep this locked?'

'I didn't think I needed to with alarm sensors everywhere and the rear door locked, bolted and alarmed,' he said sourly, pushing open the door.

So the thieves had picked the most vulnerable entry point, indicating that they must have previously surveyed the house from the inside.

Clements picked up a remote control and the room was suddenly filled with sophisticated lighting, strategically placed to show off an impressive and clearly highly valuable collection. Horton was impressed by the layout and design of the room and by the quality of the items arranged within it. He was no antiques expert but he had seen enough of them during his years of crime to recognize the genuine thing when he saw it. From Walters' description he had envisaged a few shelves dotted around the walls with something just a little more upmarket than bric-a-brac displayed on them. This looked more like a high-class art gallery or museum.

There were two sets of arched alcoves on the walls to Horton's right and another two on the opposite wall. The two on the right contained porcelain antiques – plates, jugs, figurines. The two on his left were bare. It was where the pistols had been displayed. Through the centre of the room ran a wooden plinth with cupboards beneath. On top, tastefully arranged and lit was a row of oriental-decorated vases, more figurines and plates. The window opposite was covered by slatted shutters, behind which was a grill. To the right was a tan leather wing chair and a small table. Horton could imagine Clements sitting here sipping a whisky or a glass of wine, admiring his collection. He wouldn't mind betting soft, classical music was piped into the room. Whoever had done this job was one hell of a careful burglar, and a very particular one.

'You were comfortable with having such a valuable collection here?' Horton asked, concerned and inflecting a tone of incredulity in his voice.

'What's the point of owning it if you can't look at it? I thought the security was adequate. The insurance company seemed to think so.'

'Have you ever shown anyone your collection?'

'No.'

Horton wasn't sure if he believed him. Surely the joy of owning this type of collection was to show it off. He caught a sense of unease about Clements. There was something he was holding back. Horton crossed and examined the collection of oriental objects on the plinth. There was a handsome yellow and blue decorative vase, another blue and white one and two iron-red and gilt shell containers on four tiny feet about five inches high, which looked like egg cups.

'They're intended to be used on a desk, by scholars, probably for ink, late Qing Republic and worth about five thousand pounds,' Clements explained.

'I recommend you move your most valuable items or all your collection to a secure location. A vault, perhaps.'

'Isn't that a bit like locking the stable door after the horse has bolted?' Clements rejoined sourly.

'I'm concerned that having seen this collection, the thieves might return.'

Clements shifted uneasily. 'I've re-set the alarm.'

'They managed to bypass it once. Do you employ cleaners?'

'My wife does but nobody is allowed to clean this room. I do that myself.'

'But they could have access to it because you said it isn't locked.'

'It isn't but how would a cleaner know what to steal and, even more pertinent, how to get rid of it?' he answered pompously.

'It's dangerous to make assumptions, sir,' Horton stiffly replied. 'They could easily have told someone. When was the last time you let any workmen in?'

'Two years ago, shortly after we moved in, when the room was decorated. I had the cabinets and lighting installed and none of my collection was in here then. I moved it to a secure lock-up.'

Horton noticed a thin film of perspiration on Clements' brow.

'Have you sat with the shutters open when someone has come to the house or the front door?'

'How can I remember that?' he cried tetchily and ran a hand over his hair.

Horton held his gaze for a fraction then said, 'Why do you collect the pistols?'

'Why shouldn't I?' Clements replied defensively.

'They weren't oriental and they're very different from the other items in your collection,' Horton persisted.

'It's just something I'm interested in.'

'How do you source and buy them?'

'Usually through the Internet and from reputable dealers. I can give you their names,' he quickly added. 'I also attend specialist auctions.'

'And this is where the pistols were displayed?' Horton crossed to the bare alcove. There was nothing to see. Fingerprints had been taken but there was no trace of them. Either Clements or his wife had cleaned up. Horton turned and said, 'Where were you and your wife last night?'

Clements looked taken aback. 'Why do you want to know that?'

Horton made no reply, just held Clements' hostile stare.

After a moment, Clements said tautly, 'We were here. Neither of us was in any mood to go out. We were still tired and in shock.'

Horton nodded. 'Thank you.'

'That's it?'

Was that relief he heard in Clements' voice? Horton said he would send a photographer round to take pictures of where the thieves entered and of the collection room.

They returned to the kitchen. Horton nodded at Cantelli, who rose. 'Thanks for the tea, Mrs Clements.'

'You're welcome. Will you be back?' She fingered her rather ornamental necklace.

'DC Walters will keep you up to date with any developments,' Horton answered. But they would be back whether or not it transpired that one of the stolen guns had been used to kill their victim last night, because Clements had still failed to comply with the law on gun ownership. Antique or not, historic or not, he should still have informed them.

She showed them to the door but not before Horton caught her exchanging a glance with her husband that he couldn't quite interpret.

In the car, Horton said, 'Well?'

'She's nervy, tired and unhappy and I'd say that was before the burglary. The only time I saw her eyes light up was when she was talking about her interior design business in London, which she clearly misses and I'd say regrets giving up.'

'Did you ask her where she and her husband were last night?'

'At home, still exhausted after their cruise and the robbery. Went to bed early.'

'He said more or less the same.'

'Do you want to talk to the neighbours?'

'No point if Walters and uniform have done that.' Horton glanced at the clock on the dashboard. They were due at Evelyn Lyster's apartment.

Cantelli started the car and pulled away. Horton continued, 'Clements' collection is very impressive and very valuable. He's also very uncomfortable about something but I can't see him nipping out last night and killing our supposed vagrant with one of his allegedly stolen pistols.'

'Insurance job?' Cantelli indicated right.

'Possibly. It's too neat. And why just the pistols?

85

He claims the cleaners never went in the room and it was never locked.'

'Mrs Clements said the same. She's used the same cleaning company for the last eight months – Valentines. They've got an office in Fawcett Road not far from Fratton railway station. The cleaners go in twice a week, Mondays and Fridays. On Mondays they do the downstairs and the basement, not the collection room, but they clean Vivian Clements' study, and Fridays the bedrooms and bathrooms. It's usually the same two women, who Mrs Clements says are very friendly and nice.'

'They might also have criminal contacts.'

'The cleaners wouldn't know the security code.'

'Not unless they'd seen the Clements set it or he had it written down somewhere in his study.'

'I guess that's possible. Or one of them could have planted a skimming device on the alarm to obtain the code and then removed it the next time they came.'

'We'll check them out, but my money's on Clements.' Horton stared across the Canoe Lake where a middle-aged couple with a young child were feeding the swans. 'It has to be an insurance fraud, except why the guns and why risk exposing himself to being prosecuted? Even if they are exempt from the firearms act he still failed to notify us and could be charged. It would have been much simpler for the Clements to have said the oriental objects had been stolen.'

'Maybe they're not worth as much.'

'Maybe there isn't such a ready market for them.'

Cantelli turned on to the road by the pier. 'And is Mrs Clements in on the insurance fraud?'

'Bound to be.' Horton looked at the grey, swirling Solent as they made their way west towards Old Portsmouth and Evelyn Lyster's apartment. In the distance he could see the Wightlink ferry heading into Fishbourne. To the left of the ferry terminal, rising above the trees was the abbey where he had found Antony Dormand, and to the right, tucked away around a bay and out of view was Richard Eames' Isle of Wight property, rarely used except for the international sailing regatta of Cowes Week in August and occasionally at Christmas. It backed on to a private beach, where Horton had met a beachcomber, who had said his name was Lomas.

He recalled the solidly built man in his late fifties scrutinizing him with curious and intelligent grey eyes in a bronzed, weather-beaten face, the close-cropped greying beard, shabby shorts and old leather sandals over bare feet. He'd come from nowhere. He'd certainly not been in Eames' private woods when Horton had trekked through them to reach the beach and neither had he seen a dinghy on the shore. He'd tried to locate him since then but couldn't. He had vanished and it had occurred to Horton that maybe Dormand had been masquerading as a monk at the nearby abbey because his mission had been to silence Lomas, who was in fact no beachcomber but one of those five men in that picture Ducale had left on his boat and which he'd shown Violet Ducale. They were all supposed to be dead but Horton was beginning to wonder if one of the five was still alive or had been before Dormand had got to him. Dormand hadn't been in the monastery to make peace with his God before his impending death from cancer. Horton wasn't even sure if Dormand had died in the Solent after he'd watched him climb into the small dinghy on the dark, windy night. His body had never been found but the sea didn't always give up its dead. It might have been Jennifer's final resting place. And what of the man who had taken that 1967 photograph? Was he still alive? Was it Andrew Ducale?

Cantelli's voice broke through his thoughts. 'Are the Clements hard up?'

'Doesn't look that way but who knows? They could be mortgaged to the hilt. And why take that cruise lecture job unless he needed to? He didn't sound too keen on it.'

Horton rang Walters and gave him instructions to talk to the Clements' insurance company to see if they'd made any previous claims. 'Also, check their credit rating,' he added.

Walters said he would when he returned from Treadwares. 'I'm on my way there now, guv. Trevor Lukein's back in the office for lunch.'

The parking spaces lining the road opposite Evelyn Lyster's apartment were full, which was unusual given the time of year. But the reason for it became evident when Horton saw a van with Bellman's Catering written on the side and several people in naval dress uniform making their way inside the building where Evelyn Lyster had an apartment on the top floor. The building had originally been a bank and then had become an exclusive sailing club for gentlemen from the higher echelons of the armed forces and the banking and business world, before opening its doors to their wives in the 1970s and then business and professional women in the 1990s. It was still a club and maintained its exclusivity, but also offered its high-ceilinged, chandelier-lit, sumptuously decorated function rooms to those who wanted to celebrate their anniversaries, weddings, birthdays and other special events in taste and style. Horton had been here with Catherine and his in-laws on three such occasions. He'd always felt out of place. He wasn't sure now whether that was because of the exclusivity of the club or the fact that his in-laws had always looked down on him. He'd never been considered good enough for their only child, a fact that they now believed had been proved. The middle floor of the building comprised of a members-only bar, lounge, games room, library and viewing room while the top floor had been converted into two luxury penthouse apartments.

Cantelli eventually managed to find a space around the corner in Grand Parade close to the statue of Nelson looking out to sea. They walked the short distance back towards the building in time to see a small sports car swing into a space that had just been vacated and a woman with fair hair clipped high on her slightly tanned, chubby face climb out. She was texting on her phone. She glanced up, looked uncertain for a moment and then, pushing the phone into the pocket of her fleece jacket, headed towards them with a nervous smile. Gina Lyster, Horton assumed.

Seven

'Do you always keep a key to your mother-in-law's apartment?' Cantelli asked as they stepped into the hall that smelled of paint and new carpets. Ahead was a staircase covered in a thick-pile pale blue carpet and, to their right, a lift. Horton couldn't hear a sound from the function rooms. No alarm sounded. And he couldn't see one.

'It's Rowan's key. He left it with me before he flew to Guernsey,' she answered, studying them with light-blue tired eyes, not surprising given the fact she'd received tragic news about her mother-in-law, thought Horton. He noted that her skin was pitted from scars on her high forehead and around the cheeks, the legacy of acne, he guessed, and although she couldn't be more than in her mid-twenties, there were fine lines stretched at the corners of her eyes and mouth, which, coupled with her tan, to him betrayed the fact that she spent a lot of time in the open air. The logo on her fleece jacket confirmed that: Winner Watersports. Horton knew it. He'd seen the hut set back off the beach not far from his marina and close to the swimming baths and caravan holiday centre at the eastern end of Southsea promenade, although he couldn't recall seeing Gina Lyster there. But then he hadn't really looked that closely, just run past it during the summer months.

She headed for the stairs. Horton was glad. He didn't use lifts unless he had to.

'I'm not sure what you expect to find,' she said over her shoulder. Horton noted she spoke well without any accent, local or otherwise. 'But I guess you have to look. Is there any more news?' She was understandably anxious.

Horton avoided answering. Instead he asked her the same question Guilbert had asked her husband. 'Do you know why your mother-in-law was travelling to Guernsey?'

'No. She never said she was going away, not even on Saturday when we had dinner with her here. I suppose she could have business associates there but she's never mentioned them.'

'What did she do?' asked Cantelli.

'She was a freelance translator. She spoke fluent French, German and Spanish.'

'What type of clients?'

They came out on to a landing. There were several doors leading off it.

'All sorts. Doctors, lawyers, accountants, brokers, dealers in jewellery, gems, art, the pharmaceutical companies. She travelled a lot to conferences, seminars, exhibitions and trade shows until Dennis died. Since then she's been busy selling their apartment and buying this one but she did say she was keen to get back to work. Not that she needed to financially but I guess she missed the buzz of it. She always liked to have a lot on the go.'

Horton wondered if Evelyn Lyster had perhaps been intending to visit a client in Guernsey, only she'd had nothing on her to indicate that, and there was the fact she'd had no luggage and no one had yet come forward or called her phone to ask where she was.

'How long has your mother-in-law lived here?' he asked.

'She bought the apartment last September and moved in in October. The lounge is through here.' Gina Lyster indicated the door in front of them.

It was a wide, open-plan living area with an ultra-modern kitchen beyond. To the right, three steps led up into a small dining area surrounded by floor-to-ceiling windows on three sides with French doors on the fourth giving on to a small balcony. There were also wide windows in the lounge which gave splendid views across the Solent to the Isle of Wight. Everything in the lounge looked brand new – a fact Gina Lyster confirmed.

'Evelyn put a lot of time and energy into decorating and furnishing this. She got rid of everything in the apartment which she and Dennis lived in in Clarence Parade overlooking the common. I guess she wanted to start afresh.'

And obliterate everything that reminded her of her husband? wondered Horton, including any photographs of him, although there might be some in her bedroom. Perhaps the relationship had been strained.

'She also helped me and Rowan to get the business up and running – Winner Watersports. We started it last March in order to catch the main summer period. Rowan is a European champion windsurfer,' she said proudly. 'I've done a fair bit myself and I paddle board. We give

92

tuition to groups and individuals and hire out equipment.' Her eyes swept the room before coming back to Horton. 'We'll miss her. Rowan's devastated. I can't really believe it. Rowan saw her, you know, in the mortuary.' She gave a slight shudder. 'I wished he'd let me go with him but he said someone had to stay here and see to things in the business. Not that there is much to see to at this time of year. What would you like to do here?'

Cantelli answered, 'We'll just take a look around, if you don't mind.'

'Of course.' Her mobile phone rang. She glanced at it. 'It's Rowan.' She stepped back on to the landing to take the call.

Cantelli left to check out the bedrooms while Horton gazed around the living room. It was expensively furnished and plainly decorated in white with splashes of red in the cushions and curtains, and in a rug as well as on the tasteful modern paintings which even to his untrained eye looked very expensive. The kitchen units were also white with a black granite top, with the latest kitchen gadgets on display. It reminded him of the Clements' kitchen. Everything was clean and neat. Had Evelyn cleaned the apartment herself or, like the Clements, did she engage cleaners, he wondered, crossing the room and flicking through the magazines on the low, glass-topped coffee table. They were a mixture of fashion and home furnishing; three were dated for the month of January, another February. He couldn't see any books. There was a large plasma television on the wall.

He crossed to the kitchen and opened the fridge and freezer. Both were well stocked and there was milk, cheese, butter and eggs in the fridge. There was also a loaf of bread, opened, in another cupboard. She certainly hadn't intended to be away for long. Guilbert said she hadn't booked a return flight or ferry home so why had she left food here? And why not buy a return ticket?

The cupboards were neatly stacked with crockery and in one he found six cup flasks of the same kind that she'd had on her. He turned as Gina Lyster entered. She looked upset – understandably so, given the circumstances.

'Rowan wants me to contact the undertakers to arrange to bring Evelyn home. He's hoping the coroner will issue a burial certificate tomorrow at the inquest. It's tough on him having only just lost his father, and now this.'

'Was Evelyn upset over her husband's death?' asked Horton as Cantelli returned with a slight shake of his head.

'She couldn't understand why he did it. None of us could.'

'Did what?' asked Cantelli.

'Dennis killed himself. Didn't you know?'

Horton hid his surprise. 'How?'

'He walked into the sea. We don't know where but his body was found by Ryde Pier on the Isle of Wight. He didn't leave a note or, if he did, it got washed out to sea or blew away.'

Her hands played with her phone agitatedly. She seemed less at ease than previously. Whether that was because of what she was saying or her phone conversation with her husband, Horton didn't know. He guessed the latter. Perhaps they'd argued on the phone or snapped at each other under the strain of the bereavement.

She continued, 'Dennis was depressed because he'd been made redundant and he couldn't get another job. He was fifty-eight and companies want younger people, especially in his line of work. He was a civil engineer but he was hardly ever at home. He spent most of his time working overseas.'

And suddenly there had been no more travelling, no more work, no sense of purpose and no company, just an apartment. Dennis had been stuck at home and that's when depression had set in.

'Do you know if your mother-in-law kept any personal papers or any correspondence here?' Horton hadn't found any and neither had Cantelli by that slight shake of his head.

Gina looked around as though searching for them. 'No idea.'

'Could they be with her solicitor along with her will?'

'They could be. Yes, I guess so. It's Makepeace in the High Street, just around the corner.'

Horton knew them. 'Did your mother-in-law use a computer?'

'She had a laptop.' She gazed around. 'It's not here unless it's in her bedroom.'

'It's not,' answered Cantelli.

'Then she must have taken it with her.'

But it hadn't been found with her body. Maybe she'd ditched it in the sea. Perhaps she had committed suicide after all and the toxicology tests would show that because the single ticket, the lack of luggage, the absence of anything personal on her phone and now her missing laptop computer, and the fact her husband had killed himself seemed to be all pointing to that. Perhaps when the whirl of purchasing and decorating this apartment had worn off she'd gazed around it and felt lonely and depressed. According to Gina, Evelyn Lyster had worked with doctors and the pharmaceutical industry, which could mean she knew where and how to obtain drugs. But why do it on the Guernsey ferry?

'Does anyone else have access to the apartment?' Horton asked as they made their way down the stairs.

'Not unless Evelyn gave someone a key. We came in through her private entrance. There is another apartment on the other side of the tower but that also has its own entrance.'

'Would it have been normal for Evelyn to have taken a ferry instead of a plane?'

'She'd travel by either but she didn't much care for flying. If she went to Europe on business or for a holiday she'd go by train, or by ferry and train. If it was America or South Africa she'd fly and then she always travelled business class or first class.'

They stepped outside. 'Your mother-in-law had a driving licence but no car.'

'She used to drive but after an accident two years ago decided to give it up. She'd been held up in a horrendous traffic jam on the A34 heading south towards the M3, which was blocked because of an accident, so as soon as she could get off it she took the A272 across country to Petersfield where she came off the road on a sharp bend. You see, she'd been stuck for a very long time without a drink and because she suffered from low blood pressure she passed out at the wheel. Fortunately the motorist behind her saw it happen and called the ambulance which arrived very quickly. She was very lucky not to have been seriously injured. In fact, she had hardly a scratch on her.'

'Is that why she carried a cup flask?'

'Yes. She now has . . . had a bit of a phobia about always making sure she had a flask made up with coffee to act as a stimulant.'

Hence the row of them in her cupboard and one of them on her when she had died. The flask had been empty so she'd obviously had a drink. The drop in her blood pressure couldn't have been caused from lack of fluids. But she could have taken drugs with the liquid.

Horton said that they might need to look around the apartment again.

'Why?' she asked, surprised.

'It's just routine.' He handed over his card. Cantelli did the same. They crossed the road, watched her climb in her sports car and drive away.

As they walked back to the car, Cantelli said, 'The bed was made up, the room clean and neat, and the same for the shower room. Looks like something out of a show home. No note and no personal correspondence. No laptop computer or any computer device. No landline, no book beside her bed and no photographs, not even of her husband or her son, and not a wedding picture in sight. You'd think she'd have some baby pictures of her boy, or one of the wedding.'

'Perhaps she does but stored elsewhere, although I shouldn't think with her solicitor. Or perhaps she had them on her laptop. Maybe she didn't go in for photographs.'

Cantelli looked dubious.

Climbing in the car, Horton said, 'She seems to have stripped back her life since her husband died. Get hold of the coroner's report on Dennis Lyster's death. I'm curious, that's all,' he added to Cantelli's quizzical look.

'Her clothes are good quality and expensive. The same for her shoes. She's got six pairs. She's very neat. Nice underwear. Not your sexy stuff, but tasteful and newish.' Cantelli started up and reversed out of the space, adding, 'I may be wrong, but to me she didn't have enough clothes and shoes. Not that Charlotte's got stacks of stuff, but there's her summer clothes stored away in a cupboard and a bunch of clothes in another cupboard that she might wear again and probably never will. And even Charlotte's got more than six pairs of shoes on a sergeant's low pay.'

Horton ruminated over Cantelli's remarks as they headed into the centre of the city. 'It sounds very much as though she has another property where she keeps more clothes, her personal belongings and possibly a computer. A property which her son and daughter-in-law know nothing about.'

'In Guernsey?'

'Looks possible, although Guilbert can't find any trace of her owning one there and it's not an easy commute if she doesn't like flying. But given that was where she was heading maybe she has and he hasn't found it yet. Or she's living with someone there who hasn't come forward.'

'Because he's married. That might be why she didn't mention it to her son.'

'And it could explain why Dennis Lyster became so depressed that he took his own life – he'd discovered that his wife had been having an affair. I'll ask Guilbert if he's checked whether she's previously booked on flights from Southampton, or the ferries from both Poole and Portsmouth.'

Cantelli pulled into the station car park and silenced the engine but Horton made no attempt to alight.

'OK, so if we rule out suicide, she sets off to meet her lover in Guernsey but not to stay with him for long because she hadn't cleared out the fridge. Why not?'

'She forgot?'

But Horton shook his head. 'That doesn't seem to fit with what we saw. She seemed very fastidious. And why buy a single ticket – why not a return?' He answered his own question. 'Because she intended returning with him.' And Horton knew there were two ways she could have done so, apart from using the ferry or commercial aeroplanes. 'Lover boy might own a private plane or a boat. I'll get Elkins to circulate her picture to the staff in the marinas in case she ever came back with him on a boat. When you've got a chance get on to the private airfields – Goodwood near Chichester, Sandown and Bembridge on the Isle of Wight – see if anyone recognizes her flying in with someone.'

A figure loomed large beside Horton and a fist tapped none too gently on the window. Horton let it down.

'Is this a private meeting or can anyone join in?' Uckfield growled.

Horton climbed out. Cantelli followed suit.

'Fingerprints have got a result on our dead man.'

'That was quick,' Horton said with surprise. But perhaps not if he'd had a previous conviction, which Uckfield confirmed.

'He's not an actor and he's not an undercover cop. But he was a vagrant. He's also an ex-con. He's got convictions for drink driving, being drunk and disorderly, vagrancy and assault. Once on a uniformed officer and twice for fights, the last one when he smashed a bottle in a man's face and was in possession of a knife, which he fully intended to use, and which copped him a custodial sentence of six years. He served four years, during which time he dried out, took a degree in neuro-linguistic programming, gained qualifications as a life coach and found himself a lucrative business as some kind of motivational guru giving public talks about changing your life.'

'That's where I've seen him.' Cantelli clicked his fingers, delighted. 'There was an article about him in the local paper about a year ago. He was holding a public lecture in the Guildhall.'

'Wish you'd remembered before,' Uckfield grunted. 'His name's Peter Freedman. Come on.'

He threw Horton his car keys. 'Let's see if anything in Mr Freedman's flat can tell us why he decided to dress up like a tramp and get himself shot. You're driving. I'm likely to sneeze and blow us off the road.'

'Thanks,' muttered Horton.

Eight

The area where Freedman's flat was located was far more impressive than Horton had expected. It was a tree-lined, narrow, twisting street set back off the seafront, comprising of large Victorian villas that had once housed the influential, rich and professional people of Portsmouth, and still did judging by the expensive motors parked in front of some of the properties. He counted two Bentleys, a Porsche Cayenne and a Ferrari, the last of which caused Uckfield to cast an envious glance before he sneezed loudly. Horton had made sure to keep his window open in the vain hope he could avoid catching Uckfield's cold but Uckfield's window was securely shut. Horton didn't rate his chances of escaping the germs. In fact, he thought the entire incident suite would probably go down with colds.

On the way, Horton had briefed Uckfield about the Clements' robbery, expressing his view that he believed it was an insurance job, which meant the pistols were stored away somewhere, probably in the house or in the boot of the Mercedes and,

101

by the descriptions of them, it seemed unlikely they could have been made to fire. Which, worryingly, meant someone on their patch had a gun and was prepared to use it. He asked if the house-to-house in Ferry Road or the press briefing had yielded anything more on the murder of Peter Freedman.

'Sod all,' was Uckfield's answer. 'And we're still waiting on Dr Clayton's report. The bus driver's been interviewed but she doesn't remember Freedman getting on the bus and she didn't see him walk down Ferry Road. By the time she reached the houseboats she had no passengers on board and nobody got on the bus at the ferry. She doesn't remember seeing anyone hanging around or any cars parked up by the houseboats either.'

Horton had anticipated as much. But it was disappointing. 'He could have walked along the seafront from here to the houseboats. It's about two and a half miles and he'd have been used to tramping.' But Horton didn't think they'd pick up any sightings of Freedman on the CCTV cameras along the promenade because the bad weather would have obscured the images. 'Where are his keys?' he asked, pulling up in front of a set of electronic gates outside the large house that had been converted into apartments. 'They weren't found on the body.'

'Maybe the killer took them.'

And that meant they might find the flat ransacked.

A patrol car waiting further down the road moved off to come behind them as Uckfield pressed the intercom.

102

'Does he own or rent this?' Horton asked.

'Owns it, according to the council rates department.'

'On a mortgage?'

'Trueman's checking.'

'Life coaches must do very well.'

'It's all the crap they spout, filling people with the idea that with the flick of an eyelid they can turn their lives around.'

'He seems to have turned his around.'

Uckfield grunted.

Horton said, 'Neuro-linguistic programming isn't just about body language, it's about the way we think and how that affects our behaviour and actions.'

'It's all bollocks.'

Horton smiled. 'It's what we were told on those courses.'

'Yeah, and a waste of bloody time and money they were too,' scoffed Uckfield, again pressing the intercom for Freedman's apartment. 'Trying to tell us that the nasty bastards we have to deal with are just highly creative individuals and if we were only to see that we'd understand them better. I don't want to understand them; I just want to lock them up. It's a load of pseudo-science shit which some poor sods believe in. And, judging by this place and Freedman's website, there's quite a few of the suckers who do. His company's called Ascend. Trueman's getting the background on it and his finances but Freedman's mobile number was on the website. The line's dead.'

'Like Freedman,' muttered Horton. So where was his phone?

There was no answer to Uckfield's summons at the intercom. 'Looks as though he lives alone,' Uckfield said, making it sound as if there was something obscene or abnormal in that.

'Perhaps his partner, *if* he has one, is working.' But no one had come forward to say he was missing.

Uckfield pressed the buzzer of apartment number one and this time got a disembodied female voice. Uckfield assumed his most sugary tone. Horton wondered if he'd remain so sweet if the female turned out to be seventy. There was a camera over the gates and as Uckfield introduced himself, he held up his warrant card so that the woman could see it. That and the patrol car behind them persuaded her to buzz them in. She had the main entrance door open before they had climbed out. PCs Keating and Allen followed them, Keating carrying the ramrod.

'Is this a raid?' she asked excitedly rather than alarmed as she let them in. Horton took in the luxuriously decorated wide hall with its sweeping staircase, brass stair rods, highly polished brass rail, pale green carpet and an impressive chandelier. To the right of the stairs was the kind of lift that Horton only ever saw in television dramas set in the 1930s. Not that he watched TV – he didn't have one on the boat and he didn't miss it – but the programmes he'd seen when he'd lived at home with Catherine and Emma.

'Should it be a raid?' Uckfield asked. Horton put his gaze back on the lady in front of them. She was well into her seventies, slender, well dressed, well spoken and with a distinct twinkle in her eyes.

'Not unless one of my neighbours has done something illegal.'

'Would they have?'

'You never know.' She smiled. 'But I think you'll find us a very law abiding lot, if not a little boring.'

'And you are?' Horton asked, also smiling.

'Mrs Stella Nugent. I've lived here since the building was refurbished five years ago. It's very quiet and handy for the shops, especially John Lewis, just around the corner.'

Into Horton's mind flashed the picture of the dead man's boxer shorts and Gaye's remark that they had been bought from John Lewis. But then there were a lot of John Lewis's around the country.

Mrs Nugent was still in full flow. 'There are only ten apartments here, two on each floor, so it's quite select and most of us have been here since it was refurbished. I was the first in.'

'And Mr Peter Freedman?' Horton interjected as Uckfield shifted impatiently while Keating and Allen stood silently behind them.

'He moved in, now let me see, yes, it must be two years or perhaps eighteen months ago. That's right, because he bought the apartment from poor Mr Randall. He had a heart attack right where you're standing. Dropped down dead, just like that, and only seventy-two. A lovely man, so kind and very polite.'

'Who? Mr Randall?' interrupted Uckfield.

'No.' She beamed at Uckfield. Horton thought she was almost flirting with him. She gave a small laugh and said, 'Mr Freedman.'

'When did you last see him?' Horton asked.

'Tuesday morning, I think it was. Yes. He was walking across the driveway. I looked out of the window.'

'How was he dressed?'

'Smartly, as usual,' she answered, looking quite bemused by the question.

Uckfield threw Horton a slightly impatient glance that had a hint of exasperation in it. 'He'd hardly have gone out dressed as a tramp,' he muttered nasally.

Stella Nugent looked confused. 'Is there something wrong? Has Mr Freedman had an accident?'

Horton broke the news that he'd been found dead but didn't say how, where or the circumstances surrounding it, but she'd been listening to the news. Her eyes widened with surprise.

'The man found by the houseboats. Is that poor Mr Freedman?'

Horton said it was.

She looked sorrowful but Horton saw the gleam in her eyes that betrayed her excitement at such calamitous news. He said an officer would call on her later to take her statement and police officers would be speaking to the other residents. She returned to her flat, where no doubt she'd be on the phone in an instant to her friends and family, relaying the news.

Uckfield pressed the button for the lift.

Horton said, 'Freedman could have left his flat when it was dark. No one would have seen him dressed as a tramp.'

'He'd have been taking a chance going down in the lift or the stairs and crossing the hall.'

106

'Not if he said he was going to a fancy dress party or a tarts and tramps ball.' And if one of the occupants had seen him they'd be able to confirm that. 'He might have used the fire escape. There are CCTV cameras in the shopping precinct and there's a camera over the front gates – we might pick up a sighting of him.'

Uckfield removed a large handkerchief from the pocket of his trousers and sneezed into it, then blew his nose loudly. The lift arrived. Uckfield stepped inside it. Horton had no intention of joining him. Quickly, he said, 'I'll meet you at the top.'

'Me too,' Allen rapidly agreed, stepping out, leaving a startled and wrong-footed Keating to travel in the lift with Uckfield's germs.

Horton arrived on the landing just after the lift, Allen a little later and breathing more heavily. Uckfield was blowing his nose noisily as he stepped out and Keating was looking resigned to the fact he'd probably end up with the Super's cold.

'Go on then,' Uckfield growled at Keating. 'Don't just stand there like you're holding your cock.'

'Chance would be a fine thing if it was this big,' Keating muttered, and with one swift movement the door sprang open. Horton asked Allen to find out if there was anyone at home in the flat opposite while Keating remained on the door.

'Did Freedman drive?' Horton asked, stepping into a small lobby, noting there was no post on the mat. There hadn't been in Evelyn Lyster's flat either. He wondered if Freedman had changed his clothes in a car.

107

'There's no record of him with the Driver and Vehicle Licensing Agency.'

But he could have owned a car without registering it and been driving it illegally. It might be parked behind the building or perhaps he kept it elsewhere.

The carpeted hall gave on to two doors. Only silence greeted them. The door on the left opened into a cloakroom. Two coats hung on hooks: a man's overcoat and a waterproof jacket. Uckfield put his hands in the pockets and shook his head. 'Empty.' He pushed open the door ahead and they entered a modern, clean kitchen which led through to a dining room and into the lounge. There was a door beyond, which Horton assumed must lead to a bedroom and a bathroom. The floor was covered throughout with good quality light oak. A table and four chairs in the dining area were also modern and light oak. Beyond, in the lounge, was a TV fixed to the wall, a large three-seater sofa covered in a striped fabric and an oak-style coffee table in front of it. The windows to Horton's right were draped with blue-and-green-striped Roman blinds and looked out over the front of the building.

Uckfield strode to the door ahead. 'He's got a study area here,' he called back. 'And a computer.'

Horton joined him. It was an inner hallway which gave on to a bedroom and, as he had suspected, a bathroom.

Next to the desk were some built-in cupboards. Uckfield opened them. Inside were some books on neuro-linguistic programming and personal motivation, the sort that told you how you could change your life in sixty seconds. 'Took Freedman six years to do it,' Uckfield grunted.

'Four,' corrected Horton.

'Still bloody longer than sixty seconds.'

There were a couple of lever-arch files. Above the desk, pushed up against the wall, were some framed certificates that declared Peter Freedman had qualified in neuromuscular programming, had various coaching qualifications and had completed a course in mindfulness.

'What the hell's that?'

'Something to do with focusing on the present rather than the past,' muttered Horton, thinking he'd be a prime candidate for that. 'It's said to help people with mental ill health and those who want greater well-being.'

'Can it cure the common cold? Because if it can't it can sod off, along with all the other airy-fairy claptrap.'

'Maybe the power of positive thought can stop you from getting one.'

Uckfield snorted. 'Then I must have been thinking about Wonder Boy the day the germs decided to attack me. Looks like someone loved Freedman – there's two messages flashing on his answer machine. Let's send out some positive thoughts and hope it's the killer confessing to having shot the poor bugger and leaving his name, telephone number and address.'

With a latex-covered finger, Horton pressed the play button.

'Peter, it's Glyn Ashmead. Sorry I missed you yesterday. I had a conference in Southampton which went on for ever and ended up in drinks in the pub. There's someone I'd like to discuss with you. Give me a call when you've got a moment.'

Horton explained to Uckfield's baffled scowl, 'Ashmead runs Gravity, the homeless charity, around the corner from the station.' He'd had occasion to visit it many times in the course of investigations and he'd referred people to it. Glyn Ashmead was very well-respected by both his customers and the professionals he liaised with. Given Freedman's background, Horton could see the connection between the two men but not the exact nature of it. They'd get that, though.

The second message played. 'Hi, Peter, it's Rosie Pierce. Just wanted to say a huge thank you for everything. It seems to be working. I'm having a great month, my sales are up by thirty-five per cent and the boss is happy. Buy you a drink or two. Give me a call.'

'Sounds like he was on a winner there,' said Uckfield. 'Could be a disgruntled client who killed him, who didn't get the life-changing results they were expecting.'

'Why would he dress up as a vagrant to meet a former client?'

'No bloody idea. You take the bedroom and the bog; I'll look through these files.'

The double bed was made up. The room was immaculately tidy, a habit perhaps Freedman had picked up in prison. Horton crossed to the built-in cupboards where he found a row of very good quality suits, some ties and some casual clothes, again good quality, and some designer labels. In the drawers were half-a-dozen shirts of varying

110

colours, socks and boxer shorts, all neatly folded and arranged. Most of these, he could see from checking the labels, were from John Lewis. There was nothing, he noted, from the Savile Row tailor, Gieves and Hawkes.

Swiftly he searched among the clothes for any personal items and correspondence but didn't find anything. The drawers weren't removable so there couldn't be anything stashed under them or at the back.

He turned his attention to the bedside cabinets. He found a pair of shop-bought reading glasses, a packet of over-the-counter painkillers and little else. The window faced the rear of the building and he looked out on to the fire escape to his left and down on to the waste bins and car park, which contained four cars. They'd check the registration numbers with the occupants. Directly opposite was another block of flats – modern ones this time with some windows facing this way – but given that it had probably been dark when Freedman had left here, Horton didn't think anyone would have seen him climbing down the fire escape. There was no view to the sea as there had been in Evelyn Lyster's apartment.

The shower room was spotlessly clean like the rest of the flat. As he briefly examined Freedman's shaving gear and toiletries he could hear Uckfield's laboured breathing, occasional sneeze and nose blowing as he skimmed through Freedman's files. This wasn't a crime scene so there had been no need to preserve it, but Horton didn't think it helped having Uckfield's DNA spattered over everything. He was certain Uckfield would get SOCO in here because Freedman's killer might have visited him at some stage.

He joined Uckfield in the small office area. 'Anything?'

'No client list, no blackmail letters, no death threats. Sod all except some lecture notes.'

'Where would he have changed into those clothes if not here?'

'A public toilet?'

'Possible. And he stashed his other clothes inside it waiting to retrieve them later, but he wouldn't have left his wallet and keys.'

'The killer took them.'

'But the killer hasn't been here unless he's the neatest one we've ever seen. Or he came specifically to look for something, removed it then left. You'll have to get SOCO in.'

'You don't need to tell me how to do my job,' Uckfield said bad-temperedly.

But maybe Horton did. 'Why don't you go home, Steve? You're clearly not well.'

'I'm fine. OK?' thundered Uckfield before breaking into a coughing fit.

'OK.' Horton held up his hands in capitulation.

'I'll ask Dennings to instigate a search of all the public lavatories in Portsmouth,' Uckfield croaked.

'Where is Dennings, by the way?' Horton asked, following Uckfield back through the lounge to the kitchen. He'd wondered why Dennings hadn't joined Uckfield here, or had been sent instead of coming himself, although Uckfield had said earlier that Dennings and Bliss were working the investigation from the incident suite.

'At the houseboat. Trueman finally got the information out of the rates office. That old wreck is owned by a Mrs Cecily Thomas. She's in her mid-eighties, lives alone and seems to have all her marbles, according to Dennings. He's sent someone round with a picture of Freedman taken off his website to ask if she recognizes him. She gave Dennings the key to the houseboat. Took her an age to find it and he's over there now with a unit. Packman also said he'd meet Dennings there. Dennings will re-interview him and see if the name means anything to him.'

Horton pulled open the kitchen cupboards. They were clean, neatly arranged with crockery, cutlery and glasses and the food cupboards were well stocked.

'Maybe the killer is someone he knew while a vagrant,' he said. 'Or while in prison?'

'Trueman's getting hold of his prison record.'

The fridge was also well stocked. 'No notes, correspondence or photographs,' Horton said, turning to gaze around the open-plan room. He thought it very much like Evelyn Lyster's apartment in that respect, but then many people kept their pictures on their phones and computer devices these days rather than on display or stashed away in photo albums. And given the former lifestyle of Freedman, he wouldn't have had any belongings from his past.

Uckfield said, 'I'll get all these files bagged up and taken back for a proper examination and the same for the computer.' He detailed Keating to call the locksmith and to wait for a scene of crime officer to arrive, then to bag up everything from the study area. Allen reported that the occupant of the opposite flat was out.

Uckfield addressed Horton. 'I'll send Marsden and Somerfield over. They can oversee things this end and start interviewing the residents.' He stepped into the lift. Horton said he'd meet him on the ground floor and took the stairs. This time he beat the lift and Uckfield emerged with his phone clamped to his ear. By the time they reached the car Uckfield had come off the phone.

'Freedman's registered as self-employed. For the last three years he's filed a tax return that shows his income steadily increasing. The first year he earned twenty-eight thousand pounds; the second year he doubled that and last year he declared earnings of seventy-three thousand pounds.'

Horton gave a low whistle. 'Must have been damn good,' he said with surprise. And perhaps on that kind of track record he had been given a mortgage to buy the apartment.

'I told you these suckers will pay for any kind of twaddle,' Uckfield said, climbing in.

'Should have gone into business ourselves.'

Uckfield snorted. 'All Dennings has found in the houseboat are insects, woodworm, damp and dust. Nothing in Packman's houseboat either. And Packman swears blind he's never seen or heard of Freedman but we'll see if he shows up on Freedman's computer.'

'I wouldn't have thought a self-employed carpenter would be able to afford him.'

'You never know – he might have been desperate to change his life.'

114

'To what?'

'A plumber?'

Horton smiled and eased the car through the open electronic gates. 'Did it say on his website where he held coaching sessions for his clients?'

'No. Could have been in his flat or perhaps he has an office somewhere or hired an office by the hour. His tax return will tell us if he claimed it as a business expense.'

'I'll talk to Glyn Ashmead. I know him.'

Uckfield's phone rang. He listened. 'We'll be there in five minutes.'

'That was Bliss. Dr Clayton's finished the autopsy.'

Horton thought Uckfield's five minutes was rather ambitious. It would take at least twenty to travel from the southernmost tip of the island to the hospital on the hill slopes on the northern edge, and that was barring any hold ups. But Uckfield reached into the glove pocket. Horton anticipated him. He dropped a gear.

'No point in having a blue light if you can't use it,' said Uckfield.

Nine

'The victim was alive when shot as opposed to being unconscious or already dead having been killed by another method,' Gaye announced in her small office off the mortuary. Horton had taken the seat opposite Gaye, who had divested herself of her mortuary garb and was wearing her customary jeans and T-shirt, while Uckfield stood leaning against the filing cabinet. Gaye had ordered him to keep his distance, saying that on Friday she was travelling to Denmark to attend an international conference on forensic research and technology and would be tacking a week's holiday on the end of it to visit friends in Europe; she didn't want to be infected by his germs. Horton felt a stab of disappointment that she wouldn't be around but then he'd probably be busy on this case.

'Let me explain,' she continued. 'As a bullet perforates the skin it scrapes the epidermis, creating an abrasion around the bullet hole. Because the abrasions in the victim are reddish brown, that indicates he was alive when he was shot as opposed to being already dead, because then the abrasion would have been yellow, tan or greyish brown. The entrance wound is round with a margin of abrasion surrounding it of uniformed thickness, which means the bullet penetrated the skin nose on rather than at an angle.'

Her eyes rested on Horton and connected, causing his pulse to skip a couple of beats, and then swivelled to Uckfield.

'As to range of fire, well, the shape of the entry wound, the stippling – a pattern of tiny abrasions in the skin around the wound – and my examin-ation of the clothes, matching the tears in it to the entry and exit wounds, and the absence of soot on them indicate he was shot at intermediate range, between two feet and two and a half feet, possibly three feet.'

'I'd call that close range.' Uckfield sniffed noisily.

'Not as close as the muzzle of the gun being placed against the skin or the clothes,' Gaye answered. 'He was shot face on while standing.'

She left a pause while they assimilated this. Horton visualized Freedman standing in front of his killer, perhaps looking down at the gun – shocked, terrified, or perhaps thinking it was a joke and feeling confident he could talk the killer out of his proposed action using his neuro-linguistic programming techniques. Then he pictured his expression turning to astonishment and horror as the gun was fired.

Gaye continued, 'As a bullet moves through a body it crushes and shreds the tissue in its path while flinging outward the surrounding tissue, creating a temporary cavity which then collapses, contracts and disappears, and it is the crushed and shredded tissue and any marks against the bone that gives us the path of the bullet and possible clues as to what kind of bullet. However, in the case of handgun bullets, there is very little internal disturbance and this is the case here. To cause significant injuries to an organ a handgun bullet must strike that structure directly. This is different with a high-velocity rifle bullet. So I can confirm that he was killed with a handgun.'

'What type of handgun?' Uckfield impatiently demanded.

'I'll come on to that shortly. The exit wound again confirms he was shot while standing and not while lying on the ground or sitting. But the fact that there is an exit wound means there is no bullet in the body to retrieve.'

'Great,' Uckfield scoffed. Horton knew exactly what he was thinking: they couldn't tell which weapon had been used, and that was a blow. The bullet hadn't been retrieved from the scene either, but how could it when the area was covered with stones? They could hardly dig up the entire beach.

'But I can tell you what we do have,' Gaye continued, shifting position and sitting slightly forward across her desk, her green eyes shining. 'We've taken internal X-rays to ascertain the type of ammunition and weapon used. It doesn't give us a great deal but it does tell us that he wasn't killed by a metal jacket bullet because there are traces of lead, and the pattern also indicates it was conical, so we're looking for a weapon that can fire conical-shaped lead bullets. I contacted the ballistics expert who has the pictures of the stolen pistols DC Walters sent to him. Percussion revolvers like the ones stolen have been involved in homicides and in some suicides in the USA and here in the UK.'

Horton interjected, 'Even antique ones.'

'Yes. Percussion weapons appeared in the early nineteenth century and became obsolete with the introduction of metallic cartridges. Until recently they've mainly been of historical interest, collected by enthusiasts, but the ballistics expert confirmed my findings. In the last ten to fifteen years there has been an increased interest in them and in replicas. Most are manufactured abroad.'

118

Uckfield broke in, 'You mean they're making new guns based on these old designs?'

'Yes.'

'Do we know if the Clements' stolen guns are genuine antiques?' Uckfield fired at Horton.

He didn't. 'We haven't asked to see any provenance.'

'Then do so,' he growled.

Horton saw Gaye's eyebrows rise slightly. She continued, 'Many of these guns are available as flintlock and percussion muskets, rifles, shot-guns and percussion revolvers like the ones your man had in his collection, but I can't say for certain that the victim was killed by one of the stolen guns. The ballistics expert might be able to give you more on that in due course.'

Horton wasn't certain now that they were looking at insurance fraud. But as Gaye had said, Freedman could have been shot with a replica antique pistol.

She said, 'In homicides the highest percentage of fatalities by gunshot wounds are caused by those to the head while a quarter are to the heart and aorta. In our victim, it's the latter.'

Horton interjected. 'So not a professional killer because he would have shot Freedman in the head?'

'Not necessarily,' she corrected him. 'The killer might not have been the given the opportunity to do that so he went for the next best thing – the heart. The victim was not only alive when he was shot but he didn't die immediately.'

Uckfield tossed her a horrified stare. 'You mean he didn't die where he was found?'

'The victim can incur a fatal gun wound but still be capable of physical activity. In fact, he can run hundreds of yards before dying.'

'Great,' Uckfield cried before breaking into a coughing fit.

'Would you like some water, Detective Superintendent?'

He waved an arm at her to decline.

Horton said, 'Do you have any idea of how far he could have got after being shot?'

'No. And I'm not saying the victim definitely did this but it's a possibility that has to be considered.'

'Even if he was shot in the heart?' Uckfield croaked disbelievingly.

'Yes, an individual can still function for a short time.'

'Dean's functioned for a long time without one,' muttered Uckfield.

Gaye said, 'It's the oxygen supply to the brain that's the critical factor in survival and time of death tests have proved that an individual can remain conscious and can function, he can run or walk for ten seconds, before collapsing.'

Uckfield addressed Horton. 'We need to test that out.'

'Hope that doesn't mean you're going to shoot anyone,' Gaye said.

'I could think of a few to nominate.'

Horton turned to Gaye. 'How fit was Freedman?'

'Not bad for a recovering alcoholic but even if he hadn't been very fit the instinct for survival could have taken over and spurred him to almost superhuman activity in the hope he could seek help in time to save him.'

'And the killer let him run or stagger about rather than firing again.'

'The killer might not have had time to reload and fire the pistol or he might not have had the ammunition to do so. Or perhaps he thought it unnecessary because he knew that the victim would die.'

Gaye was right. Horton knew the killer would rather use the time to get away.

'I don't have access to his full medical records but Sergeant Trueman sent me over Freedman's prison medical file. He underwent a full programme to help him recover from alcohol abuse and responded well. Fortunately he undertook it before his liver was irrevocably destroyed. And the liver can make a remarkable recovery if the disease hasn't gone too far.'

'Could he have killed himself?' Horton asked.

Uckfield looked at him as though he'd lost the plot. Maybe he had but he still thought the question worth asking.

'There is no gun residue on his hands, although the rain could have destroyed that, but if he had killed himself then he'd have pressed the gun against his clothes and it would have shown up. And usually, although not always, suicides chose the head or mouth.'

'And there was no gun found with the body,' added Uckfield pointedly.

'Someone could have picked it up, thinking it was valuable.'

'No, this is murder,' Uckfield said firmly. Horton was inclined to agree, he just thought it worth exploring all possibilities, which was what Guilbert was doing with Evelyn Lyster's death, although that was the other way around – it had been natural causes but it looked like suicide. Horton was beginning to wonder if in fact it was murder – something he knew must be crossing Guilbert's mind. Could she have been given a drug before boarding the ferry? Maybe he should check out the CCTV footage from the port? But why kill her and why did someone kill Freedman? He asked if they had a next of kin in his prison file.

'Not unless he changed it since being released from prison. His records state that he wished to leave his body to medical science. A local solicitor is named as his executor – Framptons.'

The legal firm that had handled Horton's divorce.

Uckfield said that a member of his team was checking with the General Register Office to find out if Freedman had ever been married and if he had children.

Gaye said, 'I'll let you have my full report and ballistics will hopefully give you more on the bullet and the gun.'

Uckfield hauled himself away from the prop of the cabinet, blowing his nose. As he did so, Gaye rose and began to spray the air behind him. 'Antiseptic spray,' she explained to Horton. He thought they could do with some of that in the incident suite.

As they headed down the corridor to the exit, Horton said, 'The Clements say they were in on Tuesday night when Freedman was shot but there's no one to corroborate that. The guns were missing on Monday when they returned, uniform can confirm that, but we've only got Vivian Clements' word that there were no other pistols in the house. But why report the robbery if one of them intended killing Freedman with an antique pistol? Clements could easily have done the deed or handed the gun to an accomplice and then put it back in his collection.'

'Maybe he thought if he reported it stolen it would make him look as though he was in the clear, just like when someone reports his car stolen and it's used in a raid, I know nothing about it, guv,' he said mockingly and coughed.

Yes, Clements was arrogant enough to believe the police were stupid and, from what he'd seen, Constance Clements was too timid to contradict her husband, certainly in his presence.

'Got any Panadol?'

'Not on me.'

'Stop at the nearest chemist.'

Horton did so. Uckfield returned with a large paper bag. It looked as though he'd bought every conceivable cold cure imaginable. He swallowed some painkillers and then put a strong throat lozenge in his mouth before lapsing into a silence punctuated by nose blowing, sniffing and coughing.

At the station, Horton made for the canteen, which thankfully had been spared recent police spending cuts. He bought a coffee, sandwiches, banana and a Kit Kat and returned to his office, wondering how long it would be before the axe fell on the canteen and they'd all end up buying food from a vending machine or a kebab takeaway down the road; the latter of which would please Walters, it being one of his favourite foods. He glanced into Bliss's office on the way to CID and breathed a sigh of relief that she wasn't there. She was still getting under Trueman's feet in the incident suite.

Walters greeted him with the news that the Clements had never made an insurance claim. 'And Trevor Lukein is not a thief.'

'Your view is based on what?'

'My gut.' Walters patted his rounded stomach.

'Oh, good, I'll tell the Clements that. I'm sure they'll be pleased,' Horton said facetiously, opening his sandwiches.

'But he doesn't like them.'

'Them?'

'Well, him. He says Vivian Clements is a pompous little prat. Well, OK, he didn't say that exactly, but that's the gist of it.'

'What did he say *exactly*?'

'That Mr Clements is particular to the point of fussiness and stands over Lukein while he services the alarm to make sure he's doing it properly. Clements doesn't speak, just watches and breathes heavily. Lukein says he's tried to engage him in conversation in the past, several times, but gave up when he got no response. In fact, Clements told Lukein, "You're not here to talk about the weather or the state of the country, you're here to do a job so get on with it".'

Cantelli looked up. 'Sounds about right from what we've seen of Vivian Clements.'

Walters nodded agreement. 'He struck me as a jumped-up little—'

'And what did Lukein have to say about Constance Clements?' Horton interrupted, biting into his egg and cress.

'Nice woman, apologizes for her old man. Looks embarrassed. Always offers him a cup of tea which Mr Clements disapproves of and which Lukein accepts just to get up Clements' nose.'

'Does Lukein go into the collection room?'

'Yes. He has to check the sensors in there. He says he's made some comments on the collection, you know, nice stuff and that sort of thing, but he only got a tart reply from Clements to do what he was paid to do. He remembers seeing the guns but as Clements wasn't forthcoming he didn't comment on them.'

'How often does he service the alarms?'

'Every six months. The last time was on the twenty-ninth of October as Clements claimed. But Hugh Treadware says Clements hasn't paid for it yet. He isn't a prompt payer. Treadware always has to chase but this time Clements is spinning it out even longer.'

'Financial troubles?' Horton mused.

Walters shrugged. 'His credit rating's OK. Perhaps he's just mean.'

'Check with the shipping line that they were actually on that cruise and returned on Monday. Contact the international port, ask them if they have any CCTV footage from Monday morning. If so, ask them to send it over.'

'You looking for the Clements disembarking?'

'No, I'm looking for Evelyn Lyster.'

'Why?'

125

'Because someone could have put a drug in her flask.'

'They're hardly likely to do it in the port.'

'Just do it, Walters, and while you're at it contact the taxi companies and find out if any of them picked her up from her apartment.'

'What's she look like?'

Cantelli interjected, 'Guilbert's sent over a photograph her son gave him. It was taken at his wedding last March. I've circulated it to the private airfields.'

Horton finished off his sandwich and crossed to Cantelli's computer where he studied the picture. Evelyn Lyster was taller than the man beside her, who was obviously her husband, the late Dennis Lyster. He was thin, slightly hunched and looked older than his wife. Judging by the troubled look on his narrow features he was clearly ill at ease. Evelyn wasn't exactly beaming herself but she appeared confident. She was dressed elegantly in a cream and black outfit with a wide-brimmed cream hat with black trimming. Gina Lyster, in a cream, knee-length modern wedding dress, was beaming at her husband, a tanned, muscular man with cropped dark hair and a rather solemn expression.

Horton addressed Walters. 'Evelyn Lyster is the older woman and not the one in the wedding dress,' he explained, because with Walters you never knew. He gave him a description of what she'd been wearing when her body had been found.

Cantelli said, 'I briefed Inspector Guilbert about our visit to Evelyn Lyster's flat. He says Condor

126

ferries are checking to see if she booked on any of their sailings over the last couple of years and he's got an officer liaising with the airlines. Elkins has also got her photograph and is checking out the marinas. Guilbert's officers are doing the same in the marinas in Guernsey.'

While drinking his coffee, Horton briefed Cantelli and Walters about the autopsy results and what he and Uckfield had found at Freedman's flat.

'It was very like Evelyn Lyster's apartment in that there were very few personal items in it and no photographs.'

'Well, there are a few pictures on his website,' Cantelli said, jerking his head at the computer screen. He'd called it up while Horton had been talking. Horton leaned over. He found himself studying a slender man with slightly overlong dark hair streaked with grey. He was casually but smartly dressed and smiling into camera, displaying a mouth of the cosmetically enhanced teeth that Dr Clayton had pointed out. The photograph had been professionally taken. Horton wondered by whom. He recognized the clothes as those he'd seen in his flat.

In another two photographs, Freedman was wearing a microphone head set and the picture had clearly been taken at one of his public seminars. There was another of him more serious, wearing a suit and looking into camera with bright, penetrating grey eyes and a strong-featured but ravaged face. Horton got the impression of a charismatic man full of nervous energy, with a zest for life tinged with something else that he couldn't put his finger on. Was there a slightly sardonic air about him? A superiority with a hint of danger?

Cantelli said, 'It says here that he's been down as low as any man could get, and only prison and the discovery of neuro-linguistic programming and gaining his coaching qualifications took him out of the cesspit. He knows what it's like to be at rock bottom, desperate and despairing, to suffer extreme stress, to feel a failure and by knowing this his mission in life is to help others.'

'For a fee, and from what Uckfield told me about Freedman's finances, quite a hefty one at that.' But despite that, Horton thought all credit to the man. He'd pulled himself up from the gutter, overcome alcohol addiction and turned himself into a success, which had earned him a large income. That had been no mean feat. It took guts, determination and willpower, all of which Freedman had once lacked because he'd succumbed to drink, but then that was easy when your world felt as though it was collapsing around you. He should know. What had caused Freedman's descent? Business pressures? Matrimonial problems?

He thought it time he briefed Bliss on the interview with the Clements. Uckfield would have told her about the results of the autopsy and what they'd found in Freedman's flat.

The incident suite was a hive of activity. Uckfield was in his office, the door was open and even from a distance Horton could see he was red-eyed and red-nosed, coughing and sneezing into his handkerchief. Horton was surprised Trueman hadn't set up a cordon around him.

'I was thinking about it,' he said solemnly. He reported that Marsden and Somerfield had gone into Freedman's apartment block to interview the residents and he'd requested CCTV from the area. A team were also bagging up all the paperwork and Freedman's computer. There had been a few reports from the public of sightings of Freedman which were being checked out. 'But seeing as most of them come from out of the area they're probably a waste of time.' Trueman told him that Freedman was divorced and had no kids.

'We're trying to track down his former wife.'

'Any joy with Freedman's coat?'

'Not so far. The Super's going to release a picture of it to the media tomorrow. Or rather, DCI Bliss is.'

Horton crossed to her temporary office. What they had on the Clements' robbery didn't seem to please her but then very little did. Horton said nothing about his and his team's enquiries into Evelyn Lyster's death – that would please her even less. He told her that Walters was going to interview the cleaners tomorrow and that he was calling on Glyn Ashmead at Gravity.

On his return to CID, Walters reported that the shipping company had confirmed that Vivian and Constance Clements had been on the cruise to China which had left Portsmouth on 19 December and returned to the port at six a.m. on Monday, 13 January. The passengers had disembarked at eight forty-five. The robbery had been reported at nine twenty. Uniform had attended at nine thirty-five and called CID because it involved firearms. Walters reached the Clements' house at nine fifty-five and had returned on Tuesday with the crime-scene officer. The cruise company also confirmed that Vivian Clements had been engaged as one of their guest lecturers.

Walters added, 'The port also has CCTV footage for all of Monday morning. They're emailing it over now and none of the taxi companies picked up a fare by the name of Evelyn Lyster or from that address, but I've sent round her photograph.'

Then perhaps a friend had driven her to the port. Horton didn't think she would have caught a bus. She didn't seem the type. He still needed to see the paperwork associated with the purchase of the Clements' pistols but Cantelli would get that tomorrow. He detailed Walters to interview Valentines the cleaners in the morning. 'And while you're there, ask if they clean for Peter Freedman and Evelyn Lyster.'

He turned his attention to his paperwork and to answering his messages and emails. Elkins rang in to report that the Hayling Ferry crew hadn't seen anyone hanging around at the top of the pontoon on Tuesday night and no one in the local marinas recognized Evelyn Lyster, but he'd left her photograph with them and would try the marinas on Hayling Island, Fareham and at Emsworth tomorrow and circulate it to those in Southampton and on the Isle of Wight.

It was just after seven thirty when Cantelli knocked and entered.

'Just had Ables Taxis on the line. One of their drivers, Adrian Woolacombe, remembers picking up Evelyn Lyster at the Hard on Monday morning at eleven minutes past seven.'

Horton raised his eyebrows. 'Then she didn't come directly from her apartment.'

'Looks that way. Woolacombe's on duty all night at the Hard. Want me to interview him?'

'No. I'll do it.' Horton had nothing to go home for. Cantelli had his family. He also had a sick mother staying with him. Horton sent him on his way, telling him to escape before he could be roped into the incident suite and the Freedman investigation. Walters looked hopeful but Horton told him to finish writing up his reports for the day before leaving. It was amazing how fast Walters could type when motivated in the correct way. Half an hour later, he saw from his office window that Uckfield's car had gone. But Bliss and Dennings were still here. He hadn't been summoned so he assumed he wasn't needed and that everything that could be done was being done. Before Bliss could change her mind, he quickly made his escape and headed for the taxi rank on the waterfront and Adrian Woolacombe.

Ten

'Yes, I remember her. What's she done?' Woolacombe said in answer to Horton's question when he showed him the photograph of Evelyn Lyster. Woolacombe, a stout, short man with a pale, jowly face, put down his crime novel and climbed out of the third taxi from the front of

131

the rank. The wind lifted a few fine strands of greying hair that flapped over his large, balding head. He pushed them down with fat fingers but they refused to stay put in the blustery wind that brought with it the smell of the sea and diesel fumes and the rumble and screeching of the trains on the long and sturdy pier to their left.

'What direction did she come from?' Horton asked, ducking the question.

Woolacombe looked slightly bemused. 'From the station, of course.'

'You actually saw her come out of the railway station?' And not from behind him, which was where she would have approached if she'd walked from her apartment or had alighted from a bus.

'Well, no. I didn't actually *see* that.'

'So she could have come from the Gosport ferry.' That was also in the same direction, Horton thought, glancing at the lights on the shore opposite before letting them travel back to the fat man in front of him.

Woolacombe's fleshy face puckered up as he considered this. 'I guess she could have done. She didn't say. She climbed in the back and asked me to take her to the international port.'

'What was her manner like?'

'Chilly. I chatted to her, trying to be friendly and asked if she was catching one of the ferries to France or the Channel Islands but she said, "Just take me to the port, please." I thought, well, pardon me for breathing.'

'She said, "please" though.'

Woolacombe looked taken aback. 'Yeah, she did actually.'

132

Polite, then, but not keen to engage in social chitchat. No crime in that.

'I glanced at her in my mirror a few times but she was just staring out of the window.'

'Did she seem sad or anxious?'

'Not so you'd notice. She wasn't nervy or crying or anything like that. Just staring. Thoughtful, like.'

'Did she have a phone with her? Did she call or text anyone?'

'I didn't see her with a phone or using one and no one called her while she was in the cab.'

'How did she pay you?'

'By cash. She gave a ten per cent tip, too, in cash.'

'What was she carrying?'

'No luggage, if that's what you mean. Just her handbag.'

'But you still asked her if she was catching a ferry.'

'Yes, it was just natural, I guess, taking her to the port. She could have been meeting someone, I suppose. Why all the questions? Has she run off with someone's dosh?' He smiled as he spoke.

'She's dead.'

Woolacombe stared at him, wide-eyed. 'You don't mean—'

'We just need to establish some background facts,' Horton said evasively. 'She was found dead on the ferry to Guernsey.'

'Poor woman. How did she die?'

'Did you watch her enter the terminal building?'

'No. I drove off. I didn't check my mirrors.'

'Did you see her with a cup flask or take a drink from a bottle?'

'No. Like I said, she just sat looking out of the window.'

'Have you ever picked her up before anywhere?'

'Can't say that I have.'

Horton thanked him and made for the Gosport ferry, skirting the railway station on his left where the entrance to the terminal for the Isle of Wight Fast Cat ferry to Ryde was also situated. Guilbert hadn't found a ticket for either the Gosport or the Isle of Wight ferry or a train ticket in her possessions but she could have ditched it in one of the litter bins he could see on his route. Or perhaps she had come from her apartment, approaching the taxi rank from a roundabout way. But why should she? He was becoming increasingly more puzzled by her death. There was so much that just didn't make sense.

He could see the small green and white Gosport ferry on the other side of the harbour. It only took four minutes to cross the water so he waited along with several other people. As he stared across at the shimmering lights of the town opposite he again wondered if it had been his mother's final destination. He could see the masts of the yachts in Haslar Marina to his left and those in Gosport Marina to his right. Rising between them were the lights in the tower blocks much like the high-rise flat he'd lived in for a few years with his mother but on this side of the harbour. The only visitor he could remember was a man with a big flash car, the same man he thought had taken them to Bembridge on the Isle of Wight – not by boat, he would have remembered that, so it must have been on the car ferry which

134

he could see leaving its berth to his left and swinging out into the harbour. That man hadn't been Andrew Ducale. He thought it more likely to have been Jennifer's boss at the casino, Charlie Warner, but he could be mistaken as he couldn't recall his features. Before that there had been a succession of men in the tiny, terraced house they'd lived in in a crowded area on the western edge of the city, not far from the police station. As he'd grown up he had assumed they were his mother's callers and that his mother had been a prostitute because that had been the picture painted of her by those in authority, but now he wasn't so sure. They had lived and slept in one room upstairs and shared a bathroom and kitchen downstairs so the men could have been calling on the occupant of the other room. Or had Jennifer cultivated their acquaintance because she'd been gathering intelligence on possible IRA suspects or been involved with the IRA as Dormand had said? Whose side had she been on, if anyone's? She hadn't been Irish or Catholic. Her parents had been born and had lived and died just outside Bristol.

The ferry docked and disgorged its passengers. Horton showed his warrant card and the photograph of Evelyn Lyster, and asked if the crewman remembered seeing her on board on Monday morning.

'I wasn't on shift,' came the reply. 'You need to come back tomorrow morning and ask the crew on that sailing.'

Horton said he would. He headed through the railway station to the Wightlink terminal and got

135

the same response from the staff there. He made for his marina but instead of turning into it he decided to revisit the scene of Freedman's death in the light of Gaye's findings. He pulled up in front of the houseboats. There were no longer any officers at the scene but a remnant of blue-and-white police tape was trailing on the stones, the wind lifting it like a kite and sending it flapping and falling.

It would have been dark, like it was now, when Freedman had been shot on Tuesday night sometime between seven and nine. And in the dark and the wind and rain Horton didn't think a critically wounded man would have walked, run or staggered very far.

He swung the Harley across the road and parked beside the lifeboat station. Climbing off, he removed his helmet. The wind was gusting off the sea, bringing with it the smell of salt and a fine, chilly drizzle. The killer's car could have been parked beside the lifeboat station except someone would have noticed it. There were no reports of anyone seeing a car or motorcycle. The bus stopped directly opposite. But the killer could have timed his arrival to coincide with when the bus wouldn't be here. Or perhaps the bus driver had seen a car and hadn't thought anything of it because after doing this journey several times a day she'd stopped noticing. In Horton's experience, people weren't very observant. Usually their minds were running along different tramlines just as his kept jumping back to Jennifer's past, and the thought now occurred to him that perhaps those numbers on the envelope he'd been bequeathed by Dr Quentin Amos, who had worked at the London School of Economics at the same time as Jennifer, weren't a location at all but the code to a safety deposit box and one kept in a private bank in Guernsey. The bank that Violet Ducale had once worked for, Zuber's, which had become Manley's. Was that what the former lecturer, Amos, and Andrew Ducale had been leading him to? Would Violet Ducale recognize the numbers or rather the format of them? He could return and ask her and he would but that would have to wait for a few days, unless Guilbert wanted him back there sooner for the Evelyn Lyster investigation but he couldn't see why Guilbert should for a natural death, or why Bliss would permit it while they had a definite murder investigation on their patch. Which brought him back to Freedman.

He crossed to the slipway in front of the wide doors of the lifeboat station. The sea was a black, swirling mass in front of him, crashing on to the shore. The icy wind buffeted him, growing colder by the minute, it seemed.

He turned and scrutinized the sizeable modern building. Was it possible that Freedman had met his killer here? They would have been completely hidden from the view of anyone in the road. And no one would have heard the shot. Here the killer had shot Freedman, then what? Had he expected Freedman to drop dead in front of him? What had he done when Freedman hadn't? Surely Freedman would have used his strength to try and plead with his killer for help. Or perhaps not – perhaps he'd seen that course of action was hopeless and instinctively knew he had to get away, to get help before risk being shot again.

He put himself in Freedman's shoes. In pain, shocked, desperate to get help, the wind buffeting him, the stones impeding his progress, he staggered up to the road. It was heavy going walking and running on stones in daylight let alone on a dark, wild night with a bullet in you. But desperation can drive people to extraordinary lengths, as Gaye had said.

Opposite were the houseboats. Why would Freedman have made for the last one in the row of five? Why not head back towards the marina where there was a chance of help? But when you have a bullet in you you'd hardly be thinking straight. Maybe he'd seen Packman's car parked beside the second-to-last houseboat and reasoned, despite his injury, that it was his best hope? Packman hadn't heard the shot or Freedman's cries for help because of the roar of the wind, but he would have seen or heard a boat or car and Dennings said he hadn't.

Then when Freedman had finally fallen, had the killer calmly gone through the dead man's pockets and taken his wallet, keys and phone? Or had Freedman, with the gun pointing at him, been asked to empty his pockets before he was shot? In both scenarios the killer hadn't wanted Freedman's identity discovered, or at least not for some time. Perhaps the killer hadn't known that Freedman had a prison record and that his identity would be traced that way. But Horton remembered that Cantelli had said the newspaper article had mentioned it and Freedman

138

had made no secret of it on his website, so perhaps the killer was someone from outside the city who hadn't read the local article, or someone who didn't have access to the Internet or know how to use it so hadn't seen his website. Taking the keys and wallet could have been used as a tactic to delay identification while the killer got away. Freedman's murderer could be out of the country by now.

But on Tuesday night had the killer returned to his vehicle parked close by? Or perhaps he had returned to a boat on the shore. The weather had been atrocious and if the killer had come by boat Horton didn't think he had crossed the turbulent racing currents that separated Portsmouth from Hayling Island, or motored further up into Langstone Harbour. But, as he'd previously considered, he could have arrived and left by a small boat or RIB across the more sheltered waters of Eastney Lake to the shore at Milton.

He thought of the pistols stolen from the Clements and of the pompous little man. He couldn't see Vivian Clements risking his life in a RIB or small boat on a stormy night but had he travelled here by car, shot Freedman and then returned home?

Horton returned to his boat, his mind speculating on Freedman's death for which, as yet, they had no apparent motive. Why would Vivian Clements kill him? Jealousy? Did Constance Clements know Freedman? Horton reckoned Vivian Clements, a man full of his own self-importance, would be unable to stomach the thought that his wife found another man attractive or vice versa, but why was Freedman dressed as a vagrant? It was hardly the kind of clothes he'd wear for a secret assignation with Constance Clements on her return from a cruise.

And what of Evelyn Lyster? Why had she caught a taxi at the Hard? It was late but not too late to call Guilbert on his mobile. He came on the line almost at once. Horton asked if he'd discovered anything more or if someone had come forward claiming to know her. The answer was no on both counts. Horton told him about the taxi driver.

'She could have stayed with a friend,' he added. 'Except there were none listed on the phone we found on her body.'

'Maybe she had another mobile phone.'

Horton had already considered that. 'If she did it's not in her apartment and there was nothing of a personal nature in it. She puzzles me. There's a lot about her death that's not right.'

'I know,' Guilbert said with feeling in his gentle voice. 'I'll talk to Rowan Lyster tomorrow before he flies back, see if he can tell me who his mother's friends were. She must have had some.'

'And clients. Gina Lyster said she had stopped working as a freelance translator after her husband's death but she might have had some clients in Guernsey who she'd kept in touch with.'

'They're in no hurry to come forward.'

'Maybe they just haven't heard the news yet.'

'Yeah,' Guilbert said sceptically.

'Her client records could be with her accountant, which could be the same one that Rowan Lyster uses for his business.'

'I'll ask him.'

Horton said he'd return to the Gosport and Isle of Wight ferry terminals in the morning. 'And I'll see if the British Transport Police have any CCTV footage of the station for Monday morning in case she got off a train.' But again he came back to that same question. Why was she travelling with no luggage?

He pushed away all the questions about her death and Freedman's murder and tried to sleep. Surprisingly he did, rising early, which meant he had time for a run and after it time to call in at the Hard before heading for the station. He didn't expect to gain any new information so he was astounded when a crew member of the Isle of Wight Fast Cat ferry remembered her. She had been on the second sailing of Monday morning, the six forty-seven from Ryde Pier. The Solent crossing took approximately twenty-two minutes so the timing tallied with that of the taxi driver, Woolacombe, who said he'd picked her up at eleven minutes past seven. She wasn't a regular commuter. The crewman knew all of those but he did think he had seen her before. The booking office clerk didn't remember selling her a return ticket from Portsmouth to the Isle of Wight but she could have bought it online or perhaps she'd travelled to the island by the car ferry or the hovercraft and had returned by the Fast Cat. Did it matter? he wondered. Maybe she had come straight from a friend's house on the island. He was curious to know what Guilbert would discover from Rowan Lyster. He called him with the latest news before heading for the station.

141

Bliss's car was in its allotted space but there was no sign of Uckfield's. Perhaps he'd called in sick, but somehow Horton doubted it. Knowing Uckfield as he did, he thought he'd rather crawl into work than miss out on a major investigation and, although Uckfield might have faith in Bliss's ability, he certainly didn't in the burly, squat DI Dennings, who Gaye Clayton had nicknamed Neanderthal Man.

He found both Cantelli and Walters in CID. It was just after eight o'clock.

'How's your mum?' Horton asked, stopping at Cantelli's desk.

'Not too good. Charlotte called the doctor last night and he's prescribed some antibiotics, but unless Charlotte can get mum to drink more she's going to dehydrate and that means a drip and hospital. Charlotte hopes that will put the fear of God in her and make her take more fluids.'

Horton said he hoped it worked. He told Cantelli and Walters what Woolacombe and the Wightlink crewman had said and asked Cantelli to get on to Wightlink and Hovertravel to find out if Evelyn Lyster had bought tickets to the island and when. 'Also get on to the Isle of Wight council rates office and see if she owns a property on the island. Maybe she keeps most of her clothes and shoes, and her photos and personal papers there.'

He detailed Walters to look through the video footage from the port for Monday morning and to see if Evelyn Lyster showed up on it.

'I was just going to the cleaning company.'

'OK, do it when you get back.'

Walters scooped up his newspaper, stuffed it in the pocket of his shapeless suit jacket and padded out.

Horton dumped his helmet and leather jacket in his office and picked up his sailing jacket. To Cantelli, he said, 'I'm walking over to Gravity to talk to Glyn Ashmead about Peter Freedman.' The centre opened at eight and, unless Ashmead was attending a conference or had a day's holiday or was sick, Horton knew he'd find him there.

Eleven

The two-storey building, erected in the mid-1960s, had been many things over the years – shops, offices and an amusement arcade. Now it was a day centre for the homeless and those struggling to make ends meet, funded partly by the council but mainly by donations. It gave food and drink free to its rapidly expanding clientele. The catering supplies were donated by generous individuals and supermarkets offloading their out-of-date stock. At the rear were a communal laundry and a couple of shower rooms, which were available free of charge. There was also a clothing bank. Horton had donated many of his clothes to it, especially after Catherine had thrown him out. He didn't have much space on his boat.

He pushed open the door and stepped into the steamy café that smelt of sweat and fried food and something else not quite definable, but, as he surveyed the forlorn, weatherworn and hardened faces at the tables, he thought it a mixture of dirt, diesel and decay, while defeat hung in the air. Hostile eyes watched him warily as he headed towards the counter. He was too clean, too well-dressed and too self-assured. His demeanour smacked of the 'authorities'. It was as though he had *police officer* emblazoned across his chest.

It was busy even this early, but then, he thought sadly, there was no shortage of homeless people and those in need in the city and their numbers were shamefully growing. They spanned all age groups. Not all were victims of alcohol, drug or gambling addictions – many had mental health issues, some had become homeless as the result of abusive and failed relationships, ruined businesses and health problems. And some had lost or had their benefits frozen through stringent changes to the system and had been kicked out of their homes by private landlords increasing rents to extortionate amounts which they couldn't pay. They had very few places to turn for help. One was the Salvation Army, the other was Ashmead's charity. It wasn't such a big step down but it was a bloody huge one up. Freedman had managed it though and so had Glyn Ashmead, and for that Horton admired them.

He smiled a greeting at the two women behind the counter and addressed the older, thinner woman, whose sallow cheeks were crisscrossed with a myriad of tiny fine lines while deeper ones were scored into her forehead and around her mouth.

She, like the other younger woman beside her, was wearing a short, light-blue nylon overall over black trousers. The younger woman was serving a man in rough, soiled clothes who could have been any age between forty and sixty. She was new to Horton but over the last eleven months from his occasional visits here he'd got to know the older one, Martha Wiley, who, like others at Gravity, with the exception of Ashmead, was a volunteer. Horton asked Martha if Glyn was in.

'Yes. Go through and I'll bring you a coffee, Andy.'

She knew how he liked it. Black and strong. No sugar.

Horton entered the narrow corridor behind the café and knocked on the door of an office on his right. It was open but he didn't like to walk straight in.

'Come in,' a voice called out.

Glyn Ashmead looked up from his untidy desk, laden with paper, and smiled a weary greeting. His heavily lined face was like a knife, his hazel eyes sharp but kind and intelligent. He'd been down as far as you could get and, like Peter Freedman, he'd managed to climb out of the cesspit and claw his way back up. But, unlike Freedman, he hadn't made a fortune. Instead, he'd used his experience to help others who had suffered hardship and homelessness as he had done, and three years ago he'd been given the position as paid manager of the charity. He gestured Horton into the worn seat across his desk and after exchanging a few pleasantries

Horton broke the news about Freedman's death. Ashmead looked shocked then sorrowful.

'You left a message on his answer machine.'

'Yes. He used to volunteer on Tuesdays but I was at a conference in Southampton and I just wanted to catch up with him about one of our customers who I thought he might particularly be able to help. I heard something on the local radio about a man being found dead by the houseboats but I never imagined it would be Peter. How did he die?'

Before Horton could answer there was a tap on the open door and Martha entered. She handed Horton his mug of coffee and put the second she was carrying on the desk in front of Ashmead.

'Is it OK if I break the news to Martha?' Ashmead asked.

Horton nodded. He watched her lined, narrow face register alarm before she sank heavily on to the chair next to Horton. He knew from Ashmead that she was in her mid-fifties but whatever life had thrown at her it had made her look at least ten years older. Her light brown eyes were slightly bloodshot and ringed with fatigue. She studied him anxiously.

'Peter, dead? I can't believe it.'

'When did you last see him?' Horton asked her gently. He could hear voices outside. They grew louder as two men headed past the office towards the showers. Ashmead rose and quietly pushed the door to but didn't close it completely.

'On Tuesday,' she answered. Her voice was soft, her accent local.

The day he'd been killed, thought Horton.

'Tuesday was his day for helping us unless he was away on one of his lecture tours, but that wasn't very often.'

'How did he seem?'

'Fine, his usual self. We chatted about the weather, the news. He joked, as he usually did, asking me if I'd found a good man to whisk me off to the continent. I said chance would be a fine thing.'

'And his love life?'

'He told me he was single. He said no one would put up with him. All I know about him is that he had been homeless, was a recovering alcoholic and that he'd been in prison. He made no secret of it, which was why he was able to relate so well to some of our customers. He never preached at anyone. He just listened and if they asked for advice he gave it if he could.'

Horton noted the slight flush under her skin and how her eyes dropped. He guessed she'd asked Freedman for advice. Maybe she had also experienced homelessness and drink problems.

She continued, 'Peter sat in the café, as he usually did, drinking tea and chatting with anyone who stopped by him. Some of them came to talk to him specifically. He arrived at about ten and stayed until four, his usual hours.'

Ashmead explained, 'Peter was generous with his time. He was also generous with his money. He donated ten per cent of his earnings to us.'

So Freedman hadn't been all talk.

Ashmead added, 'I wish I'd seen him but the conference went on for ages and then I stayed on for drinks – a mineral water in my case. It

147

was about attracting funding and sponsorship. It raised some interesting ideas but equally it was rather depressing because we're all chasing the same pot of money, which is getting smaller despite the increase in the number of people getting wealthier. They seem to want to hold on to their wealth. The same for the big corporations, and despite what we're told there is no trickle-down effect to the poor. Some benefactors see medical charities, and those connected with children and dogs – donkeys, even – as being far more important and vital than helping a bunch of down-and-outs, drug addicts and drunkards, with many believing it's our own fault.' Horton heard the bitterness in Ashmead's voice. 'I left Martha my office key in case Peter needed to use my office to talk to anyone privately.'

'He didn't,' Martha said. 'How did he die?'

It was the question Ashmead had asked earlier. Both were looking at him eagerly as they awaited his answer but Horton hadn't been authorized to give it. 'I can't say, sorry,' he apologized. Then added, 'Only that we are treating his death as suspicious.'

Martha's skin paled. She dashed a frightened glance at Ashmead and then back at Horton. 'Who would want to kill him? It wasn't one of our customers, was it?'

Could it be? he wondered. He kept coming back to that one question above all others that nagged and gnawed away at him: why had Freedman been dressed as a tramp?

'Was there anyone he disagreed with or who threatened him?'

148

Martha shook her head. 'Not that I have ever heard or seen.'

'Me neither.'

Horton showed Ashmead a photograph of the coat, which had been touched up so as not to reveal the bullet hole and blood. 'Peter Freedman was wearing this when he died. It's of exceptional quality and from the Saville Row tailors, Gieves and Hawkes, but it was worn and the lining was torn. Had you seen him wearing it?'

Ashmead answered, 'No. Peter was always casually but immaculately dressed when he came here.'

'Do you know if such a coat was donated?'

'I don't recognize it but then I don't handle clothing donations. Martha, have you seen it before?'

She scrutinized it carefully and shook her head. 'No. Sheila Broadway might have done – she usually deals with the clothing donations. She works Mondays and Fridays and sorts through them. Those that need washing go into the machines and those that are beyond repair get bundled up for the recycling company. If it was clean then it would have been handed out but if grubby and needing dry-cleaning, which a coat like that looks as though it would, then we would have passed it on to another charity – Oxfam or the British Heart Foundation. We haven't got the machines here or the money to dry-clean clothes.' She looked puzzled. 'But why would Peter want to wear a coat that was donated?'

Why indeed? But before Horton could continue with his questions, Ashmead, looking thoughtful, said, 'There could be a reason. And it could have been Peter's coat.'

'Go on,' Horton said keenly.

'He could have kept it as a memento of when he was on the streets. A reminder to him not to go down that route again.'

Horton hadn't considered that. 'Would someone do that?'

'Yes,' Ashmead answered with conviction.

'What did you keep?'

There was a moment's pause before Ashmead answered. 'A brown leather belt.' A shadow crossed his hawk-like features. 'It started off around my trousers as normal and ended up wrapped around my outer clothes, with each passing year going in a notch and getting more worn. I'd removed it a few times with the intention of using it to hang myself but never had the courage to go through with it. Instead I'd take another drink, then another. I can barely look at the thing now, but when things get tough, and when I think what harm would it do to have a small drink, it's there reminding me of where that might lead. Maybe Peter needed the same reminder.'

And perhaps the belt had also been Freedman's of old. Horton could check Freedman's arrest record to see what he'd been wearing when he'd been booked and what he'd taken into prison and been discharged with.

There were more voices from outside. Martha rose. 'I'd better get back, Glyn. We're very busy and Sarah's only been here a few days.'

'Did Sarah speak to Peter on Tuesday?' asked Horton.

'No, she wasn't here. She's a volunteer covering Thursdays and Fridays. I was on my own on Tuesday. We used to have another volunteer, Angela Daneton, but sadly she died a couple of weeks ago and we haven't found anyone to replace her yet.'

'I'm working on it,' Glyn said a little wearily.

'I know you are,' she replied, bestowing a kind and worried smile on him. Then she addressed Horton. 'Can I tell the customers that Peter's dead, if they ask?'

Horton nodded and added, 'If anyone tells you anything that might be helpful, no matter how insignificant it seems, or if anyone reacts in an unusual way to the news, would you let me or Glyn know? It might help us find his killer.'

'Of course.' She seemed about to say something then smiled sadly and left.

Horton turned to Ashmead. 'Did Peter ever talk to you about his experiences?'

'We rarely spoke about our drink problems and our life on the road. We didn't need to; we both knew what it was like. But I've never been convicted of a crime or been sent to prison, thank the Lord. I saw the light before it got that far.'

'What changed things for you?' Horton asked, genuinely interested. He wondered if Ashmead would tell him. Perhaps it was too painful for him to talk about but he answered.

'I was sleeping rough in a hedge in a car park in Southampton. It was early morning in winter and this smart young woman parked her new car there. She was on her way to work in one of the modern offices close by. She saw me emerge from the hedge as she was putting her ticket on the windscreen. She looked at me candidly without any trace of horror, disgust or alarm. She headed towards me. She delved into her bag and gave me five pounds. She said, "It's not much but I hope it helps," then she smiled and left. It was as simple as that. I looked at that money and I watched her walk away, nice clothes, smart suit. She turned back, waved and smiled again before disappearing into the office block. One simple act of kindness and humanity from a young woman. She didn't sneer or revile me; she treated me as a fellow human being. I felt ashamed and shocked. I stared at that five-pound note for some time. Then I shoved it in my pocket, headed for the nearest Salvation Army centre and asked for help.'

'It couldn't have been easy.'

'It was easier than I expected, mainly because I had so many people to help me and all the time the picture of that young woman stayed in my mind. I can still see her now though I have no idea who she was or where she is. We all need help and compassion and I like to think I've given some of that back to those less fortunate than me. And let's face it, Andy, it's bloody tough out there and it isn't getting any easier. To lose someone like Peter . . .' He shook his head sadly.

'Did he talk about his time in prison?'

'He said it was hard especially as he was also drying out but he got a lot of medical assistance. He also got help from the prison officers. Studying gave him the strength and focus he needed in order to cope. He told me that neuro-linguistic programming gave him skills that not only helped him to understand his past failed relationships, both personal and professional, but also how he could forge ahead. He certainly made a success of it.'

'Did he see clients at his apartment?'

'He might have done. I don't know.'

'Did you visit him there?'

'No. Our relationship was friendly but also professional.'

'Did he talk about friends or were you aware of him having any relationships?'

'No. It didn't come up in the conversation and I wasn't going to pry. Peter was very charismatic and had great empathy not only because he'd been down there but his studies helped him to get the best out of those he was trying to help. He didn't preach to anyone – you and I both know that doesn't work – but listening, trying to understand, just showing that you're trying is often all it takes. Being non-judgemental.'

Just as that young woman had been when she'd seen Ashmead emerge from that hedge, thought Horton. And that had changed his life.

'Was there anyone he used to see here regularly?' he asked. 'Anyone he was particularly friendly with?'

'He never mentioned anyone but there might have been. I can ask around for you. They won't talk to you but they might to me and to Martha.'

Horton heard raised voices in the corridor. It sounded like one man was accusing the other of pinching something. Glyn looked beseechingly at Horton.

He rose. 'You've got a lot to do and a lot of customers.' Sadly there would always be many.

'I'd happily spend all day talking about Peter if it helped to find his killer,' Ashmead answered, rising and moving to the door, where he halted. 'Peter was pleased to be able to help others. He was clever and funny, yet there was a seriousness about him and I think there was a darkness inside him – or at least something dark inside – that he kept a hold on and was afraid of. I'm not sure but occasionally if I caught him alone and off his guard I'd see something in his eyes that looked not like sorrow but more like anger.'

Horton asked if he'd be prepared to formerly ID the body. He knew that Ashmead was sadly no stranger to that particular task. Ashmead agreed. Horton said they'd let him know when and that they'd send a car to take him to the mortuary. As he headed back to the station, he mulled over what he'd been told. He had a clearer picture of Peter Freedman now but nothing that could pinpoint his killer or the reason for his murder. And that made him think again of Evelyn Lyster. He had no mental image of her except what he'd seen in that apartment which showed her to be a smart, fastidious woman, but what had she really been like? Secretive was the word that sprang to mind.

He reported into the incident suite, noting that there was still no sign of Uckfield or his car. He relayed to Bliss, Dennings and Trueman what Glyn Ashmead and Martha Wiley had told him and gave Trueman Sheila Broadway's address which Ashmead had given him before he'd left.

154

Trueman said he'd tracked down Freedman's GP. 'He was registered with the surgery closest to his flat. The receptionist has confirmed that he hadn't named anyone as next of kin and that he last saw the doctor eighteen months ago, and then only for some inoculations.'

'What kind?'

'For the nasty buggers you need when you travel to foreign parts – hepatitis B and A, tetanus and Japanese encephalitis.'

Dennings said, 'Must have gone there on holiday.'

But Freedman wasn't the only one to go there. Through Horton's mind flashed Vivian Clements' oriental collection and what he'd told Cantelli: *I've cruised with Constance to Japan, China and Asia.*

Trueman continued, 'We've spoken to Rosie Pierce. She last saw Freedman two weeks ago. According to her Freedman either met his clients in hotels or coffee shops or if they wanted somewhere more private he'd hire a room in a business centre for a couple of hours. We're checking that out but from the initial look at his computer and his accounts he did quite a lot of work with companies on their premises. He also ran training courses, probably in hotels or at conference and training centres. We've checked the vehicle licensing numbers registered with the occupants of his flats and they all match up. And none of the residents saw him on Tuesday, except Mrs Nugent in the morning. There's nothing so far from the house-to-house or from the search of the public toilets for his clothes or personal

155

belongings, so unless someone has stolen them he didn't change in the toilets.'

Horton still thought Freedman had changed into those tramp's clothes in his apartment.

Trueman was saying, 'His prison record is exemplary and bears out what Ashmead told you, Andy. We're still waiting for the ballistics report to see if we can get anything further on the type of gun that was used and if those stolen from Clements could be made to fire, but apart from those pistols there are no other reports of stolen guns that fit the description which Dr Clayton gave us, but one could have been purchased either online or from someone importing them. No motive as yet. And we still can't find his ex-wife.'

Horton asked what Freedman had been wearing, what he'd had in his possession when he'd been arrested and when he'd been sent to prison. Trueman called up the file but said that neither the coat nor the belt was logged.

Once Bliss and Dennings were out of earshot, Horton asked if Uckfield had phoned in sick. He hadn't.

'He'll probably show up soon.'

'Bliss will be disappointed.'

'Well, I won't be,' Trueman said with feeling. 'Can't you take her back to CID with you?'

'Not if she doesn't want to come. But it's where I'm going.'

'Lucky you.'

Cantelli greeted him with the news that he had the coroner's report on the death of Dennis Lyster. 'It wasn't suicide – the coroner gave a verdict

156

of undetermined death. DCI Birch oversaw the investigation, which was why the name, Lyster, didn't ring any bells with me.'

Birch was head of CID on the Isle of Wight and not a fan of Horton's, but then Horton didn't much rate the dried-up stick insect of a man either. Birch disliked anyone who challenged his views and his method of policing, which was taking the line of least resistance by bullying the most vulnerable of suspects into a false confession and then somehow making the evidence fit. Birch had got away with it for years but the paper trail they were now required to fulfil was fast catching up with him and Birch had gone sick for more months than he'd worked over the last two years. He'd be retiring in April. And good riddance, thought Horton, wondering who would be lined up to take over on the Isle of Wight. Not Bliss – she wouldn't want the job. The island's crime rate was a lot lower than the mainland's. She'd set her sights higher. He bet even now she was eyeing Uckfield's large leather chair in his office. Maybe even sitting in it.

Cantelli continued, 'An early morning commuter reported seeing Lyster's body wedged between the pylons under Ryde Pier just before six forty-two a.m. Ryde Inshore Lifeboat and the fire service attended and retrieved it. There was no suicide note and Evelyn and Rowan Lyster claimed there had been no sign that Dennis Lyster had been suffering from depression, but Evelyn Lyster acknowledged her husband was finding it hard to cope after being made redundant. He was also a diabetic and there's the possibility that he

157

fell into a coma close to the sea and his body got washed out on the tide. There was no evidence to confirm that he travelled to the Isle of Wight but he could have fallen into the sea somewhere along the coast here. And neither Wightlink nor Hovertravel have a record of Evelyn Lyster having travelled with them over the last year. I've asked them to check back further. I could ask them if Dennis Lyster had travelled there before his death.'

'Did Birch check that out?'

Cantelli shrugged. 'The coroner's report doesn't say if he did. But there's a bit more in the report. Evelyn Lyster said that she and her husband had once owned boats and that Dennis always loved the sea. It would be natural for him to end his life by choosing to drown. The pathologist said it was difficult to estimate how long he had been dead, but the fact that the body was bloated and had risen to the surface, and that it was greenish black and gloving of the hands and feet had occurred indicated he'd been in the water for days rather than hours. Evelyn Lyster didn't report him missing for five days. I thought you might find that interesting,' Cantelli added with a wry grin. 'She only contacted the police when she heard about a body being found and after trying his mobile and getting no signal.'

'She didn't try it before then?'

'She says not. She admitted that their relation-ship was strained. They'd spent a great deal of time apart over the last eighteen years and they were both finding it hard to adjust to being together. Her husband had told her he needed time to think through what he wanted to do with the rest of his life, so she didn't think anything of him going off and not being in touch.'

Horton looked sceptical.

'Yeah, I thought that. They probably had a row or she told him she wanted a divorce. He took off and she was glad he was gone, probably even happier when the poor man turned up dead.'

'And she quickly sold up and moved into the penthouse apartment where everything is new so that she doesn't have to think of him. No photographs of him either. Was Dennis Lyster insured?'

'It doesn't say here but DCI Birch might have asked the question.'

Horton was doubtful about that. 'Did Lyster take his medication with him?'

Cantelli again scoured the report. 'Evelyn Lyster says he did but that doesn't mean he continued to take it. His body was clothed but he wasn't wearing shoes or a coat. No personal belongings, keys, wallet or phone were found on him so they could have been left in his coat. I've checked with lost property both here and on the island but nothing was handed in. Evelyn Lyster couldn't give a description of what her husband had been wearing on the day he left, only what she'd last seen him in: casual trousers, a shirt and jumper. ID was confirmed by fingerprints because the gloved skin came off intact, and by dental records.'

Horton said, 'Well, that seems to scotch the idea she was taking a sentimental trip to Guernsey because it was a special place for them and that she intended ending her life either there or on the ferry. But I'm curious to know what she was doing on the Isle of Wight before travelling to Guernsey.'

'Nothing from the council rates department to say she had a property there.'

'I'll update Guilbert then we'll head for the Clements'. We need the provenance of those pistols and I'd like to know if either of them knew Freedman. Trueman's discovered that Freedman had inoculations for travelling to Japan and Clements told us he'd been on lecture cruises to there.'

Cantelli's phone rang. As he answered it Horton entered his office, calling Guilbert on his mobile as he went. While he waited for him to answer he saw Uckfield's car pull in and smiled as he imagined the look of disappointment on Bliss's face.

Horton told Guilbert what he'd discovered, adding, 'Ask Rowan if his mother and father had life insurance. See if you can get anything out of him about his parents' relationship and what he thought of his father's suicide. Cantelli will send over the coroner's report on Dennis Lyster's death.'

'I'm driving Rowan to the airport later today after the inquest. I'll get chatting to him in the car.'

As he rang off, Cantelli appeared in the doorway with a worried frown. 'That was Constance Clements on the phone. Vivian Clements went out last night and hasn't returned. She has no idea where he went but she says he was very agitated. I've told her we're on our way.'

Twelve

Constance Clements had the front door open before they could reach it. Horton noted that she was dressed as carefully and elegantly as before and wearing make-up but there were dark circles under her eyes showing a disturbed night and her mouth looked tighter and harder than before. As they stepped into the hall, she said, 'I've tried his mobile phone several times but there's no answer.'

'Could he have gone to a friend or a relative?' asked Cantelli.

'No. There's only an aged aunt who lives in Worthing and he wouldn't go there.'

Horton didn't ask why. Perhaps they didn't get on.

'And Vivian doesn't have any friends.'

Horton raised his eyebrows. 'None?'

Her eyes dropped before coming up again as she said, 'He's a very private person. He sees enough of people when he's working so prefers to keep most relationships on a business level.' She headed towards the kitchen, assuming they'd follow her. They did.

Cantelli exchanged a pointed look with Horton. 'Could he have gone to see one of these business contacts?' Cantelli asked.

She tossed them an anxious glance. 'I don't see why he should and he would have told me if that were the case. And before you ask,' she continued as they entered the kitchen, 'I've called the hospital three times, the last just before you arrived, to ask if he'd been admitted or if anyone answering to his description had and they said he hadn't. I wondered if he'd been taken ill or had an accident. He might be lying somewhere and hasn't been found yet.'

'Mr Clements mentioned that he used to have a flat in London. Could he have gone to anyone he knows there?'

But she was shaking her head a little too vigorously. 'No.' Her hands were restlessly playing with the silver bracelet on her wrist.

Gently, he said, 'Shall we sit down?'

She perched on the edge of the chair as Horton took the seat opposite and Cantelli next to him. There was no offer of refreshments this time. Constance Clements was far too agitated to think of that. Cantelli removed his notebook from inside his jacket as Horton asked her what time her husband had left the house.

'I don't know. I wasn't here. I'd gone for a walk along the seafront to clear my head.' She glanced down at her hands in her lap.

'You'd rowed,' Horton said, interpreting her manner.

Her head came up. She looked as though she was about to deny it, then nodded. 'It's my fault. I should have been more understanding. If anything has happened—'

'Let's just take it one step at a time,' Horton quietly interjected.

She took a deep breath in an effort to get her

emotions under control. After a moment, she continued more evenly. 'Vivian has a bit of a short fuse at the best of times so when we arrived home from the cruise and he discovered some of his collection had been stolen it sent him right over the edge. Well, you saw him, you know what he's like.' Her eyes flicked between them.

Horton recalled the pompous little man. He agreed but made no comment and neither did Cantelli.

After a short pause, she continued, 'It got worse. Yesterday he ended up shouting at me. Normally I'd just ignore it or try to mollify him but I'd had enough. I told him . . . I told him to go to hell and walked out.' She took a breath and eyed them as though beseeching them to understand and perhaps also looking for approval, fiddling with her bracelet and then with the ring on her left hand.

'I needed some air and space, some time to think. I walked along the seafront to Southsea Castle and back. When I got in he wasn't here. His car was gone. I made myself something to eat, even though I didn't feel much like it. I had a couple of glasses of wine and then another. I went to bed, expecting him to come back, listening for the sound of the car, getting angrier with him every minute until I eventually fell asleep. I woke up at four and discovered he still hadn't come home. That's the first time I rang his mobile. He didn't answer it. I sent him a text, thinking that maybe wherever he was he might not be able to take a call or there might not be a signal, although I have absolutely no idea where

163

he might be. I then called the hospital. I tried his mobile again at six o'clock. Nothing. I got dressed and went for a walk along the seafront. I rang him again at eight and then called the hospital. Then I rang you.' She turned her gaze on Cantelli. 'And as I said, I rang the hospital again before you arrived.'

'Does he own a boat?' Horton asked, wondering if he'd taken off on one or was sleeping over on it. His thoughts flicked to Freedman being shot on the shore and his killer possibly having got there by boat. But somehow Horton couldn't see the squat little man as an expert seaman, although he knew he shouldn't judge by appearances.

Constance Clements looked startled at the question. 'No.'

So that probably scotched that idea unless he'd kept that secret from his wife.

'Is there anywhere special he's likely to go when upset?' asked Cantelli.

She ran a hand through her hair. 'Not that I know of, except to his collection room.'

Horton had some questions to ask about that but he'd do so later. First he wanted to explore his idea of a possible connection between Clements and Freedman because of the information Trueman had given him. 'Was your husband on a lecture cruise about eighteen months ago to Japan?' The time when Trueman said Freedman had received the inoculations for Japanese encephalitis.

'Yes. Why? We both were,' she said, taken aback before Horton caught a hint of wariness in her eyes.

'Do you know a man called Peter Freedman?'

164

By her reaction she obviously did. He watched with a quickening pulse as her face flushed deep red and her eyes dropped to her lap. She twiddled her bracelet. Horton said nothing and neither did Cantelli, forcing her to look up and search their faces for a meaning behind the question. 'Do you think Vivian's gone to see him?' she asked nervously.

'Why should he?'

'I don't know – you just said . . .'

Horton held her frightened gaze. The name of the dead man hadn't been given out. 'Is there any reason why your husband should be jealous of Peter Freedman?' He could sense Cantelli's heightened interest but he remained silent.

'Jealous? Vivian? No, of course not. There's nothing between me and Peter.'

'But you have seen him since returning from that Japanese cruise?'

'Well, yes.' She shifted. 'But in a professional sense. I was interested in learning more about mindfulness techniques. I thought it might be something I could pursue,' she added almost defiantly. It was so obviously a lie.

'And was it?' Horton asked evenly, holding eye contact.

After a moment, her body slumped and she let out a sigh. Dejectedly, she said, 'Not really.'

'When did you last see Peter Freedman, Mrs Clements?'

'What has this got to do with Vivian missing?' She again ran a hand through her short, high-lighted fair hair. It reminded Horton of Evelyn Lyster. They were both of a similar age. But he was convinced from what he had discovered about Evelyn, which was precious little, that she had been far more confident in life than Constance Clements was and possibly had ever been.

'If you'd just answer the question.'

'About six months ago.'

Another lie? He wondered. 'Where were you and your husband on Tuesday night?'

'I've already told you that. We were both here. Vivian went missing last night not Tuesday. Look, I don't understand all this.'

'Are you sure you were *both* here?' He held her stare.

Her lips twitched nervously. Her eyes restlessly flicked between them and finally rested on Horton. After a moment, she muttered, 'I was here. Vivian went out.'

'Where?'

'I don't know. He didn't say.'

'What time did he leave and return?'

'He went out at six thirty and came home just after nine o'clock.'

'By car?'

She nodded.

'How did he seem?'

'Angry, upset, distracted. I don't understand why you're so interested in Tuesday night . . .' Her words trailed off. She frowned as she thought. 'You think he might have gone to see Peter Freedman on Tuesday and last night and something's happened? There's nothing between me and Peter – there never was – and I can tell you now, Inspector, that Vivian never thought there was either.'

Maybe she had refused to see that or her husband had fooled her into thinking he believed her when she denied it. But Horton was beginning to think that Vivian Clements had staged the robbery and had used one of his pistols to kill Freedman and make it appear that someone else had. And after killing Freedman and hearing about the investigation on the news, he'd taken fright and taken off. Horton thought it time to break the news about Freedman's death and gauge her reaction.

'Peter Freedman is dead. He was killed on Tuesday night,' Horton announced rather brutally. He watched the expressions cross her face as she took in the news – first puzzlement, then surprise and finally horror. Her eyes widened and her skin blanched. 'You can't think that Vivian killed him! That's impossible. Vivian couldn't kill anyone.'

Horton wished he had a pound for every time he'd heard that. 'What time did you leave the house last night?'

'What? Oh, just after five thirty,' she answered distractedly.

Horton could see her mind trying to grapple with the fact that Freedman was dead and her husband missing. It would have been dark when she'd left the house. 'Did anyone see you or did you speak to anyone?'

'Why are you asking about *me*, it's Vivian who is missing!' she cried, frustrated.

'We're just trying to fix the time he went out. He could have left shortly after you and a neighbour might have seen him.'

167

'Oh, I see. No, I didn't speak to or see anyone. It was cold and drizzly. The seafront was deserted.'

'And you got back when?'

'About seven o'clock.'

'Have you checked if your husband took anything with him – his laptop computer, for example?'

'Well, it's not here,' she said, waving at the table.

'Could it be in his study?' asked Cantelli.

'I don't know. I haven't been in there.'

'Not even to see if he has left you a note?'

'He wouldn't leave one there. He knows I never go in his study or his collection room.' There was an acid tone to her voice.

'Then you haven't checked if anything from his personal collection is missing?'

She shook her head.

'Or if any of his clothes or personal belongings are missing?'

'No.' She looked deeply troubled. 'You think he's killed Peter and run away? Well, I can't believe that.' But she sprang up and set off for the hall without asking them to follow her. She knew they would. Cantelli asked if she had the combination to the safe.

'Yes.'

Good. That meant they could check the contents. She pushed open the door to the collection room and switched on the lights. Horton saw exactly what he'd seen last time. Nothing was missing and Clements wasn't here.

'Do you have an inventory of everything that was in the collection?'

'The insurers have that.'

'But your husband must have a copy.'

'It'll be in his study.'

She made to leave but Horton forestalled her. 'I'd like you to take a good look around. Is there anything missing?'

She looked baffled. 'I don't really know. I don't come in here.'

'But your husband must show you a new acquisition. He'd be excited, pleased with it.'

'Yes. But that's before he puts it in this room and there haven't been any purchases for about a year.'

'Why not?'

'I don't know.' Her eyes fell to the floor.

She was clearly lying. 'Did he buy anything on the last cruise?'

He noticed that she was looking even more harrowed than when they had arrived.

'You mean an antiquity or weapon? No.'

'Did he buy anything while in Japan?'

'Those inkwells.' She pointed to them on the central plinth.

'Had he already arranged with someone in Japan to purchase them?'

'I don't know. I suppose he must have done. He has lots of contacts all over the world.'

And Horton wouldn't mind seeing a list of them. He surveyed the room again. Wherever Clements had gone, he hadn't taken anything from here.

They followed her along the short passageway to her husband's study. Horton surveyed the neat room with its quality mahogany desk, low-level matching bookcases, burgundy leather swivel chair and a leather two-seater Chesterfield sofa. It was the archetypal gentleman's study, he thought, crossing to the desk while Cantelli scanned the bookshelves. There was a blotter on the desk, a tray of pens, a telephone of the antique variety but obviously functional, and space for Clements' computer. There was also a Wi-Fi router on a cabinet behind the desk. There was no sign of Clements' laptop computer and no note for Constance Clements.

He asked her where the safe was. She opened the cupboard doors of the sideboard behind the desk to reveal a sturdy-looking, dark grey safe. 'It's bolted to the floor. This is a fake cupboard front, as you can see.'

He watched her open it. Inside were several files, some jewellery and their passports. So Clements hadn't skipped the country.

'Could you check whether he's taken any clothes or other personal belongings with him?' he asked.

She hesitated, obviously wondering whether she should leave them alone, then nodded and left.

Horton reached for the files from the safe while Cantelli went through the desk drawers.

In the first file Horton found the paperwork for the collection. He flicked through it, mentally noting that the stolen pistols had been purchased from an online specialist as Clements had told them. Some of the other items gave the name of the individual buyers, which included several from the Far East. And there were certificates and paperwork which seemed to authenticate them. He'd need someone more expert to look through this lot and to match the paperwork to the items in the collection. He'd ask Constance Clements for permission to do both. She might refuse but in light of her concern over her husband's disappearance he couldn't see how she could.

Another file contained personal items such as birth and marriage certificates. He assumed the deeds of the house were kept with the solicitors. There was a copy of their wills, each naming the other as beneficiary. A further file contained details of Clements' talks, including the contract for the recent cruise. It was a sizeable fee.

Cantelli looked up from his search of the desk. 'There's a file here with a list of antiques including pistols with circles around some of the items. There are details pulled off the Internet and some photographs, and notes and names of individuals, websites and contact details. It looks like a shopping list.'

'Might be worth looking into, especially his notes on any pistols,' Horton said. He caught the sound of footsteps on the stairs. Constance Clements entered, looking disturbed.

'He hasn't taken any clothes with him.'

Horton asked if they could keep the paperwork on the antiques.

She shifted, uneasy. 'I don't think Vivian would like that.'

She seemed a little afraid. Why? Clements was pompous but was he also violent? Horton couldn't envisage that but it didn't have to be physical abuse. Mental torment was just as damaging.

Cantelli's phone rang. He dashed a glance at it

171

and excused himself to answer it. Horton turned to her.

'I'd appreciate it if you left everything here as it is. We'll put a call out for your husband. If you could give us his vehicle details and a description of what he was wearing the last time you saw him . . .'

'Of course.'

'And if he should return in the meantime, let us know immediately.'

'I will.' She closed the study door behind her and they made their way back up into the hall where Cantelli came off the phone. Horton knew instantly that something had occurred but no one else would have detected it. Swiftly, he made his farewells to Constance Clements after she'd relayed details of her husband's car and the clothes he was wearing.

Outside, Cantelli said, 'That was Sergeant Stride. A woman walking her dog has found a body on Milton Common on the edge of Swan Lake and, before you ask, it's not wearing a Tutu.'

Horton gave a grim smile at the black humour.

'It looks like suicide but the description of the pistol beside the body given by the uniformed officer in attendance prompted Stride to call us.'

Horton felt a cold chill run up his spine. He knew what was coming. Cantelli didn't have to tell him but he did.

'It sounds very much as though we've found Vivian Clements.'

Thirteen

'So Clements killed Freedman and then shot himself?' Uckfield pronounced as they stood at the entrance to the canvas tent which had been erected over the body of Vivian Clements.

The area had been cordoned off and they were waiting for Dr Clayton to arrive. Uckfield had given instructions to bypass Dr Sharman, who would only state the bleeding obvious. SOCO were examining the wider area outside the tent, while Clarke was snapping away inside it. Phil Taylor of SOCO had told them they'd found nothing suspicious in Freedman's flat such as blood traces, which Horton hadn't expected. There were several sets of fingerprints he'd said, mostly Freedman's but there were others which could belong to the cleaners, clients or friends. Horton had already asked the fingerprint bureau to match them with the Clements' prints. Uckfield had released the touched-up picture of the coat Freedman had been wearing when shot to the media, which had set up a frenzy of phone calls but nothing relevant so far.

Two four-wheel drive police vehicles straddled either side of the scene. One had brought the scene of crime officers with them while the other had transported Uckfield over the rough terrain. Cantelli had parked in the residential area bordering Milton Common, where they had found

Clements' car. Leaving an officer to watch over it, they'd walked to the scene, much as Clements had done last night, thought Horton.

He understood Uckfield's reasoning and on the surface it looked like murder followed by suicide. They had a possible motive too – jealousy. Not that Constance Clements had admitted an affair but, reading her body language, Horton thought it highly probable. They also had the means – a pistol. And according to Constance Clements, her husband had certainly had the opportunity. But although Horton could see Clements shooting Freedman he couldn't see him killing himself. He thought him too arrogant to have taken such drastic action but it looked as though he was wrong.

He turned to survey the area. They were on the seaward side of Swan Lake, one of three small lakes, in an area of wild grassland, reed beds and shrubs. The entire area had once been Milton Lake until the land had been reclaimed in the 1960s by filling it with domestic rubbish and any other conceivable bit of junk nobody knew what to do with. In the mid-1970s the land had been capped and grassed and was now a Site of Importance for Nature Conservation.

The wind was blasting off the sea of Langstone Harbour, bringing with it the smell of seaweed and a cold easterly wind. He caught the call of a flock of Brent Geese flying overhead and he could see some grazing along the shore line in the harbour. It was an hour after high tide. To the west, behind him, was the dual carriageway that led out of Portsmouth on its eastern boundary.

To the south was the densely populated area of housing called Milton, which wasn't far from Eastney Lake and Horton's marina, and where Freedman's body had been found.

Horton, like Uckfield, was wearing a scene suit, which they now both climbed out of. He'd called the Super on his way to the scene, giving him a swift update, and had rung him again as soon as he and Cantelli had set eyes on the dead man. There was no doubt it was Vivian Clements, despite the fact the top half of his head was a bloody mangle of bone and brains where he must have put the gun to his temple. The pistol lay beside him. It looked old, or rather antique. It might have been on Clements' list of stolen pistols but until he could get a closer look at it he wouldn't know. He said as much.

Uckfield popped another throat lozenge in his mouth. 'We'll see what Dr Clayton comes up with and how Clements' wife reacts to the news when we tell her that her husband's dead. If she doesn't give us permission to search the premises I'll apply for a warrant.'

'She denies any affair with Peter Freedman.'

'She would,' Uckfield scathingly replied.

It would have been dark when Clements had come here, if Constance Clements' account could be believed, and raining lightly. There were no lights. The nearest were on the dual carriageway and that was too far away to illuminate this area. It was a very private place to kill yourself, Horton thought. There was a heavy-duty torch beside the body. Clements was wearing ordinary shoes not boots, the ground was soggy and there was mud on the bottom of his khaki trousers. But what was a bit of mud when you were intent on killing yourself? He was also wearing a heavy duty raincoat.

He looked up to see the petite figure of Dr Clayton heading towards them. Her large waterproof sailing jacket swamped her tiny figure and she looked almost childlike in the bright pink and yellow floral-patterned wellington boots. Cantelli's were the more traditional green. He always kept them in the boot of his car while Horton's shoes and the bottom of his trousers were mud spattered like Uckfield's. Cantelli was carrying Gaye's medical case and they were deep in conversation. She smiled broadly at something Cantelli was saying and he grinned back. Perhaps he was describing the antics of the twins or one of his other three children. Horton watched with an all-too-familiar feeling of being an outsider, of glimpsing a life from which he was for ever to be excluded. He had no reason to believe that the future would hold the same as the past but believing and feeling, in his experience, were two very different things.

She locked eyes with him. He took a silent breath, knowing that his feelings for her were deepening and he believed hers were for him, but he didn't want anyone to know that. Certainly not Uckfield, who, if he discovered it, would announce it to the entire Hampshire Constabulary and make endless jokes and snide remarks about it. And Horton wasn't prepared to take that. Not that he cared for himself, but he wasn't going to have Gaye made the nudge, nudge, wink, wink innuendo of the police force.

He turned away but not before catching her puzzled glance, and nodded at Taylor who hurried across with a scene suit as Clarke emerged from the tent.

'We'll leave you to it,' Uckfield said to her.

They stepped further away from the tent. Horton could see a couple of walkers talking to a uniformed officer on the outer cordon, probably asking why this area of the common had been sealed off. News would travel fast and probably already had. Leanne Payne and the photographer from the local newspaper might already be on their way. Two suspicious deaths in a short space of time would certainly be newsworthy, especially if Leanne Payne discovered they had both been caused by gunshot wounds. Uckfield was still keeping that, and Freedman's identity, quiet for the time being, but Horton knew it wouldn't be long before it was leaked. Anyone in the apartment block where Freedman lived could put it out on the Internet. He'd have to announce it very soon. He looked happier now that he thought these two cases might be neatly signed off as murder followed by suicide but Horton still had some questions that didn't fit with that scenario.

'Why would Freedman arrange to meet Vivian Clements on Tuesday night?'

Sucking heavily on his throat lozenge, Uckfield answered, 'Perhaps he thought he was meeting Constance Clements. She'd arranged the meeting but her old man overheard her on the phone and they had a row. Then Vivian Clements slipped out before she could warn Freedman and killed him. She knows her husband killed Freedman or suspects it which was why she was nervy and upset.'

'But why would he meet Constance Clements dressed as vagrant?'

Uckfield sniffed. 'Perhaps she'll tell us when we question her.'

'Is there anything in Freedman's flat or on his computer to indicate they were lovers?'

'Not so far but the computer's still being examined. Dennings has sifted through the paperwork from Freedman's flat. There's no birth certificate or anything of a personal nature – just a few bills, details of his accountant and a copy of his will leaving his body to medical science, as Dr Clayton told us. His worldly goods are to be split fifty-fifty between the Salvation Army and Gravity.'

Horton wondered how much that was. Ashmead would be pleased with the legacy, especially if it was a substantial one, but he thought Ashmead would have preferred Freedman alive not just for the continuous contribution of ten per cent of his income but, more importantly, for the vital work he had done for the customers of the centre.

Horton thoughts flicked to Evelyn Lyster. His enquiries that morning at the Hard seemed an age ago but he wondered how much her estate was worth. It looked as though Rowan Lyster was going to be a fairly wealthy young man if only on the proceeds of the sale of that flat, which had to be worth about half a million pounds.

Gaye emerged from the tent with Clarke following. She was holding a plastic evidence bag. She crossed to them and handed the bag to Uckfield, saying, 'The contents of his trouser and coat pockets.'

Horton could see a wallet, a set of keys, a white handkerchief and a mobile phone. The latter might prove interesting.

'Is it suicide?' Uckfield asked eagerly.

'You know as well as I do, Superintendent, that I can't tell you that until I've examined him.'

'But suicides usually shoot themselves in the head,' he insisted.

'Some do, not all. It has been known for suicides to shoot themselves in the back of the head or in the back.'

'He'd have to have been a bloody contortionist,' Uckfield grunted.

'It's incredible what people can do if they're intent on killing themselves. I once had a corpse who had shot himself but had also put his head in a noose in case he failed to kill himself with a gun.'

'Talk about belt and braces,' Uckfield muttered.

'Most suicides, though, shoot themselves in the temple – right-handed people in the right temple and left-handed in the left temple, although there are exceptions. Other than that, in descending order they shoot themselves in the mouth, under the chin and the forehead. But it has been known for some to even shoot themselves in the eye or ear, or on the top of the head.'

Cantelli was shaking his head in wonder.

'From my brief examination, though, I'd say he was shot in the forehead, using the gun in his right hand. He then fell back and the gun dropped from his hand to land a short distance away. But,' she emphasized, stilling Uckfield's reply, 'I can't say yet for certain if *he* used the gun or indeed if it was that gun found lying beside him that killed him. The pattern of injuries show that he was shot at close range but he didn't press the barrel of the gun to his temple and fire. *If* he held the gun then he did so about a foot away. I'll be able to confirm the distance once I take a closer look.'

Uckfield sneezed loudly into his handkerchief.

Gaye continued, 'My initial estimate of time of death puts it about eighteen to twelve hours ago. It's difficult to be more accurate because of the environmental conditions but you're looking at some time between say five p.m. and eleven p.m.'

And that fitted with what Constance Clements had told them.

'Why come here to kill himself?' Cantelli mused. 'Why not walk across the road from where he lived to the beach and do it there?'

Horton answered, 'Maybe that would have been too public. Or perhaps as we'd thought for Freedman' – and Evelyn Lyster, he mentally added – 'this place had a special meaning for him.'

'You mean he was a birdwatcher?' sniffed Uckfield dubiously.

No, Horton didn't have Clements down as a twitcher. 'Perhaps he and Constance liked walking around here.' But he didn't see Vivian Clements as a walker either.

Gaye said, 'I can't confirm if the bullet exited the body, not without examining him, but you'd do as well to search for it just in case. I'll perform the autopsy as soon as you get the body to me.'

Taylor emerged from the tent carrying the gun encased in an evidence bag. He handed it to Cantelli, saying in his usual glum manner, 'We've managed to lift some prints from it but they're very smudged.'

'Any bullets lying close to it or the body?' asked Uckfield.

'No, sir.'

Horton judged the pistol to be about twelve inches in length with a barrel that he estimated to be about six inches. It had a dark-coloured, finely chequered walnut grip and he could see the name of the manufacturer and the serial number on it – Adams Patent No. 30088. He seemed to remember from his firearms training and studies that there had been a Victorian British gun manu-facturer called Robert Adams. He said as much, adding, 'If I remember correctly Adams revolvers were used during the Crimean War, the Indian Mutiny and the American Civil War.'

'So unless we've got a ghost who's returned from any of those conflicts to kill Freedman it fits with Clements and his antique pistols,' Uckfield said a little sourly.

And mention of a ghost made Horton think of one who had walked into the casino where Jennifer had been working shortly before she had disappeared. According to her colleague, Susan Nash, the appearance of this person had shaken Jennifer so much that she had gone 'deathly pale

181

as though she'd seen a ghost'. She'd left the gaming table – strictly against the rules – and after she had returned, and in the days following this apparition, she'd been elated. Was this person someone she had believed dead? Was the 'ghost' her killer?

'It wasn't on the list of stolen items.' Cantelli's voice brought Horton up sharply. Cantelli would see that the pistol reached their firearms expert very quickly – the same expert who was studying Freedman's wound. And neither had it been on Clements' wish list obtained from his desk, thought Horton. That paperwork had been given to a uniformed officer to take back to Trueman in the incident suite.

'How many more guns has he got that he's not notified us about?' growled Uckfield. 'Let's see what's in his car.'

With Gaye they walked back to the road where Clements had left his car. A wide cordon had been set up around it and beyond it a gathering crowd, most of whom were taking pictures with their phones.

'The ghouls are here,' Uckfield muttered.

'And the press,' Horton added, spotting Leanne Payne's lean figure. He heard her calling Uckfield. The latter ignored her and turned his attention to the car. Gaye stood beside him, making no effort to return to her Mini parked within the outer cordon. Extracting the keys from the evidence bag she'd handed Uckfield, Horton watched as the Super opened the boot. There was nothing inside except a rug and a large golfing umbrella. Uckfield told Cantelli to get the car towed away for forensic examination and to call the under-takers. Uckfield reached for his mobile phone and stepped away. He'd be ringing through to the incident suite and to ACC Dean.

Horton turned to Gaye. 'I hope this won't delay your trip to Denmark.'

'I don't leave until tomorrow evening. I'll get everything tied up my end by then, but you can still reach me by phone and email, and I'll have my laptop with me just in case you or Superintendent Uckfield need to discuss it further. I'll have to inform the coroner that I'll be away and I'll pass all the information over to a colleague, unless the coroner agrees to delay the inquest.'

'He'll probably open and postpone it,' Horton said.

She eyed him curiously. 'You don't think he shot himself, do you?'

'I'm not sure.' Horton told her what he and Uckfield had discussed earlier about Clements possibly killing Freedman and then himself, adding, 'If Clements was murdered though and the same person killed them both wouldn't he or she have aimed for the same part of the body?'

'Not necessarily. Perhaps Clements stepped backwards, alarmed to see someone approaching him with the gun. He tried to reason with the killer, slipped in the mud or stumbled over a bramble and fell, landing on his back. Or the killer pushed him hard so that he lost his footing and fell. Before the victim had time to recover the killer aimed and fired at the head.'

Horton suppressed a shudder. 'Must be a hard bastard to have done that.'

'Hard, calm, cold, dispassionate, angry, desperate . . . who knows, but I have every confidence you'll find out.'

'Thanks.' Now was the time to ask her for that dinner date on her return from Denmark but there was something else he wanted to discuss with her, maybe over that dinner, maybe not, and it had to do with his past, or rather his mother's, and possibly the identity of that 'ghost'. Uckfield was still on the phone and Cantelli was talking to a uniformed officer. They were alone but wouldn't be for long. 'There's something I'd like to discuss with you,' he began.

'Concerning work?'

'Yes and no.'

She raised her eyebrows. 'Sounds intriguing.'

'It's about a fire that occurred in 1968 at a psychiatric hospital in Surrey.' He registered her surprise but before he could elaborate Uckfield was steaming towards them. Hastily, Horton said, 'We'll talk later.'

Uckfield said, 'I'll give a brief statement to Leanne Payne if only to shut her up. You'd better break the news to the widow.'

Uckfield would withhold information on the identity of the body until they had told Constance Clements. Horton watched Gaye cross to her Mini and climb in. He wondered what she was making of his comment. Perhaps she thought him slightly mad. Maybe he was. Perhaps he shouldn't have said anything because he'd have to explain why he was interested.

'How do you think Constance Clements will take the news?' Cantelli asked, interrupting his thoughts.

Horton focused his mind on the unpleasant task that lay ahead. He didn't know. Losing her husband and her lover would be tough, but how tough they were about to find out.

Fourteen

'Vivian would never kill himself,' Constance Clements firmly declared.

'Why do you say that?' Cantelli asked gently. They were in the drawing room where the burglars had allegedly entered.

'Because he has a very low pain threshold and, if he was ever going to kill himself, then it would be by a much less painful method.'

As evenly and as kindly as he could, Horton said, 'Shooting yourself is a very quick and painless way of dying.' Unless it went wrong, of course, and maybe it had for Clements. He could have lain there and bled to death for some time before eventually dying. Gaye would be able to tell them if that was the case. But he wasn't going to tell the widow that. He studied the confused expression on her harrowed face.

'Are you certain it is Vivian?' she asked.

'There's no doubt, Mrs Clements,' Cantelli reiterated.

But they would need her to make a formal identification. Time to tell her that later.

She sank on to one of the sumptuous chairs in front of the fireplace. Bewildered, she said, 'This doesn't make sense. Vivian. Dead?'

Horton took the chair opposite across a heavy dark oak chest that doubled as a coffee table. 'Did he give any indication to you that he intended taking his own life?'

Alarm registered in her dazed eyes. 'No. Never. Oh, he's been moody, but never depressed. And apart from being furious about the robbery . . . I didn't think . . . I can't imagine . . . to shoot himself.' Her words trailed off. She clasped her hands tightly in her lap, as though trying to control her emotions by controlling them.

'This is a picture of the weapon that was found beside him. Do you recognize it?' Horton handed her his mobile phone. Jim Clarke had emailed one of the photographs he'd taken of the pistol. Horton wondered if she'd be appalled or if she'd shrink back, frightened and distressed at the sight of it. Or would seeing it prompt her to tell them about the fake robbery? But she only stared at it, baffled.

'I don't think I've seen it before,' she answered hesitantly. 'One gun looks very much the same to me. Is it on the list you got from the safe?'

No, but he wasn't going to tell her that yet, not until they had thoroughly checked. He said, 'It's not one of the stolen pistols and yet it was in your husband's possession.' But had it been? wondered Horton, recalling what Gaye had said. If Clements *had* been killed maybe the killer had brought the gun with him. Clements had been a gun collector. Perhaps he'd bought his guns from dubious sources. He could have come across some nasty bastards whom he might owe money. Or perhaps he'd been asked to supply guns to a criminal. But a criminal or a collector wouldn't have left it behind, unless he wanted it to look like suicide.

He'd given her another chance to tell them about the phoney robbery. She didn't take it. Maybe she didn't know about it. Perhaps he was wrong and there really had been a robbery and one that her husband had colluded in, not for insurance purposes but to allow the pistols to get into criminal hands.

He said, 'I know this must be very difficult for you, but do you know of any reason why your husband was at Milton Common?'

'Was that where . . . where he was found?'

Horton nodded.

She looked baffled. Her hands unclasped and began to fiddle with her bracelet, turning it round and round. 'I've no idea. Why would he go there?' She appealed to them with pleading in her blue eyes seeking the answers, but they had none to give.

Cantelli took up the questioning. 'Was your husband in financial difficulties?'

Horton remembered that Treadware had said that Clements hadn't been the most prompt of payers and he hadn't settled his account for the servicing of the alarm in October.

'Not that I'm aware of.'

'You have a joint account?'

'Yes, but Vivian deals with all the finances. He never said anything was wrong. You think he could have shot himself because of that?' Her eyes scoured their faces for explanations.

'We'll need to look into it,' Cantelli said.

'Yes, I suppose you must.' She glanced down at her hands and then pressed them together and held them tightly in her lap.

'Was he in good health?'

'Yes.' Her voice was strained and her face was growing more haggard by the minute. Cantelli, noticing this, asked her if there was anyone they could call who could comfort her but she shook her head.

'No. I'll be OK. I just can't take it in. I can't believe he'd do this. I should have understood. I shouldn't have said such dreadful things.'

'You mustn't blame yourself,' Cantelli said.

'But I do.' She rounded on him. 'If I hadn't shouted back at him he wouldn't have left the house and . . .' She rose and turned away from them towards the fireplace. Cantelli exchanged a glance with Horton. After a moment, she turned back, clearly with an effort to control her emotions.

'Will I need to see him?'

Horton answered. 'We'll need you to make a formal identification.' The mortician would make sure to cover the top part of the head which had been blown away. And perhaps then she'd be ready to tell them what had really happened.

'When?' she said a little harshly.

'Detective Sergeant Cantelli will arrange it and let you know.'

She nodded solemnly.

Horton continued, 'Did your husband give you any indication of where he went on Tuesday night?'

'No. He went straight into his collection room and came to bed about midnight. He'd been drinking.'

'And on Wednesday?'

'He was very short-tempered and edgy. As I told you, we began arguing. I walked out and when I came back he was gone.' Her set expression told Horton she was not prepared to go into details of what they had been arguing about. He believed it was over the phoney robbery. They'd get it from her later but he didn't think now was the time to put pressure on her to reveal it. Uckfield would probably disagree but Horton thought it would only make her more determined to say nothing. He could also probe her about her relationship with Freedman and ask if she'd called him and arranged to meet him on Tuesday night, but if she had he was back to that same old question: why would Freedman dress up as a vagrant?

He rose. 'Are you sure there's no one we can call for you?'

'No. Thanks. I'll manage.'

Before leaving, Cantelli obtained her bank details and the name of her husband's doctor.

In the car, Horton said, 'Was she having an affair with Freedman?'

Cantelli did a three-point turn and headed towards the seafront.

'I'm not sure. She didn't make the connection

189

and she seemed genuinely confounded that her husband could kill himself. She's holding something back, though, and once she's over the initial shock it'll be interesting to see what her reaction is. I certainly don't think her marriage was a very happy one. Perhaps she'll be glad she's rid of him and she'll probably be quite wealthy if she sells the collection and the house, unless Clements is mortgaged to the hilt. I'll check that with his bank.'

Perhaps, like Evelyn Lyster, she'd get rid of everything that reminded her of her husband and start afresh. Evelyn Lyster's marriage had by all accounts been a part-time one with her husband abroad so often. Horton glanced at the clock on the dashboard and was astounded to see it was almost three o'clock. The day was racing away and so much had happened. They'd had no chance to eat. The inquest into Evelyn Lyster's death must be over by now and Guilbert would have dropped Rowan Lyster off at the airport for his fifteen fifty-five flight home. Horton switched on his phone and saw he'd missed a call from Guilbert. Horton returned it as Cantelli drove through the busy streets towards the station.

Horton asked first about the inquest on Evelyn Lyster and got the expected reply.

'Open and adjourned for a fortnight to give us more time. Rowan Lyster didn't seem very happy about that, but that's understandable. The coroner issued a burial certificate. And before you ask, Andy, I'm still waiting on the toxicology results.'

Horton asked how his chat with Rowan had gone.

'Dennis Lyster was insured but Rowan has no idea if his mother was. He doesn't know why she visited the Isle of Wight. They don't have any relatives there and his mother never mentioned having friends on the Island. He was uneasy when I mentioned his father's body being found by Ryde Pier, but when I suggested that his mother might have gone to the Isle of Wight as a way of getting close to the deceased or in an act of remembrance, he stared at me as though I had a screw loose. He says his parents led quite separate lives and he didn't see a lot of them growing up because he'd been away at school.'

Horton said he'd let him know if he came up with anything his end. Walters would have been back from the Clements' cleaners long ago and would have had time to view the footage from the port for sightings of Evelyn Lyster there on Monday. There had to be a reason why she had travelled to the Isle of Wight the day before travelling to Guernsey and it wasn't because she liked ferries. By the time he'd updated Cantelli they were pulling into the station car park. Horton stopped off in the canteen to buy some sandwiches while Cantelli headed for the CID operations room to eat his homemade ones.

Horton needed to report back on how Constance Clements had taken the news of her husband's death but first he returned to CID to eat his lunch and get an update from Walters, who was busily munching his way through a packet of Jaffa Cakes.

'June Valentine confirmed that her company has been cleaning for the Clements for eight months.

The cleaners go in twice a week, Mondays and Fridays. Monday they do the ground floor and the basement, not the collection room, but they clean Vivian Clements' study, and Fridays the bedrooms and bathrooms on the first floor. There are a couple of rooms on the top floor used for storing things but they only do that once a month. The last time was in November before the cruise.'

Just as Constance Clements had told them, with the exception of that top-floor room, which was interesting.

'I had to hang around to talk to the two women who regularly clean the Clements' house, Shirley Yardley and Patricia Richmond, because they were out working, which was why I was so long.'

Knowing Walters, he'd have found the nearest café and filled his face.

'They said that Constance was friendly and let them get on with the work but he was a pain in the proverbial. He never smiled, said good morning, kiss my arse or nothing. Stuck up.'

'Well, he's not any more.'

'Yeah, I heard he's dead. Top himself, did he?'

'That's what we're waiting for Dr Clayton to confirm. When were the cleaners last at the house?'

'December, before the Clements went on their cruise. They were due to go in tomorrow but Mrs Clements telephoned yesterday afternoon and cancelled it. They're still scheduled to clean on Monday.'

'Did she give a reason why she'd cancelled?'

'Said she didn't need them, having just returned from the cruise. She didn't mention the robbery. I've run Shirley Yardley and Patricia Richmond's details through criminal records. They're both clean, as June Valentine was at great pains to tell me. She said all her staff are criminally checked before they're engaged and come with excellent references.'

Cantelli looked up from his computer. 'They could have lied and faked their references.'

'That's what I said and wish I hadn't. I thought Ms Valentine was going to knee me in the balls for even suggesting it. She's built like a sumo wrestler. She made it clear that if any of her employees lied then they'd better look out for their kneecaps.'

'And if the clients don't pay their bills?'

'She doesn't need to send in any heavies – believe me, she's scary enough to frighten anyone into coughing up. The Clements paid on time because they pay by standing order.'

Horton polished off his sandwich. 'And do Valentines clean for Peter Freedman or Evelyn Lyster?'

'Neither. They've got two other clients in Darrin Road: a toffee-nosed naval captain and his equally snotty blonde bimbo wife – the cleaners' words, not mine – and an elderly couple who wax lyrically about their son, Derek, who lives with them and is some kind of computer nut. They're not allowed to touch his office either, which is in the basement. I asked if the cleaners had seen any vans or cars parked outside the Clements' house or in their driveway at any time they were on their cruise but they both said they hadn't.'

'And the CCTV footage from the port?'

With his mouth full, Walters said, 'She's on camera, sitting in the waiting lounge. Smart, good-looking woman.'

'Doing what?'

'Nothing. Just sitting. She's not reading or on her phone. She doesn't look nervous or excited. And she didn't buy anything while waiting.'

'Did anyone talk to her?'

'No. And no one sat near her either.'

'Did anyone approach her outside after the taxi driver had dropped her off?'

'No.'

'Did she drink from her cup flask?'

'Not while the camera was on her. And as far as I can see, she didn't visit the ladies' room either.'

But perhaps she'd taken a drink from that cup flask in the minibus on the way to board the ferry and finished drinking it in her cabin.

Horton asked Walters to get on to the cruise company to check what Constance Clements had told them about the cruise to Japan and to find out if Freedman had been on the same cruise, either as a passenger or a guest lecturer. 'Check with the Border Agency to see if he's travelled abroad, where and when.'

Horton reported into the incident suite where Uckfield, seeing him, beckoned him in to his office. A few seconds later, Bliss entered, prob-ably scared she was going to miss out on something, but maybe Uckfield had already instructed her to join them because he buzzed through to Dennings and Trueman and ordered them in. The phones were ringing constantly. Horton didn't need to be told that the world and

194

his wife were calling in about the coat Freedman had been wearing. Even the usually implacable Trueman looked slightly harassed. He reported that the fingerprint bureau had rung to say that the prints in Freedman's flat were neither of the Clements.

Horton relayed Constance Clements' reaction to the news of her husband's death and that she denied ever having seen the gun.

Trueman said, 'It's a Victorian British Robert Adams Patent Large Frame .54-inch Bore Five Shot Double Action Percussion Revolver.' As Horton had already said but Trueman had obviously got more details. Horton mentally noted that Freedman had been shot with a percussion revolver and knew that the others around Uckfield's conference table were also thinking the same, Bliss by her usual scowl, Dennings by his smug look and Uckfield by his sniff.

Trueman continued, 'It was retailed by Maynard Harris & Grice, London. The markings are on the pistol. Robert Adams was a nineteenth-century British gunsmith who patented the first successful double-action revolver in 1851. This revolver,' he stabbed at the pictures he had spread out on the table in front of them, 'was manufactured in 1861. Adams' revolvers were a popular private purchase weapon for British Army Officers. It fires moulded lead balls and conical bullets. Yeah, so it fits with what Dr Clayton said about Freedman being shot with a lead-based conical shaped bullet. It's worth about four thousand pounds and doesn't require a licence as it's classed as an antique as long as it's kept as part of a collection or display.'

195

Horton said, 'Except it doesn't seem to have been in Clements' collection – or rather, in his display.'

'And he got ammunition for it and made it function,' said Uckfield.

'And he never notified us or a firearms officer about any of his weapons,' added Bliss.

Dennings said, 'Perhaps he'd only just bought it on that last cruise. The National Ballistics Intelligence Service say there are no incidents matching the Clements' MO or of anyone being shot with any of the guns stolen from Vivian Clements.'

'Ask them if they've got anything that matches this Adams gun,' Uckfield commanded.

Trueman continued, 'Our ballistic expert claims that Clements' stolen antique pistols could be made to fire if someone was hell-bent on making bullets for them but it would take someone who knew what they were doing and had the equipment to do so and in-depth knowledge of the guns. He says the Adams revolver has been fired and he's conducting tests on it to see if it matches the wounds inflicted on Freedman and Clements. That and Dr Clayton's results on Clements' autopsy should give us more.'

'Have you got anything from Clements' mobile phone?' asked Horton.

'His log of recent calls received confirms his wife rang him when she told you she did. She left a message each time. The last call he made was to his insurance company on Wednesday morning. There's no record that he phoned Freedman or Freedman called him but he could

196

have deleted it from his log. I've applied for his mobile phone records but they'll take time to come through.'

'Didn't phone the Samaritans then,' Uckfield said with heavy cynicism.

'Seems not,' Trueman answered, treating Uckfield's remark as genuine though he knew it wasn't.

Dennings reported that the search on Milton Common hadn't retrieved any bullet. 'Just drink cans, sweet wrappers, empty fag packets, dog shit and those bags dog owners put their pooch's crap in and then leave lying around or suspended from bushes, all of which have been bagged up,' he added, though by his tone he clearly thought it a waste of time. Horton was in agreement. That part of the common would be the cleanest it had been for years. The search was still continuing but there was only an hour of good light left. Perhaps Gaye would find the bullet in Clements' body.

'Did SOCO find anything at the scene?' Horton asked.

Dennings answered, 'There are several footprints close to the body. Harris, the footwear mark examiner, is comparing them with Vivian Clements' shoes. But it's too muddy to lift clear enough marks.'

Uckfield's phone rang. He hauled himself up from the conference table and crossed to his desk. Glancing at the caller display, he said without picking it up, 'It's the press – Leanne Payne.' He nodded at Bliss. 'Call her and tell her you'll give her an update as soon as we have anything to say.'

Horton returned to his office to find Walters on the phone. Cantelli reported that he had an appointment with the Clements' bank on Monday. Constance Clements had given the bank permission to divulge the financial information they required. He'd also spoken to Clements' GP.

'Apart from his inoculations for his travels abroad, Vivian Clements rarely saw the doctor and he's never been treated for depression.'

Walters replaced the receiver. 'That was the cruise company. Peter Freedman wasn't on the same cruise to Japan as the Clements and neither has he been on any of their other cruises to Japan or anywhere else.'

Horton threw Cantelli a puzzled look. 'Didn't Constance Clements tell us she'd met Freedman on that cruise?'

Cantelli quickly consulted his notes although Horton didn't think he needed to. Horton was rapidly mentally replaying their conversation. Cantelli said, 'She confirmed that she and her husband had been on a cruise to Japan and the timing fits with when Freedman had his inoculations for Japanese encephalitis, but she didn't actually say that she'd met him on the boat.'

Walters chipped in. 'I'm still waiting for the Border Agency to tell us where Freedman travelled to and when.'

'Did they meet in Japan by accident or by design?' wondered Horton. 'We know that Freedman must have gone there, otherwise why have the inoculation? What was Freedman doing there?'

'Learning some new oriental practice like meditation or something?' suggested Walters. 'To

198

go alongside his coaching skills and that mind-fulness crap.'

Maybe. Horton would like to know. He entered his office and checked his messages and emails. He answered those that were urgent or had been waiting a while for an answer, made a few calls and then ran through the reports. There was still nothing from the Clements' neighbours. He checked the cases that had come in over the last few days – some burglaries, an assault – but his attention was distracted by the sound of a car pulling into the car park. Looking out of the window, he saw Gaye climb out of her Mini. Returning to CID, he hastily gathered up Walters and Cantelli and, without waiting to be invited, made for the incident suite, eager to know the results of the autopsy on Clements.

Fifteen

'It's not suicide,' Gaye announced. 'There is no evidence that Clements ever held that gun.'

Uckfield glared at her. Bang went his neat and tidy end to the investigation.

'Let me explain.' She perched on a desk at the front of the incident suite and addressed them. The phones were still ringing and being answered by civilians and officers but Uckfield had called Marsden and Somerfield over and Horton and his team had been joined by Bliss, Dennings and Trueman.

'When the deceased contemplates suicide, he or she usually holds the gun for a while, leaving a yellow- to orange-brown area of discolouration on the skin in the palm of the hand. With Clements there is no evidence of this or of residue on the back of the firing hand or of back spatter – blood droplets – there or on the other hand which is sometimes used to steady the muzzle. I called George McGann, the ballistics expert, who confirms that there is no blood or tissue on the gun either outside on the muzzle or inside the barrel, which doesn't preclude it being fired at close contact but that, along with the other factors, confirms it was fired from an intermediary range.'

'As in the Freedman case?' asked Cantelli.

'Yes, between two to three feet.'

Horton stretched out his arm as he said, 'That's pretty close quarters – arm's length. The killer must have been looking Clements in the eye.'

'Yes. It took some nerve. And this time I found the bullet embedded in the skull, which I've despatched to McGann – the bullet, that is, not the skull – and he'll be able to confirm if the barrelling on it matches that of the Robert Adams' revolver found at the scene. The shape of the wound in this victim matches that of the first. I can't say for certain though that they were both killed with the same gun. McGann will need to confirm that.'

Uckfield said, 'So Clements' death was made to look like suicide in order to make us believe he'd killed Freedman and then couldn't live with that knowledge.'

Bliss said, 'Perhaps Vivian Clements killed

Freedman, told his wife about it and she killed him.'

'But why would she lure him to Milton Common to do so?' ventured Horton.

'Because it was dark and no one would see or hear them.'

'So she said, "let's take a walk on the common, darling, in the dark and rain" and he said, "oh, yes, please"?' Uckfield mocked, drawing a grin from Dennings and a scowl from Bliss.

Undaunted, Bliss continued, 'He obviously arranged to meet someone there, someone he wasn't afraid of and who had a strong enough hold on him to get him there. And who he faced with a gun. He didn't turn or run away.' She glanced at Gaye to confirm this.

'He didn't.'

Dennings said, 'He might have stood there and pleaded with his killer for his life.'

Gaye answered, 'He didn't put his hands across his face or in front of him to instinctively protect himself. However, the gun might have been raised and fired at the last moment and taken the victim by surprise.'

Recalling Clements' manner, Horton said, 'He might not have considered it possible that this person had the nerve to fire the gun. Or maybe seeing the type of gun being pointed at him, he felt confident the killer wouldn't have ammunition for it. We've no evidence that it was Clements' gun. He could have gone there to meet someone who told him he had the Robert Adams for sale. Or perhaps Clements was supplying antique, or almost antique, guns to a criminal. Clements got scared when he saw he'd been robbed and told this crook he wanted out. Clements had become a liability so was shot.'

'You're saying Freedman's killer is not the same person who killed Clements? And we've got two nutters running around the city shooting people!' cried Uckfield, horrified.

Horton shrugged. He sincerely hoped not but it was possible. If ballistics came back with the evidence that the same gun had been used to kill both men then it would rule out the two-killer theory but not necessarily a criminal who had expertise in weaponry. And if that was the case then somehow and somewhere along the line, Freedman was connected with it. It was possible it was someone he had met in prison. Someone he might have met while a vagrant who he'd then met again in prison. Perhaps that explained why he'd been dressed as a tramp. He said as much but Bliss wasn't going to give up on her theory of Constance Clements as the killer.

'She could have telephoned her husband using a payphone, disguising her voice, saying she knew the robbery was phoney and that Freedman had been shot with one of his guns, and that unless he met her on Milton Common she'd tell the police. Then she shot him.'

Cantelli said, 'From what I've seen of Vivian Clements, I don't think he'd believe for one moment that his wife was capable of firing a pistol. He would have stood there mocking her, telling her not to be stupid. And bang.' Cantelli fired two fingers. 'But her shock seemed genuine when we told her about her husband's death and she held up well when we questioned her.'

'See if she cracks when she views the body. When can she do that?' Uckfield addressed Gaye.

'Tomorrow, whenever you're ready.'

'And tomorrow we'll have a search warrant for her premises. See to it, Trueman. DCI Bliss, you can front the media tomorrow – we'll discuss the statement. I can't face the TV cameras looking like Rudolph the red-nosed reindeer.'

Bliss followed Uckfield into his office. Gaye stopped to talk to Trueman. Horton headed down the stairs with Walters and Cantelli. There was nothing more they could do that night. He told Cantelli and Walters to go home. As he reached the bottom of the stairs his name was called and he turned to see Gaye behind him.

'You look tired,' he said as she joined him.

'I am.'

'Would a drink help?'

She smiled wearily. 'I'm whacked but—'

'Another time,' Horton said hastily.

'Coffee is rarely refused, though. It's just I can't be bothered to go home and change and then go out to a pub and I don't fancy any of the ones around here.'

Horton understood. He wasn't keen on being seen in a tête-à-tête with her either by any of his colleagues who happened to be in the local pubs. Not because he was ashamed – on the contrary – but he knew the gossip it would fuel. Here on the premises, though, it was different. It would be classed as work. 'The canteen?'

'Perfect.' She smiled and his heart lifted.

He bought them both coffee and they installed themselves at a table in the far corner. He thought it unlikely that Bliss would poke her beaky nose in here but Uckfield could saunter down, although his latest conquest, Alison, wasn't working and his cold was still raging so maybe he'd simply go home, a fact that was confirmed as Horton took their coffee to the table and saw Uckfield's car leave through the slightly steamed-up windows.

'I haven't forgotten I owe you a dinner.'

'Probably several.'

'When you get back from Europe?'

'Sounds good to me.'

He was pleased. She sounded as though she meant it.

She added, 'Let's hope no more suspicious deaths prevent it.'

He hoped so too.

She said, 'OK, so you wanted to know about the fire at the Goldsmith Psychiatric Hospital in 1968.'

'How did you know?' he said, startled.

'You mentioned it earlier on Milton Common.'

'Not the name of the hospital, I didn't.' Through his mind flashed the thought that Eames must have told her, then equally rapidly he dismissed the idea as ludicrous. Why would Eames discuss it with her? 'How do you know about it?' he asked warily.

'I could ask you the same question but I won't, for now,' she added. She sipped her coffee. 'Everyone in my line of business knows about it. But I have an extra-special reason for being interested.'

Horton's heart seemed to skip several beats. What possible involvement could Gaye Clayton have in Jennifer's past? His mind raced with thoughts, each one seemingly more outlandish than the last. He wanted to trust her. Surely he could. He didn't have to tell her everything anyway – certainly nothing about the photograph from 1967.

Seeing him hesitate, she continued, 'It was a case that fascinated my father.'

Horton hid his surprise. If the fire had intrigued Dr Samuel Ryedon, an eminent Home Office forensic pathologist and a living legend in police circles, it meant there was a great deal more to it than the inquiry had found.

Concealing his excitement, he said, 'I didn't see his name mentioned in the inquiry or the autopsy reports.'

'That's because it wasn't. He was in America at the time. He didn't return to the UK until 1974, long after the inquiry had been concluded. It was one of the cases he looked at while researching for one of his books.'

Horton's interest quickened. He should have looked that up. He cursed himself for not researching it more thoroughly.

'I've examined the case myself and my father and I discussed it many times before he died. That and other notable autopsies.' He could see from her tired eyes that she was recalling those days with her father with tenderness.

He thought of Bernard and Eileen Litchfield. 'You must miss him a lot,' he said gently.

'I do. It would have been good to talk over my cases with him.'

Did she talk them over with someone? he wondered. A boyfriend, a partner? He didn't know and hadn't asked. She'd told him once that she had been married, but not for long, and that was all she'd said. He hadn't questioned her about it. It was none of his business.

He sat forward eagerly. 'I'd like to know how thoroughly the autopsies were conducted.'

'Not very. It wasn't necessarily the pathologist's fault – there was only one appointed along with three morticians and it was a huge workload. The pathologist, Dr Jocelyn Jennings, was under extreme strain and things were overlooked. He died three months after completing the examinations.'

'How?' asked Horton.

'Car accident in the Brecon Beacons in Wales. No other vehicle was involved.'

Horton took a breath. He hadn't discovered that information anywhere. The Brecon Beacons was an isolated spot where bad weather could descend in an instant. Had it really been an accident or designed to look like one?

She continued, 'Dr Jennings was an experienced forensic pathologist but he was suffering from depression following the death of his only child, a son, aged fourteen. Dr Jennings found his son hanging from a tree in their garden.'

Horton stifled a shudder and his thoughts flicked to his daughter, Emma. 'The poor man.'

'He should never have been appointed. At the inquest following the car accident it was discovered he'd been drinking heavily. But despite that he should never have been left to handle such a huge workload alone and that was just one of the cock-ups.'

But Horton was beginning to wonder if Jennings' appointment was a genuine error. Perhaps someone had made sure that a vulnerable man had been chosen, a man under pressure. And therefore a man who could make mistakes or find what he'd been told to find.

Gaye eagerly continued, 'There were other interesting factors. Not necessarily unusual for the period – this was 1968 and there was no sealing off the crime scene like there is today and, of course, this being a fire also made it difficult to amass evidence. The scene was contaminated from the start. The firemen, desperate to get the blaze under control, had poured water all over the place. That's understandable – what else could they do? And although they found some charred remains of patients against the door, frantic to escape the flames, they'd walked over them and some of the other remains not realizing they were doing so. Some had perished in their beds.'

'Drugged?'

'Probably. To help them sleep. There were no toxicology tests carried out on the bones to determine if drugs had been used but it was common practice to sedate mentally ill patients and lock them in.'

Horton had discovered that. He swallowed his coffee, noting that the canteen had emptied. It was getting late. He thought of that fire and the patients hammering on the door in desperation, terrified as the clawing black smoke of the fire constricted their throats and stung their eyes, as the heat burned their flesh before smoke inhalation mercifully overcame them. He didn't know where Zachary Benham's remains had been located.

He said, 'From what I've read of the reports, the remains of the victims were gathered up and taken away by the undertakers without any note of where they'd been found.'

'Correct. The room was photographed after the event but *after* all the remains had been removed. So there was no telling who had been pounding the door and who had collapsed elsewhere in the room. Those who had died in bed could be identified by matching the bed with the patient allocated to it but who's to say that one or two of them hadn't got up and someone else had laid down on the bed? Unlikely, I know, but not impossible. The police should have photographed the remains in situ, even if the remains hadn't been numbered and catalogued, but the inspector in charge gave instructions for the remains to be removed.'

'And nobody questioned it,' Horton said, surprised. 'Not even the inquiry findings.'

'No, because this was a mental health issue in the days when you didn't discuss such things unless you had to, and even then mental health was something to be ashamed of. Mentally ill patients were locked away. Out of sight, out of mind. There's still a terrible stigma surrounding mental health today – you can imagine how awful it was then. The issue of mental health coloured the case. It was said that the fire, although tragic, happened to those who had been locked up for their own good and that of the community. It was, shall we say, considered more an act of God than a crime.'

'But why doesn't the inquiry show which patients lay in which beds and which of them had been prescribed sedatives?'

'Good question, and one my father asked. He felt the relatives had the right to know if their son, brother or father had died while already asleep but he was told the record was unavailable because the relatives of those poor souls who had beaten frantically against the door before being overcome by smoke and those screaming to be let out would be traumatized by the horror of it, though that was not the word used at the time. Upset was the term. So in the interest of all it was best left out. I did say this was 1968. The authorities could get away with a lot then.'

So Horton had no idea if Benham had already been drugged or if he'd tried to find a way out, or if, in fact, he had been there in the first place. According to Dormand, he had, but could he believe the word of an assassin? If Dormand was telling the truth then who had Benham been sent to kill? Horton didn't think he stood much chance of finding out by going through the list of patients in that ward – twenty-three of them if he excluded Benham. It would be a long and arduous task and someone would make sure he never got to the truth anyway.

Gaye said, 'Police officers arrived after the fire was extinguished and they inflicted more damage to the remains of those on the floor by trampling on the bones. Dr Jennings maintained that some of the fractures might have been be caused by the fire but they could equally have been caused by the firemen and police officers. There are gaps in the autopsy reports that wouldn't be missed by any competent forensic pathologist today and should have been questioned then but, as I said, Dr Jennings was under considerable strain.'

She drank her coffee.

Horton felt a twinge of guilt at keeping her; there were dark circles under her eyes. But he continued, 'I understand that the identity of the victims was compiled from the list of patients in that ward.'

'Yes. It wasn't thought necessary to identify the patients through dental records because they knew who was in the ward and it had been locked at the start of the fire. There were no personal items or ID on the patients or in their lockers. They weren't allowed any.'

'But one of them was allowed cigarettes and matches. The inquiry found that the fire was started by a cigarette. Rather unusual, don't you think, if they were all considered to be so mentally ill that they had to be locked in.'

'They were locked in for the staff's benefit rather than the patients' welfare. It was to give the staff an easier night and there probably weren't enough staff on duty anyway. But you're right – although it was considered normal to smoke wherever and whenever you pleased in those days, both my father and I thought it unusual that one of these patients had been permitted cigarettes and matches when any one of them could have set fire to himself and the place. He could have stolen them, though, or perhaps they had been smuggled in by a relative or friend of the patient.'

The latter seemed more likely to Horton, especially in light of what he'd discovered from Dormand.

Gaye said, 'No cigarettes or matches were found in the debris but then none of it was documented. It was a very sloppy job.'

'You'd have thought someone would have asked questions.'

'Maybe they did,' she said, eyeing him over the rim of her cup, 'and that someone was told to leave well alone.'

Horton's stomach tightened. He studied Gaye closely. 'Your father?'

'He never said as much and I can't see him leaving something alone just because he was told to, unless it was imperative for him to do so.' She drained her cup.

Horton thought that perhaps Dr Ryedon had been told that it was for the good of the country that it was kept quiet. In 1968, Britain was deep into the Cold War. That would have been enough.

She added, 'I could ask you why you're interested but I don't think you'll tell me so I'll save you from making a polite excuse to fob me off.'

'I don't want to do that,' he said seriously. 'I'd like to tell you but not here or now.'

'Over that dinner?' She must have seen him hesitate. 'Or maybe when you're ready.' And she smiled to show that she understood. He wondered, though, when he would be ready. When he discovered the truth? When he got as far as he could go before the trail came to a complete dead end? Would he ever be ready though to talk about someone who had been locked away inside him for so many years and whom he had vowed with vengeance to cut out of his life, something he thought he had succeeded in doing until recently?

Gaye rose. As they left the canteen, she said, 'I never pursued it myself because if my father didn't there was a very good reason why and I certainly wasn't going to go against him. But it is interesting and it's also curious why it's never come up in all my training or at any of the conferences.' She paused and stared at him. 'Or maybe it's not so curious.'

'Why do you say that?' His heart picked up a beat.

'Someone did a very good hush, hush job on that fire. There was a lot going on in mental institutions in the fifties and sixties that governments and the medical fraternity would prefer not to have exposed and they'll make sure it stays that way.'

And they weren't the only ones, it seemed. 'Such as?'

'I'll tell you that over dinner or, better still, you can take me out sailing. No flapping ears at sea.'

There was nothing he'd like better and, with his spirits lifted, he bid her good night and returned to CID, where he wrote up his reports before heading home.

It was very late. He made himself something to eat and listened to the icy wind whistling through

212

the masts. There was plenty to occupy his thoughts – not only what Gaye had told him about that fire in 1968 but also the murder of Peter Freedman and what now appeared to be the murder of Vivian Clements. Then why did his mind keep veering back to Evelyn Lyster? Her death wasn't murder. It was either suicide or natural causes. But still it nagged at him. There were so many unanswered questions. Just as there were with Jennifer's disappearance and that fire.

Theories ran swiftly through his mind. Had Zachary Benham and the man he'd gone to help, or to kill, been locked in by someone else? Dormand? Had Benham started that fire to eliminate a traitor and then walked out to leave all those men to die? Had Benham perished and the man he'd been sent to kill walked away? Was Benham the ghost Susan Nash said Jennifer had seen walk into the casino? Was Benham his father and a mass murderer?

Horton felt a cold chill run through him and took a deep breath. Was that the secret so awful that Eames was keen for him not to discover it? Was he better off leaving things where they were? Would he be allowed to do so? Did Andrew Ducale want him to discover the truth and Eames to bury it? His head ached with it all and with the questions troubling him about the deaths of Evelyn Lyster, Peter Freedman and Vivian Clements. He'd get nowhere thinking of any of it. Best to grab some sleep, but as he retired to his bunk he wondered if sleep would ever come.

Sixteen

Friday

At four fifteen Horton gave up, showered, shaved and climbed on his Harley. He made his way along the dark and damp seafront to the harbour where he parked in the nearby multi-storey car park, crossed to the railway station and headed down into the Wightlink ferry terminal. He bought a return ticket for the five fifteen to Ryde, wondering why the hell he was doing this. The ferry office had confirmed that no one by the name of Evelyn Lyster had bought a ticket by credit or debit card and so far none of the staff remembered selling her a ticket at the Portsmouth office, but maybe she'd done the same as she had at the international port – bought a single ticket across to the island using cash and a single one again using cash at the Ryde booking office. He'd ask them at Ryde ticket office.

He bought a coffee and watched the Fast Cat ferry ease its way in to the dock. He knew this wasn't the way that Bliss policed. She'd simply lift the phone and ask an officer in Ryde to investigate. That was the correct use of resources, but hell, it was his time and money he was wasting and it had been him who had seen Evelyn Lyster's body in that cabin. And him who had been following this through. He knew what questions to ask.

214

Within thirty minutes he was stepping off the ferry at the end of Ryde Pier waiting for the passengers to embark before questioning the terminal staff. At this time of the morning it was essentially one-way traffic as far as passengers were concerned. Most were travelling from the island to work on the mainland.

He showed Evelyn Lyster's photograph to the terminal staff. No one remembered her but that didn't matter because he'd already had confirmation from one of the crew at the Portsmouth end that she had been on the Fast Cat on Monday morning. He made his way up to the railway station but halted at the coffee shop, which was in the departure lounge. Evelyn Lyster had been carrying a cup flask. It had been empty. He recalled what Gina Lyster had said and the six cup flasks he'd seen in Evelyn Lyster's kitchen cabinet. Because of Evelyn's car accident as a result of not drinking enough and further lowering her blood pressure, she'd always made sure to have a flask made up with coffee to act as a stimulant. Perhaps she'd bought one here to pour into the flask which she'd drank on the Solent crossing. He crossed to the staff serving in the coffee shop.

'Yes, I remember her – smart woman. It was early Monday morning,' one of the women unexpectedly told him. 'She didn't buy a coffee but she had one of those drinking flasks with her. She took it out of her bag, looked up, saw me then put it back again. Probably thought I was going to tell her she couldn't drink it in here.'

'Did she speak to anyone?'

'Not that I saw. After she put her flask back in her bag the ferry came in so she got up to leave.'

That didn't get him any further. He called in at the ticket office and again showed Evelyn Lyster's photograph. The clerk didn't remember her. It had been busy and they were short-staffed. He'd had a headache. Horton headed through the station towards the pier exit on the far right, feeling out of sorts. He crossed to the water and stared at the black mass of swirling sea as it slapped up against the struts. This was where Dennis Lyster's body had washed up.

The wind, though not as strong as it had been during the night, buffeted him. He was glad of the sea air, hoping it would clear his head and shake off the slough of despondency that he could feel sleeking over him. The pier was half a mile out to sea. There was no entertainment on it. It had been constructed purely as a means of enabling the wealthy of the nineteenth century to arrive on the island from the mainland on the steamer service without getting their feet wet on the sands because the tide went out for miles. Trams and trains had traversed it. Now only one small train consisting of former London underground railway carriages trundled up and down it twice an hour, along with cars and pedestrians. There were several cars parked behind him and taxis dropped off their fares for the ferry service to Portsmouth.

He gazed westwards along the coast to the wooded area of Fishbourne, where he could see the lights of the car ferry easing its way into its berth. Beyond it were more trees and a bay, above

216

which was Osborne House, once the holiday home of Queen Victoria, but between Fishbourne and Osborne House was another imposing house hidden by the trees and not as stately as the former queen's, belonging to Eames. Where was Eames now? Not there, not in January. Perhaps at his Wiltshire estate or abroad at one of his other properties. Perhaps he was sailing in the Caribbean or on a trade mission on behalf of businesses and the government. But wherever he was, Horton wouldn't mind betting Eames had an update on his movements.

He looked up to see a taxi heading towards the pier head. He crossed to it and waited for it to discharge its fare. The taxi driver climbed out and lit up a cigarette. Horton didn't expect a result that was any different from what he'd already had but Evelyn Lyster had got to this ferry terminal somehow. Maybe she'd caught the train from Shanklin or perhaps a friend had given her a lift. Or perhaps she'd caught a taxi as she had done in Portsmouth.

He showed his warrant card and then Evelyn Lyster's photograph and was astounded when the taxi driver said, 'Yeah, I recognize her. I dropped her and her friend here on Monday morning.'

'Friend?' Horton asked, startled and with a racing pulse. 'She was with someone?'

'Yeah, a tall man, collar-length brown hair, going grey, teeth like a film star, about mid-fifties.'

Horton's head whirled. My God! Was it possible? There were a lot of tall men going grey in their mid-fifties but there was only one he'd recently come across who'd had expensive dental work.

217

With a pounding heart, he rapidly scrolled through the photographs on his phone until he found the one he wanted.

'Was this the man?'

'Yeah, that's him, who is he?'

A dead man, thought Horton. Peter Freedman.

He asked the taxi driver to take him to where he had picked up his fare. The address was on the north-western edge of Ryde and within ten minutes they were pulling up in front of a large pair of wrought-iron gates, behind which was an imposing Victorian house built in the warm grey stone of the Isle of Wight quarries. It was set in a small cul-de-sac of other substantial Victorian properties just off a leafy lane. The intercom showed that it had been divided into apartments and Horton's knowledge of the area told him the property backed on to the Solent.

His head was teeming with questions since the surprising news, which he hadn't yet passed on to Uckfield. He paid off the driver after ensuring he had all his contact details and scrutinized the intercom, but it listed only the apartment numbers and no names.

The driver had told him that the couple hadn't spoken a word in the taxi and they hadn't appeared close or in the middle of a row. The woman had ordered it on Sunday night for Monday morning at six thirty and had given the address, but not the flat number, and her name as Smith. After dropping her off at Ryde Pier Head the driver had then taken the male passenger to the hovercraft terminal to catch the hovercraft from Ryde to Southsea. Freedman had paid the taxi fare in cash. So why not travel across the Solent together? Why the false name? Had Freedman known that Evelyn Lyster was travelling on to Guernsey? What had he done the rest of Monday while Evelyn was on board the ferry? Had he been expecting to hear from her? If so, how did he feel when he didn't? Or did he know she'd be dead before she arrived because he'd killed her? But how? It had to be poison – something in that flask she'd drunk and which had taken effect on board the Guernsey ferry. Guilbert's toxicology experts must be able to find traces of it in her blood and forensics in the flask lining. But if Freedman had killed Evelyn Lyster then who the devil had killed him on Tuesday night? Was it the same person who had then killed Clements?

So many questions assailed him as he studied the house. Had they come from this property? he wondered, glancing around the area. Maybe they'd just asked to be picked up here. There were two large houses behind trees opposite the converted Victorian building. They'd had no need to think anyone had followed them here but they had been cautious enough to pay by cash and give false names. Why? Had they been lovers? Had the relationship been active when Dennis Lyster had been alive? Had Freedman killed Dennis Lyster in order to be with Evelyn? That had been ten months ago – time enough for them to reveal it now. So why the secrecy? Not because Rowan would object. No, there was something more.

He pressed the intercom for flat one. He'd work his way through each of the seven numbers, hoping he'd get an answer from one of them and praying that they weren't all holiday apartments. He struck lucky on flat five when a disembodied man's voice said rather querulously, 'Yes?'

Horton introduced himself and held up his ID to the CCTV camera, which he'd seen to the right of the gates. He was buzzed through and met by a man in his mid-sixties who introduced himself as Edwin Godley. Horton showed him the photograph of Evelyn Lyster and asked if he had ever seen her.

'Of course I have. She has the penthouse apartment,' Godley promptly answered. Then added warily, 'I hope there's nothing wrong.'

'How well do you know her?' Horton asked, making sure the excitement coursing through him didn't show on his face or in his voice.

'We speak when she's here, which is about two or three times a month. A very pleasant lady.'

'How long have you known her?'

'Since I bought the apartment eight years ago.'

'She's been here that long?' Horton said, this time unable to conceal his surprise. Her son had denied any knowledge of why his mother should be on the Isle of Wight. Was that a lie?

'She sold me the apartment, or rather, I should say her agents did.'

Horton looked at him, mystified.

Godley explained, 'Mrs Brookes bought the building, had it renovated to a very high standard, kept the top floor for herself and sold off the other flats.'

'Mrs Brookes?'

'The woman in the photograph.'

'You're absolutely sure that it is the same woman?'

'Positive. Is everything OK?'

'Have you seen this man before?' Horton showed him the photograph of Freedman but Godley shook his head.

'No. I hope she's all right and hasn't met with an accident.'

'Thank you. You've been most helpful,' Horton politely and evasively replied.

Godley looked taken aback by the fob off but shrugged an acceptance as Horton made his way across the tiled hallway and up the wide sweeping staircase. Godley was correct – everything here was tastefully decorated and maintained to a high standard. A property management company was obviously engaged to ensure the fabric of the building and the grounds were meticulously maintained.

He came out on the top landing which had an arched window to his right giving splendid views across the Solent to the lights of Portsmouth, which were gradually fading as a weak winter sun rose. In front of him was the door to her apartment. He didn't have a key but he suspected one of those on her key ring would be to this flat. And those keys, along with her other personal effects, had been given to her son by Guilbert. Had Rowan Lyster queried what each key was for? Or had his grief and shock blunted his curiosity? But perhaps Mr Godley was mistaken and the woman who owned this apartment only looked like Evelyn Lyster. Horton quickly scotched that idea, though, when he put it together with the taxi driver's evidence. He could get an officer over here to affect a forced entry or he could wait for someone to collect the keys from Rowan Lyster and send them over with an officer on the hovercraft. The latter would alert Rowan and delay entry, and the former could be considered excessive because he had no suspicion that a person lay dead or ill inside the apartment or that any crime had been committed inside it, but one had certainly been committed on someone who had in all probability been here, and that was the murder of Freedman.

He rang John Guilbert on his mobile phone, who expressed no surprise at the early call. Swiftly Horton told him what he had discovered and suggested that he look for a property on Guernsey registered in the name of Evelyn Brookes and a bank account in that name, although there was always the possibility she had used yet another identity. He didn't know why but if he put that with her desire to pay by cash when travelling and the fact the man accompanying her on Monday morning was dead he strongly suspected a connection with some criminal activity.

'I'll instigate enquiries but the banks aren't obliged to give us that information, even in a murder investigation,' Guilbert said. 'I'll also ask for the toxicology tests to be given top priority, chase up the analysis of the flask and recirculate her picture with the new name to all the landlords and estate agents. Keep me posted.'

Horton said he would. Next he called Newport police station and requested assistance, hoping that DCI Birch wouldn't get wind of it. He didn't fancy the acid-tongued head of CID breathing down his neck. Hopefully he was still off sick.

Then he rang Gaye, apologizing for disturbing her so early. 'There's something I'd like you to do for me if you have time before you jet off to Denmark. There's another autopsy report I need you to review, that of a Dennis Lyster. I want to know if anything was missed.'

'Who performed it?'

'A Dr Sealing ten months ago, in the mortuary on the Isle of Wight.'

'I'll access it my end and call you as soon as I can.'

Finally he rang Uckfield on his mobile phone and rapidly explained where he was and why.

'How the blazes did you know they were connected?' was Uckfield's shocked response.

'I didn't. I was just curious as to why she got off one ferry and went straight on to another one.' He didn't have time to explain all his other queries regarding her death. 'I'll get Cantelli to check with the Isle of Wight ferries and the hovercraft for any details of when Evelyn Brookes and Peter Freedman travelled during the last year, but it sounds as though they both used cash to avoid being traced. We know that Guernsey is very advantageous for those who have capital to invest and don't want to pay huge amounts of tax.'

'Or *any* tax?'

Uckfield was referring to money laundering, which could be why this Victorian property had been purchased. It was Horton's thought exactly. He told Uckfield he was going to affect an entry. He then rang Cantelli, who was at home, brought him up to speed and asked him to check with the ferry companies.

With growing impatience, Horton returned to the hall, left the front door open and headed up the drive to the gates as the patrol car drew up. He pressed the release switch and the gates swung open. With the two officers, PCs Tom Wilkinson and Sean Palmer, Horton returned to the top-floor apartment where, with one swift thud on the door, Evelyn Lyster's apartment was opened. Horton stepped into a generous hall. To the right was a door that gave on to the living quarters while to the left were three doors that he guessed must be to the bedrooms and bathroom.

He detailed Wilkinson and Palmer to take the sleeping quarters, instructing them to look for papers, photographs, computers or any mobile phones. He stepped into the north-facing living quarters that gave on to the Solent. It was one long, very wide open-plan room exquisitely decorated and furnished, with a balcony that spanned the entire width and at the far western end widened out on to a large patio area with a black wicker table and chairs.

The sea looked a grey green in the morning light and he could see the ferries crossing. A fishing boat was heading out towards the English Channel but there were no leisure yachts yet in the dull and windy January morning. He wasn't here to admire the view, though. He turned back to survey the apartment. It was spotlessly clean and contemporarily furnished, just as her Portsmouth penthouse had been. There was some good quality light oak furniture, large leather sofas, an expensive plasma television and music system, and some very tasteful and if he wasn't mistaken expensive paintings on the walls. Again, just like her apartment in Portsmouth, there were no photographs, not even of her son.

He turned to the only low-level cupboard in the lounge area but there was little in it except some magazines and the remote control for the lighting and the television. The kitchen cupboards contained what he expected – crockery, kitchen implements, food but nothing perishable. There were four cup flasks and a wine fridge under a central kitchen unit which was well stocked. Both the dishwasher and washing machine were empty.

He crossed the hall and entered one of the two bedrooms, where a king-sized bed was made up. The room gave on to a shower room and a dressing room. Inside was a mixture of smart- and casual-wear hanging on rails, drawers on one side of the rails which revealed T-shirts, jumpers, cardigans and another set of drawers the other side of the hanging rails which contained underwear, stockings, socks and tights. Several pairs of shoes were also stacked to the right of the rails. Cantelli would have been impressed.

Wilkinson entered from the bathroom. 'Nothing but a couple of towels, soap and hand cream.' He jerked his head at the clothes. 'Do you want me to go through the pockets?'

Horton said he did. 'And her handbags.'

He entered the second smaller bedroom where Palmer had the wardrobe doors open to reveal some men's clothing. No suits, just two pairs of trousers, a waterproof jacket, five shirts and some ties. Palmer was going through the pockets. The drawers were open, exposing some underwear, socks, two jumpers and a handful of T-shirts. They probably belonged to Freedman. He asked Palmer to note down the sizes. In the shower room were men's toiletries.

Horton returned to the living area and gazed around. There was no phone and he hadn't seen one in the bedrooms. He suspected then that she didn't use a landline and there hadn't been one in her Portsmouth flat. The taxi driver said she had called the office to book the taxi but Guilbert had gone through Evelyn Lyster's call log and so had he on the Guernsey ferry and hadn't found the taxi company's number. She had obviously deleted it and any calls made to Freedman. Her phone records would show it up unless the phone was a pay-as-you-go one, which he was now beginning to suspect it was. Perhaps she had another mobile phone on a contract but for someone as cautious as Evelyn Lyster he was beginning to think not.

His mobile phone rang. He expected it to be Trueman or Uckfield but was surprised to see it was Gaye Clayton.

'The autopsy on Dennis Lyster,' she said.

'That was quick.'

'It didn't take me long to spot the flaws. It's complete as far as it goes.'

'But?'

'It doesn't go far enough. The pathologist assumed death was caused by drowning and didn't look

226

for anything else. But then, maybe he didn't need to. I don't have the police files.'

And Horton was very keen to see those. Birch wouldn't relish him requesting them and he certainly wouldn't be happy if Horton found holes in the investigation. But tough. He wasn't in the job to make officers like Birch happy. Horton crossed to the window as Gaye continued.

'Remnants of clothing were found on the victim but I can't find any note to say they were X-rayed before being removed or sent to the forensic lab. The body was photographed both with and without clothes. There was substantial damage to the head, which is not unusual because as the body lies face down in the water with the head hanging it can produce post-mortem head injuries which are difficult to distinguish between those inflicted when alive. And as the body was found washed up against the pier it was concluded that the damages to the head were caused by it being bashed against the underwater structures, but I've studied the X-rays and it's also possible that the deceased was bludgeoned. I'm not saying he was, just that it should have been considered.'

Perhaps Birch did consider it, thought Horton, and ignored it.

Gaye went on: 'The pathologist looked for fine white foam or froth in the airways and exuding from the mouth and nostrils which can deter-mine if the victim was alive on submersion in water. It's not always evident if the body has been in the water for some time. He notes that the deceased had been in the water for approxi-mately five days. So again, I am assuming that the deceased was last reported being seen five days before his body was found. There is nothing in the report to say this and there should have been. Evidence of foam was found which shows he was alive when he went into the water, thereby adding to the verdict that he intended committing suicide by drowning but foam can also be caused by head injury, a drug overdose or a heart attack. There was an absence of water in the stomach which the pathologist claims was due to rapid death by drowning, thereby strengthening his probable cause of death, but it could also mean the subject was dead before submersion. Then we come to diatoms.'

Horton watched a motorboat crossing the Solent from Portsmouth and saw the hovercraft riding the waves to the mainland.

'Diatoms were found in the deceased. They're a class of microscopic algae of which about fifteen thousand species are known. Half live in fresh water, the other half in sea or brackish water. The hypothesis is that diatoms will not enter circulation and be deposited in organs such as bone marrow unless the decedent was alive in the water. Therefore the pathologist concluded that Dennis Lyster was alive when he entered the water. However, there is the issue of contamination. Diatoms can be found in the environment, for example in the building industry.'

Horton broke in: 'Dennis Lyster was a civil engineer.' Then he added, 'But he'd been made redundant some time before his death.'

'Diatoms can also enter circulation as contaminants of foods such as salads, watercress and shellfish so it's not conclusive proof that finding them in the deceased is evidence that he was alive when submerged. And I can't find any record of a sea sample being taken from where the body was found to match it against those diatoms found in the decedent's system, unless that is on your files.'

Horton would check but he had a feeling he wouldn't find it either.

Gaye said, 'To my mind the evidence is insufficient to claim death was caused by drowning or that it was suicide and clearly the coroner thought the same, which is why he gave the verdict as undetermined death. But I'd happily review it again alongside the case file and discuss it further with you or Uckfield. Only you'll have to be quick. I leave this afternoon at three.'

'I'll call you back later.'

He was about to ring Uckfield when PC Wilkinson appeared.

'Nothing in any of the pockets, sir, or the handbags,' he reported.

Horton asked him to call a locksmith and seal off the apartment, then headed down the stairs. He walked around to the rear of the building. The gardens were staggered with the upper part giving views across the Solent to Portsmouth five miles beyond. There were three steps which led down to the next tier and two more leading to a high brick wall bordering the shore. In it was a wooden gate. It was locked and no doubt the flats' occupants had keys to it. One of those keys was on Evelyn Lyster's key ring, perhaps. The gate gave on to the beach, which he knew from experience was inaccessible from both directions and therefore very private. Private enough for a man to be bludgeoned and then pushed into the water to end up wedged under one of the piles under the pier.

He rang Uckfield, who answered his mobile immediately. Horton quickly relayed what he'd found, ending with what Dr Clayton had said.

'Do you have to go looking for more suspicious deaths?' Uckfield cried with exasperation.

Horton told him about the garden leading on to the shore.

'As if we haven't got enough on our plates,' grumbled Uckfield, nasally, still full of cold. 'I'll ring DCI Birch and get the files.'

Horton said he'd sealed off the flat. Fingerprints and DNA would be taken from it and matched with those taken from the bodies of Evelyn Lyster and Peter Freedman. And Uckfield said he would need to get a team into Evelyn Lyster's Portsmouth flat to see if Freedman and possibly Vivian Clements' prints were there. Horton said he'd get the keys from Rowan Lyster. He was curious to meet him. Trueman's team would start to trace the property transaction on the Ryde house, Freedman's flat and Evelyn's Portsmouth apartment. They'd also interview the solicitors and estate agents who had handled the sales. This was turning into a massive investigation requiring a great deal of resources, a fact that would have ACC Dean on the verge of a nervous breakdown. His budget would be blown to pieces.

Horton made his way back inside and asked Wilkinson to drop him off at the Fast Cat ferry terminal. On the way over to Portsmouth he called Cantelli and asked him to meet him outside Rowan Lyster's house, the address of which he got from Trueman on the crossing.

An hour later, Horton pulled up behind Cantelli's car just a short distance away from Rowan Lyster's small, modern semi-detached house. It wasn't far from the seafront at the eastern end of Portsmouth, close to where Rowan Lyster's business was situated and where Freedman had met his death.

Climbing out and heading towards it, Cantelli said, 'There's no record of Peter Freedman buying a ticket on the Fast Cat or hovercraft last weekend so I guess he paid cash. Same for Evelyn Lyster or Brookes, but they'll get back to us as soon as they can check their records for the last year.'

'I'm not sure they'll find anything.'

'Sounds like they both wanted to keep it low profile. Perhaps they didn't want Dennis Lyster to find out about their affair and when he did he killed himself.'

'*If* he killed himself.' Horton gave him a quick summary of what Gaye had told him and his views that Dennis Lyster could have been killed on the shore on the island. 'Evelyn Lyster and Freedman have had time since Dennis's death to declare their relationship without drawing suspicion on themselves, which they haven't done. That and the fact that Evelyn Lyster was using another name means there is more than an affair going on here and whatever it is, Barney, it looks pretty dodgy to me.' He pressed his finger on the bell, adding, 'And I don't think her son knew a thing about it.'

231

Seventeen

'Are you sure this apartment on the Isle of Wight belongs to my mother?' Rowan Lyster said, puzzled.

Gina Lyster had shown them into the small lounge where her husband sat sprawled on the sofa. He made no attempt to rise or even shift position. He was dressed in jogging pants and a black T-shirt bearing his company name and logo. His square-set face showed the trace of a suntan, his short, dark hair was held in place with gel, he was clean-shaven but his deep brown eyes were red-rimmed either from fatigue or weeping or perhaps both. Gina was also dressed in sportswear but the tight-fitting kind that accentuated her rounded figure and a close-fitting pink Lycra top that didn't boast the corporate logo. She took the seat beside her husband and waved them into the two chairs opposite.

On the wall were two very large framed and rather spectacular pictures of Rowan Lyster windsurfing. Horton thought he'd put on a bit of weight since they'd been taken but Lyster was still fairly muscular with strong, slightly tanned arms. There was also a wedding picture of him and Gina on a shelf on a modern corner unit but no pictures of his parents or Gina's.

'Could there have been someone new in her life?

Another man?' Horton asked, watching their reactions as he knew Cantelli was.

'She didn't say,' Rowan replied. Gina threw them a baffled look and then her husband a concerned one.

'Would she have told you if there was?'

Rowan shrugged. Horton didn't know if that was because he wasn't sure whether his mother would have confided in him or because he wasn't really bothered if she'd had another man.

He said, 'Did she ever mention a Peter Freedman?'

Neither of them showed any reaction to the name but both denied having heard her mention him. And neither of them asked who he was.

'Did she travel to the Isle of Wight much?' asked Cantelli.

Rowan threw Cantelli a slightly irritated look. 'I've no idea. Does it matter? She's dead and that's the end of it.'

Gina shifted slightly, as though disturbed by her husband's harsh tone and words.

Horton said, 'I know this must be distressing for you but your mother's death is unexplained, Mr Lyster, and therefore questions have to be asked.'

'But she died of natural causes,' he cried, exasperated.

'That is not the verdict of the coroner and until it is we need to continue investigating the circumstances surrounding her death. Your mother bought and refurbished the property on the Isle of Wight eight years ago and then sold off all the apartments except for the top floor which she kept for herself. She was there on Sunday night

233

and returned from there on Monday morning before heading for the Guernsey ferry. Did she mention to either of you that she was going to the Isle of Wight either late Saturday night or Sunday morning?'

Gina answered first. 'No.'

Rowan shook his head.

Cantelli retrieved his mobile phone from his jacket pocket and stretched it across to Rowan, saying, 'This is the man your mother was with. Do either of you recognize him?'

Horton watched them closely as they peered at the photograph. Their only reaction was continued bafflement.

Putting the phone back in his pocket, Cantelli addressed Rowan Lyster. 'How did your mother seem when you saw her on Saturday evening?'

'Fine.'

But Horton noted Rowan shift perceptibly. 'Did you usually go round to her apartment on Saturdays?' he asked.

'No.'

'Was the dinner invitation at her request?'

Gina interjected: 'We asked if she could help us to buy some more windsurfing equipment for the centre. We'd been offered a good deal. She refused. She said that we had enough for our second season, which is this year, and that if bookings looked good then she'd reconsider. We said that the deal wouldn't be on the table later but she said that deals were always on the table when someone had the cash or they wanted to offload something quickly.'

I bet she did. Horton was beginning to get a

234

clearer picture of Evelyn Lyster, a clever woman used to doing deals, but in what? If her activities had been criminal then what had she been involved in? What had she been selling? Information? What kind, though? Had she been a blackmailer and Freedman one of her victims? No. His clothes wouldn't have been in her apartment if he had been. Horton had no confirmation that they were Freedman's clothes but he was certain they were. Perhaps he was party to the blackmail. Freedman had access to many people and, using his neuro-linguistic programming skills and the other techniques he practised, he could have elicited confidences which he then passed on to Evelyn Lyster to blackmail those individuals. But that still didn't stack up because she'd purchased that Isle of Wight property eight years ago and Freedman had been a vagrant then.

'You rowed,' he said.

Gina answered, 'No. We were disappointed but we knew that we wouldn't be able to change her mind. Evelyn is – was – very determined. When she said "no" you knew she meant it.'

Cantelli looked up from his notebook. 'Did she talk about any of her clients or her friends?'

'Not to me. Rowan?'

He shook his head and his brow furrowed.

'Do you have details of any of your mother's friends?' Horton asked.

'No.'

'None?' Horton probed, raising his eyebrows and injecting enough incredulity in his voice to make Rowan give him a surly glare.

'I spent most of my childhood away at school

and after that travelling the world in competitions so I don't know who her friends and clients were. And I've no idea where she kept that kind of information. It wasn't something we discussed.'

Horton wondered what they had talked about.

'I only returned here last August with Gina so we could start the business and get married.'

'Did you see much of your father?'

'No. He'd been made redundant by then but Gina and I were living together in a flat in Southsea, not with my parents.'

In a conversational tone, Cantelli said, 'What school did you go to?'

'Saint Levan's in Cornwall.'

'That's a fair distance from here,' Cantelli replied, surprised.

Horton thought that you couldn't get any further away from Portsmouth except for Scotland.

'It's where I learned to surf. I already sailed. I used to go out with Dad before I went to Saint Levan's. We had a boat then. The school was very keen on water sports, which was why my parents chose it. They knew I was very good at it.'

'But you came home during the school holidays?' Cantelli continued.

'My parents were rarely in the UK. Dad worked overseas and my mother travelled a lot with her business.'

Maybe Rowan hadn't minded but Horton wondered just how often Rowan Lyster had seen his mother and father. Why, if his parents relationship was strained and their son away at school, hadn't they got divorced? Perhaps they couldn't be bothered. They'd stayed married for convenience's sake. It had suited them both, until Dennis Lyster had been made redundant.

Cantelli said, 'How did you live? I mean money-wise after you'd left school?'

Horton knew Cantelli was wondering if Rowan's parents had supported him.

'I won competitions and I endorsed certain windsurfing equipment for which I got paid. I also worked for various water-sports organisa-tions, teaching windsurfing and other water sports: kayaking, dinghy sailing, paddle boarding. I earned enough. I was single then.'

'And now you've decided to settle down,' Cantelli said, smiling at Gina, who looked undecided about returning it. 'Won't you miss travelling?'

'Been there, done that,' he said airily.

'And now, of course, you'll inherit your mother's estate.'

Cantelli's words took a moment to sink in.

Rowan's eyes narrowed and his face flushed. 'Hey, what are you inferring?'

'Nothing,' said Cantelli neutrally, tucking away his notebook with a bland expression.

Horton rose. 'We know this must be a very difficult time for you and we're sorry to trouble you but we will need your mother's keys. We'll also need to seal off her apartment here and on the island.'

'But—'

'We will keep you fully informed.'

Gina rose and left the room. She returned almost instantly with the keys.

As Horton took them from her, he addressed

Rowan. 'When was the last time you saw your father, Mr Lyster?'

He looked stunned by the question. Gina answered before he could. 'It was at our wedding, a week before his body was found.'

Cantelli looked up. 'So you were on your honeymoon when you received the news?'

'No, we'd postponed it until the winter. It being March, we needed to get the business up and running. We had a few bookings. Evelyn gave us some capital to get the business off the ground and helped us to buy this house by giving us the deposit for it after Dennis died.'

So Evelyn Lyster had been generous. And when they'd asked for more she thought she'd already given them enough.

As Horton made to leave he asked one more question. 'Do either of you know a man called Vivian Clements?'

'No.'

'Mrs Lyster?'

'No.'

Neither of them asked why he wanted to know.

Outside, Horton said, 'Why didn't Evelyn and Dennis Lyster divorce? There doesn't seem to have been much love between them.'

'Perhaps one or both of them were Catholic. Saint Levan's could be a Catholic school. Not that I know that particular saint – there are so many. The Catholic Church is big on saints.'

'Convenient then that eight months after being made redundant Dennis Lyster decides to drown himself.'

'And suicide would have been against his

religion, *if* he was a Catholic. But if he was driven to it then the catechism offers hope in prayer. We didn't ask if Rowan had been raised in the Catholic faith. Maybe we should have done.'

'Check out his school. See if you can get more from them on Evelyn and Dennis Lyster.'

Cantelli's phone rang as he reached his car. Horton waited by his Harley for Cantelli to finish his call, which he did within a couple of minutes. 'That was the mortuary. Glyn Ashmead has identified Peter Freedman's body and they're ready for Constance Clements to identify her husband. Do you want to come?'

'No. Call round to collect her now if she's ready. Ask her if she knew why Freedman went to Japan. I'm going to have another word with Glyn Ashmead.'

Horton made his way back through the busy Portsmouth streets to the station, where he parked the Harley and once again set off on foot to Gravity. He remembered that Martha had told him that Sheila Broadway worked on Fridays. She was the lady who handled the clothing donations and Horton wondered if she'd recognize the coat Freedman had been wearing when he was killed. She didn't. And neither did she know Freedman because she had never worked at the centre on a Tuesday. Horton wasn't sure if Ashmead was back from the mortuary but Sheila said he was – a police car had dropped him off. He was in his office. Horton was about to make for it when Martha walked in.

'We're shorthanded and Glyn's not too well,' she explained with a worried frown. Martha didn't look too bright herself. He could see that she was genuinely concerned for Ashmead. He wondered if she secretly had a thing for him or perhaps they were in a relationship. 'Peter's death has really shaken him up,' she added.

Horton asked her if she'd ever heard Freedman mention a woman called Evelyn Lyster.

'No. Like I said, he never talked about anybody.'

'Has Glyn ever mentioned her?'

'No.' She offered him a coffee, which this time he refused.

He found Ashmead in his office looking tired and, as Martha had said, clearly unwell. Stress was etched on his lean face, making him look more haggard than before. Horton wondered if it was a result of identifying Freedman and said so but Ashmead, although admitting that had been distressing, said he'd also received news that a sponsor had pulled out of supporting the centre and the council were threatening to cut back their funding.

Freedman's bequest would come in handy then, thought Horton, taking the seat across from Ashmead's desk. Horton had no idea what the amount might be but if it was shown to have been gained illegally then the benefactors – Gravity and the Salvation Army – might never see it. Not that Horton had any evidence Freedman had been involved in whatever Evelyn Lyster's game had been. He could purely have been her lover, except for the fact he had been murdered.

'I won't keep you long. I just want to know if you've ever seen this woman before.' Horton handed over his phone containing the photograph

240

of Evelyn Lyster. He watched Ashmead peer at it. After a moment he looked up and handed it back.

'No. Attractive woman, though. Is there a connection between her and Peter?'

'It seems they were close.'

'He never said. But then why should he? His private life was none of my business, unless he cared to confide it to me and he didn't. Does she know what happened to Peter?'

'She's dead.'

Ashmead's tired dark eyes widened. 'Killed?'

'We're not sure yet. Does the name Evelyn Lyster mean anything to you?

'Sorry, no.' Ashmead looked disturbed and dejected. 'Do you want me to show the picture to the other staff and volunteers and ask them about her?'

Horton said he did but to do it discreetly. He told him he'd already asked Martha and Sheila. Horton emailed the photograph to Ashmead, wished him luck with his funding and left. He'd only just stepped outside when his phone rang. It was John Guilbert. 'I've just broken the news to Detective Superintendent Uckfield and, having just recovered my hearing, thought I'd ring you. Evelyn Lyster wasn't poisoned, at least not in the strictest sense, but an analysis of the lining of her flask shows the presence of a beta blocker.'

Horton quickly wracked his brain for his limited medical information. 'Used by athletes and prohibited in some sports.'

'Yes, and sometimes prescribed to those with high blood pressure. In themselves beta blockers aren't harmful but if given to someone suffering from low blood pressure they could be. It's taken a while for the toxicologist to narrow it down but from the analysis of what remains, it's a beta blocker, or rather two, Atenolol and Nifedipine. They're prescription medicines used in hypertension and angina. Atenolol and Nifedipine work together to block the effects of certain chemicals in the body and are used to lower blood pressure, reduce the frequency and severity of angina attacks and slow the heart rate.'

'And for someone already suffering from a low heart rate reducing it further could stop it completely.'

'Yes.'

'So it is murder.'

'Looks that way. Now all you have to do is find out who put it in her flask and when! Good luck.'

'I think we'll need it.'

Eighteen

Horton found Uckfield in the canteen tucking into a very late lunch. He bought himself a coffee, lasagne and chips and took the seat opposite. 'Guilbert called me.'

'I'm thinking of getting some beta blockers to give to Dean. He'll have a heart attack the way his blood pressure shot up after I told him we've got another murder. It's not doing my blood pressure much good either,' Uckfield added. 'Guilbert's sending over what he's got on Evelyn Lyster's death, including the pathologist's report, but from what he told me it sounds like he's got sod all anyway so he might just as well not bother.' He shovelled another fork of cottage pie into his mouth. 'How did you get on with the son?'

Between mouthfuls Horton relayed their interview with Rowan Lyster and that he'd drawn a blank with anyone from Gravity being able to identify Evelyn Lyster. 'Freedman could have laced her flask before they left the apartment on Monday morning knowing she'd be on the Condor Commodore Clipper ferry to Guernsey when she drank it. He had ample opportunity.'

'His motive?'

'The money she has stashed away somewhere, probably in an account in Guernsey, which was why she was travelling there.' And Guilbert was still looking for that.

'So who killed *him*? Constance Clements?'

'Or her husband, Vivian, and then she shot her husband.'

'Why?'

'To make us think he killed himself. Freedman could have killed Evelyn Lyster not only to get her money but because he was also having an affair with Constance Clements.'

'So he hopes to sail off into the sunset with Constance Clements only her old man gets wind of it and shoots the lover. When she finds out she shoots her old man for revenge.' Uckfield pushed away his empty plate. 'Can't taste a ruddy thing with this cold.'

'You don't seem to have done too badly.'

'You know how the saying goes: feed a cold and starve a fever.'

'According to Freedman's and Clements' medical records neither man was prescribed beta blockers. We'd need to check Constance Clements' medical records to see if she was but even if she wasn't we both know you can pick them up on the Internet. And both Clements and Freedman could have been buying them for themselves for some time.' Horton had called Gaye as he'd walked back to the station to get more information on the drug.

'Why the devil would they?' Uckfield said and blew his nose loudly.

'Stage fright.'

'Eh?'

Horton began to relay what he'd learned from Gaye. 'An article in *The Lancet* in 1965 explored the use of beta blockers for stage fright and since then they've been widely prescribed for musicians, public speakers, performers and even surgeons who have to steady their hands.'

'Bloody hell. Hope I don't get one of those if I ever need an operation.'

'Freedman was a public speaker and a recovering alcoholic – maybe he got the shakes before he was due to give one of his talks. He needed something to steady his nerves and didn't want to touch alcohol being a recovering alcoholic, but he didn't want the beta blockers on prescription, or perhaps he thought he wouldn't be prescribed them anyway so he went down the black market route. Vivian Clements was also a

244

public speaker. Perhaps he got the jitters on those cruises. He certainly didn't seem to enjoy them very much.'

'But Clements couldn't have put them in Evelyn Lyster's flask,' Uckfield declared with exasperation.

'No, but Constance could have given them to Freedman to do so. Cantelli's with her at the mortuary. There is an alternative theory.'

'Go on.'

'Vivian Clements agrees to meet Freedman on the shore because Freedman says he knows that Clements faked the robbery for the insurance money. Constance has told Freedman. Freedman threatens to expose him unless Vivian agrees to meet him. But Vivian takes an antique pistol with him that he hasn't declared on his insurance. He knows it can still be fired. Perhaps he doesn't intend using it but wants it so that he can threaten and frighten Freedman. Something goes wrong. He fires it and Freedman dies. Clements returns home in a state of shock and tells his wife what he's done.'

'And she kills him.'

Horton nodded and finished his hasty meal. 'Two problems, though.'

'Only two?' said Uckfield sarcastically.

'I can't see why Freedman was dressed as a vagrant and why Vivian Clements would go to Milton Common to meet his wife.'

Uckfield rose. Horton followed suit. As they made their way out of the canteen, Uckfield said, 'The council and the land registry confirm the Ryde penthouse is in the name of Evelyn Brookes.

245

It's her maiden name. We're checking out the solicitor and estate agent she used for the purchase. She used her married name for her tax returns. She filed them herself so it looks as though she did her own accounts. My betting is we'll find a complicated paper trail behind her, especially if she was crooked and canny enough to stash money away in Guernsey and possibly elsewhere.'

'Zurich, maybe. Have we got any sightings of Peter Freedman for the Monday he travelled back from the Isle of Wight?'

'We've had confirmation he boarded the hovercraft. Two of the staff at the Ryde terminal remember seeing him get on and one of them remembers seeing him alight at this end. He didn't take a taxi so he must have walked across the common to his flat. It's not far and at that time in the morning no one saw him enter it. There are no records of any appointments on his computer for Monday or Tuesday.'

'There wouldn't be for Tuesday. He spends it at Gravity and, according to Martha, he was there until four p.m.'

'There's nothing in his diary for the rest of the week either. So perhaps he deliberately kept it free so that he could travel to Guernsey on Wednesday and get access to Evelyn's account there, if she has one. But he wasn't booked on a flight or a ferry.'

'He might have been intending to turn up on Wednesday morning at the port as a foot passenger and pay cash, just as Evelyn did.' But Horton was still troubled by the fact that Evelyn Lyster had bought a single ticket. He thought back to his original idea that she intended returning on a private plane or boat with a lover. Would she have had more than one lover? Possibly. Or perhaps it was a business partner, a criminal one, which would explain why he hadn't come forward. He wondered if Elkins was having any luck asking around the marinas for anyone who had seen her. He guessed not, otherwise he'd have been on the phone to him.

Uckfield's name was called and Horton turned to see Joliffe, the forensic scientist, all teeth and legs, striding towards them. 'Looks as though we've got the report on Freedman's coat,' he said.

They headed up to the incident suite where Bliss glanced up from Trueman's desk. A frown puckered her high forehead, directed at him, Horton thought, for arriving at the same time as Uckfield and Joliffe. She probably thought they were plotting something behind her back or withholding vital information from her.

Joliffe handed Trueman some enlarged photographs of the coat, which he pinned on the crime board, and Joliffe took up a stance beside it. 'It's an excellent example of a British warm greatcoat,' he said with unusual enthusiasm, which surprised Horton because he was renowned for his lack of emotion on any subject. 'It's made from heavy taupe Melton cloth, the name deriving from Melton Mowbray in Leicestershire. The cloth, which was first mentioned in 1823, is a tightly-woven woollen fabric and has a short, raised nap which gives it a fleece-like texture. The heavy Melton fabric is often referred to as *Crombie Fleece*.'

'So how old is it?' Uckfield demanded impatiently.

Joliffe eyed him coldly. 'It's double-breasted with six woven leather buttons, an extra button under the collar so that the collar can be worn up when it's particularly cold, and has two buttons on each cuff. It has two flapped pockets and a breast pocket. The fluff from all the pockets is being analysed. Sadly the cuffs and collar show a little wear but nothing considerable and the brown satin silk lining is worn in places, mainly around the seat and under the arms and it's torn. The coat has a rear vent and epaulettes and is usually worn just below the knee.'

'I know what it looks like. I don't need a bloody description of it,' roared Uckfield. 'Just tell us how old it is and who it belongs to?'

Joliffe ignored him. Unfazed, he continued, 'The style of the British warm greatcoat dates back to the First World War but this one is considerably newer.'

Was that a joke? thought Horton. From Joliffe!

'It's difficult to date it precisely but our analysis and that of our textile expert puts it at approximately twenty years old.'

That didn't mean it had been with the same man for twenty years.

'It's a forty-six regular chest. There are several hairs on it which are being analysed for DNA and are being matched with those of the victim.'

'Victims,' corrected Horton. 'It might have belonged to Vivian Clements. Trueman will make sure you have the details.'

Joliffe nodded. 'There are also some spores and grass seeds on it, which we will examine and try and determine from where they might originate. There are some car oil stains. It will take some time before we have the results of the analysis.'

And even then, thought Horton, it might not tell them much.

'And that's it?' cried Uckfield, exasperated. 'Hardly worth coming out for.'

Joliffe left without commenting on Uckfield's remark. He was used to Uckfield's short temper. Horton asked Trueman if he had managed to check what Freedman had been wearing when he was arrested the final time, when he was sent to prison and when he was discharged.

'Not a British warm greatcoat,' came the answer. 'Or the belt. None of the clothes he was found wearing. And we haven't found his keys or wallet in his apartment or in Evelyn Lyster's Isle of Wight or Portsmouth apartments.'

'They could be in Constance Clements' house,' said Uckfield after noisily blowing his nose. 'Her husband could have taken them off the dead man after killing him.'

Horton's phone rang. 'It's Cantelli.' He listened for a couple of minutes, then said, 'OK, bring her in.' He rang off. 'Constance Clements has given us permission to search the house but says we won't find the guns there because they're in a lock-up on the industrial estate by Portsmouth Football Club.' It was only a short distance from Milton Common.

'She's confessed?' Bliss said surprised.

'To the phoney robbery yes but not to murdering her husband. She believes her husband killed Freedman.'

249

'And who does she think killed her husband?' Uckfield said sourly.

'She says she doesn't know.'

Uckfield snorted to show what he thought about that. 'Then you'd better see if you can change her mind.'

Horton joined Cantelli in the interview room. The plastic cup of tea in front of Constance Clements lay untouched with a greasy film on top of the pale brown liquid. Her hands in her lap played with her bracelet. Cantelli had said that she'd been shocked when she'd viewed the body of her husband but not upset. Outside the mortuary she'd admitted that she hadn't really believed he was dead until she'd seen him, then she'd said quite simply, 'I can tell the truth now, can't I?' And that's when she had told Cantelli about the guns.

DC Somerfield and two uniformed officers had been despatched to the lock-up while DC Marsden was overseeing a team searching Constance Clements' house.

'I'm not sorry he's dead,' she said with an edge of defiance, her eyes flicking between him and Cantelli. She'd been cautioned and offered legal representation, which she'd waived. 'But I didn't kill him. I'd like to have done, many times. I imagined doing it, especially when he showed me one of his prized pistols, but he said he didn't have any ammunition for them.'

'Did you look for some?'

She nodded and looked forlorn. 'I never found any, though, but I did find that gun you showed me a picture of. The one you say killed him. It was never in his collection room. It was in his study in a drawer. There wasn't any ammunition with it or in the safe.'

But there had been some somewhere. Maybe she was just saying she hadn't seen any. 'When was this?' he asked.

'August.'

That coincided with when she'd said she'd last seen Peter Freedman, but again he wondered if it was a lie. Had Freedman told her before she'd left on the cruise that their affair was over and she'd spent the time on the ship planning how to kill him and then to kill her husband? Perhaps the phoney robbery had been her idea and used as a cover to shoot her husband. But that didn't explain why she'd give Freedman beta blockers to kill Evelyn Lyster. Or why he should be dressed as a tramp.

Horton said, 'Did you ask your husband about the gun?'

She looked stunned at the question. 'Of course not. Vivian would have been furious if he'd known I'd been looking in his desk.'

'You were afraid of him?'

She looked up and said wearily, 'I just didn't want another row. I was sick of them. Vivian had the art of turning most of what I said into an argument so I stopped saying anything.'

'Living with him became like walking on egg-shells,' Horton said, knowing that abuse came in many guises.

'Yes,' she answered, surprised that he understood.

Cantelli said, 'When did it become like that?'

She swivelled her gaze to him. 'At first it was

fine. I thought him knowledgeable and fascinating. Yes, that just shows how stupid I was,' she added with bitterness. 'Oh, I thought him a little pedantic but I considered that to be one of his charming eccentricities.' She shook her head sorrowfully. 'And he seemed head-over-heels in love with me. I was a fool. I didn't see until it was too late that the only thing that Vivian was in love with, aside from himself, was my money and I had money, Sergeant. In fact, quite a lot of it by the time I met Vivian at an auction. My business was very successful and my parents had left me a house and a considerable amount. I was their only child. I bought an apartment in Chelsea. That, and my savings, meant I was worth almost two million pounds. Yes, a very tidy sum,' she added, reading their expressions.

'I agreed to a joint bank account. I was in love for the first time in my life and thought I was loved back. I'd had affairs but not very successful ones. My lovers were usually married. This time, I thought, no secrets. This is it. Vivian got through all my money pretty quickly. Oh, we bought the house in Southsea for cash and it's in our joint name, but the rest of our savings, *my* savings, have gone. He told you we'd both sold our apartments in London but what he didn't tell you was that he was living in a poky one-roomed flat near Earls Court, which he was renting, and he didn't tell me that either until after we were married. Even then I said it didn't matter.' She gave a hollow laugh. 'I was infatuated and I was sick of being on my own. Vivian didn't look much but like Peter he could be very charismatic.'

252

'Peter Freedman?' asked Horton, just to be certain.

'Yes.'

'You had an affair with him?'

But she looked crestfallen. 'No. I'd like to have done but I finally got the message that it wasn't me he was interested in, it was Vivian. Oh, not in any physical or emotional sense,' she hastily added, 'but for Vivian's knowledge of oriental antiquities and guns.'

Horton's interest quickened. He wondered just why Freedman had been so interested.

She said, 'We met in Japan. Peter said he was there to study Zen Buddhism. Peter was very easy to be with, a good listener. He made me feel that what I had to say was interesting.'

He would. After all, Freedman was an expert in those kind of techniques.

'After we returned home I met him a few times. We'd meet in the lobby of a hotel or in a café. He seemed very keen but . . .' She faltered.

'You discovered he was using you?'

'He asked me about my background, my know-ledge of antiques, my previous clients. I told him how much I had enjoyed my business but that Vivian didn't approve so I'd ceased trading. I'd hoped that Peter could give me the confidence to start it again. I'd come away from our meetings excited, thinking that maybe I could persuade Vivian to let me resume my career, but every time I suggested it we'd end up rowing. He was adamant that I shouldn't.'

No, thought Horton, he wanted to keep his wife completely under his thumb.

'I knew something about oriental art and antiques

having sourced them for previous clients, but not as much as Vivian knew.'

'You poured your heart out to Peter and by his clever questioning he got whatever information he wanted from you, including the fact that your husband was in financial difficulties and that he had bought items that were not in his collection or insured, in particular historic and antique guns with ammunition, which should have been declared to the police, like the gun that killed him.'

'Yes.' She looked down. Then, taking a deep breath, she put her gaze back on Horton. He could see the pain in her eyes. 'Vivian took great pleasure in saying how could I possibly believe a man like Freedman would fancy me. He told me what an idiot I was for thinking it and for trusting him.'

And Horton could see that the scars ran deep. Vivian Clements had been a bully. Horton didn't doubt she was telling the truth. It all fitted, except he wasn't certain that he believed her when she said she hadn't killed her husband, and she'd also just given herself a motive for killing Freedman.

She said, 'You're right about Vivian acquiring items dubiously. Not all of them were on the open market, hence the high prices he paid. It became an addiction. If there was something he coveted then he had to have it no matter what the price. Money began to get tight but he couldn't bear to part with any of his collection. I didn't know how tight. He took out a mortgage on the house and then he re-mortgaged it. Yes, I did sign the papers but I was stupid enough not to read them and he told me it was just a loan until he could sell something.'

Cantelli said, 'Do you know how much debt he had accrued?'

'No, but I believe it to be sizeable. Part of me didn't want to know and that's always been my problem. I've stuck my head in the sand, pretending everything was OK, but I can't do that any more.' She looked tired and was growing more drawn as the interview progressed. On Monday, when Cantelli spoke to the bank, he'd find out just how much debt the Clements were in.

She pulled herself up with an effort. 'Peter knew what our financial position was, or rather he knew that things were getting difficult, hence Vivian having to undertake the cruise lectures. I also told Peter how obsessive Vivian was about acquiring his precious oriental porcelain and antique pistols and that he'd go to any length to do so.'

'Was the fake robbery Peter Freedman's idea?'

'I don't know. Maybe. Vivian said we needed the money. We did but I said why not sell the collection? Vivian told me I was stupid. This way he could keep his precious pistols and still get the money from the insurance company.'

'And you went along with it?'

'I didn't have much choice.'

No, thought Horton, and if it was Freedman's idea then Freedman had something that he could use to blackmail Clements with. But why should he resort to blackmail when his business seemed to be doing very well? He considered again the thought that had occurred to him earlier: was blackmail Evelyn Lyster's racket and she'd got Freedman involved?

'Do you know a woman called Evelyn Lyster?' Horton asked.

'No.'

'Or Dennis Lyster?'

She shook her head and looked confused.

Cantelli put a picture of Evelyn Lyster in front of her. 'Do you recognize her?'

'No. What has she got to do with this?'

Horton thought her bafflement genuine.

'You said earlier that your husband went out on Tuesday night?'

'Yes. At about six thirty and he came home round about nine o'clock.'

'Did he say where he had been?'

'No. I think it was to the lock-up to check that the stolen guns were there.'

'Did he contact Peter Freedman?'

'I don't know. He might have done.'

'Did he arrange to meet Freedman and have it out with him?'

'He didn't say. I don't know. He was in a foul mood, like I told you, and then the next day, Wednesday, was worse. That's when I went out for a walk at tea time and he never came home.'

Horton held her troubled, tired gaze for a moment then rose. He nodded at Cantelli, who switched off the tape.

'What happens now?' she asked.

'We take a break.'

'You think I killed them both, don't you? Well, I didn't.'

But still, Horton wondered.

Nineteen

He reported back to Uckfield who then sent Bliss in to re-interview her with Horton on the grounds that it took a woman to know if a woman was lying. His remark hadn't gone down too well with Bliss, probably because she had construed it as being sexist but Horton knew there was an element of truth in it.

Bliss had let him lead the interview while she had observed. Horton had gone over the same ground and had got the same answers.

'Is she telling the truth?' asked Uckfield two hours later. They were all in the incident suite with takeaway pizzas which Walters was demolishing with vigour. Somerfield had reported that Vivian Clements had booked in at the lock-up at seven p.m. on Tuesday night and had logged out again at seven forty-five. Plenty of time for him to drive to Ferry Road and kill Freedman with the Robert Adams pistol he'd taken from his collection and hadn't declared, then return home and put away the gun for his wife to find later. And time enough for him to try and compose himself before returning home at nine p.m., if Constance Clements could be believed. DC Marsden had bagged up the clothes Vivian Clements had been wearing on Tuesday night but the coat and shoes were the same ones he'd been wearing when he'd been killed. They would both be examined for any traces of Freedman's blood.

Bliss answered Uckfield. 'She has a motive for both murders. She hated her husband, who was a bully and spent all her money, and she hated Freedman for rejecting her. She had access to the gun and she had the opportunity to kill them both. But without a confession we've got no evidence that she did it. Even if her prints are found on the gun a lawyer could claim that they would be there because she'd handled the weapon in her house on a previous occasion, as she freely admits. And we can't find any witnesses who can place her at either scene.'

Trueman said, 'The Clements' car will be forensically examined tomorrow but even if we find traces that it was parked close to the shore where Freedman was shot and evidence of her being inside the car it doesn't mean that *she* was there then or at Milton Common when her husband was shot.'

'That's right, cheer me up.' Uckfield sat back with a scowl and scratched his armpit. 'What about her clothes?'

Bliss replied, 'She's told us what she was wearing on Tuesday and Wednesday night and they've been bagged up. But she's put them through the washing machine.'

'Bloody convenient,' growled Uckfield. 'Anything at the scene of Clements' death that could tie her in with being there?'

Trueman shook his head. 'No footwear marks – certainly not enough to identify the type of shoes worn, just a muddy mess.'

'And before you ask,' Horton interjected, 'she also says she'd cleaned the shoes she was wearing on Wednesday night.'

Uckfield groaned and sneezed loudly. Horton noticed everyone – except Walters, who was too absorbed in eating – eased back.

Bliss said, 'She claims no knowledge of Evelyn Lyster.'

With his mouth full, Walters said, 'There's a sighting of Evelyn Lyster walking along the platform at the railway station towards the exit on Monday morning but no one approaches her or stops her. We don't have any CCTV footage of her outside the station as she heads for the taxi, so someone could have met her there but the taxi driver would probably have seen that.'

Horton said, 'He had his nose in a crime novel when I tapped on his window on Wednesday night. Maybe he was engrossed in the latest Art Marvik when Evelyn Lyster approached him.'

Bliss picked up on this. 'Constance Clements has a motive for killing Evelyn Lyster – jealousy. Perhaps Freedman ditched Constance to take up with Evelyn.'

Horton said, 'OK, so he bought the beta blockers online and he killed Evelyn for her money. But why suggest the phoney robbery to Vivian Clements and why dress up as a tramp to meet him?'

Bliss answered, 'Maybe he thought it would make him invisible. People don't like looking at tramps – it makes them feel uncomfortable. Freedman would know that. He thought no one would notice him.'

It was a point and a good one. Freedman would

know all about the public's reactions to vagrants. Most people would, as Bliss said, look away, except for one young, smartly-dressed woman who had changed Glyn Ashmead's life because she hadn't. He said, 'And why would Constance Clements want Dennis Lyster dead?'

Uckfield said, 'We've no evidence Dennis Lyster was killed.'

'But we have to consider it,' Horton insisted.

Uckfield grunted dubiously.

Horton continued, 'If we believe Constance's version of Peter Freedman then he sounds predatory and calculating but that's not the picture we get of him from Glyn Ashmead and Martha Wiley and it doesn't fit with a man who gave his time freely to the charity and donated ten per cent of his income to them.'

Cantelli said, 'Perhaps his weakness is women.'

No one looked at Uckfield.

Horton said, 'So he meets Evelyn Lyster—'

'When?' interrupted Bliss.

Trueman answered, 'It has to be in the last four years since he was released from prison, but no one at the property on the Isle of Wight remembers seeing him so we can't get a date from there. Freedman bought his flat in Portsmouth seventeen months ago from Ivor Randall.'

'Who dropped down dead of a heart attack in the hall,' mimicked Uckfield, quoting Stella Nugent – the resident who had told him and Horton that.

Trueman continued, 'Before that Freedman was living in rented accommodation for six months in Southsea and prior to that in Brighton after he was released from prison. While out on licence

260

he did voluntary work for a homeless charity and obtained a grant from a charitable trust to start his business. He got a training contract from the council and from a couple of companies in Sussex and gradually built up his business from there.'

'Why did he move to Portsmouth?' asked Horton.

'Don't know. He was born in Devon and his business – he owned three garages in and around Exeter – got into difficulties. He over-extended himself, took out loans but spent the money on cars and a bigger house. Finally he had to call in the receivers. He turned to drink. His wife left him. We've traced her. She's living in Great Yarmouth, Norfolk. An officer is going around tonight to show her a picture of her husband and break the news.'

Horton wondered how she'd take it.

Trueman continued, 'We've spoken to Freedman's accountant and have managed to speak to a couple of his corporate clients. No one has anything but praise for him. He was hardworking, personable, professional and, it seems, honest.'

Uckfield looked doubtful. He wiped his mouth with a serviette and then blew his nose with another before speaking. 'Maybe he was just a clever bastard and good at deceiving people, especially women who had money. He could have been at it for years only none of the women in Brighton want to come forward and admit they were conned because they're ashamed and afraid of looking foolish. It could be how he amassed enough money to put down a whacking great deposit on that apartment and get a small mortgage for the rest.'

Horton said, 'Perhaps Freedman arranged to meet Constance with the intention of killing her because she was becoming a nuisance. She might even have suspected or knew about his affair with Evelyn, and if she threatened to tell it could tie him in with her death and he couldn't afford to take that risk. Freedman had the gun. Vivian Clements had given it to him in return for his silence about the phoney robbery. Constance had told Freedman her husband had planned the robbery. Freedman took the gun with him but somehow Constance got it from him and turned it on him. Dr Clayton said he was shot at close range. Constance leaves, taking the gun with her, and then an idea occurs to her that she could link Freedman's death to her husband and stage the suicide, and so get rid of him.'

Uckfield rested his hands behind his head and spread his legs. He addressed Dennings. 'You and DCI Bliss can put that to her tomorrow.'

'We should let her go,' Cantelli said. 'Her husband has only just died and she's had to visit the mortuary. She's had a tough day and she looks all in.'

Uckfield eyed him contemptuously. 'She could be a killer.'

'Or she could be innocent. I don't think she's going to run away.'

'Cantelli's right,' Horton agreed. 'She looks on the verge of collapse.'

'Then we might get a confession from her.'

'It won't hold up, Steve. Any defence lawyer will tear it to shreds.'

262

'Then let them. We hold her for another twenty-four hours on suspicion of murder and in the meantime we charge her with intent to defraud the insurance company and being in possession of a firearm without a licence. It doesn't matter that it belonged to her husband – she's still culpable in law. If she wants a lawyer, get her one.' Uckfield hauled himself up. 'I'm going home.'

And that was the cue for them all to do the same.

Horton rode home slowly, his mind on the clothes that Freedman had been wearing when he was shot. Bliss could be right and Freedman had carefully chosen those clothes to make himself invisible, but equally he could have chosen them to throw suspicion on a vagrant if anyone saw him at the scene. He could have bought the clothes from any charity shop or, as Cantelli had said, taken a charity bag from outside a shop or house and helped himself. Equally, he could have got those clothes from Gravity and taken them – especially the coat – before Sheila had a chance to see it. He'd stuffed them in a bag or a rucksack and walked out without Martha or Glyn noticing. He could easily have got past Ashmead's office without him seeing and Martha might already have gone home or been busy cleaning up in the kitchen area behind the counter with her back to the door.

Then there was Dennis Lyster. If his death was the first murder in this chain of killings then maybe they should be taking a closer look at it and at him.

Horton pulled on to the seafront and caught a flash of lightning out to sea. What did he know about Dennis Lyster apart from the fact he'd been a civil engineer? Had he always worked overseas? No, because Rowan had said that before he'd gone away to school he had sailed with his father on a boat they owned.

Horton recalled the coroner's report. Evelyn Lyster had said that she and her husband had once owned boats, which backed up what Rowan had said about sailing with his father, but Dennis didn't have a boat at the time of his death. Evelyn Lyster had claimed that it would have been a natural choice for her husband to end his life by drowning. So where had they kept their yacht when Rowan was a boy? Where had they lived? Did it matter? He didn't think so. He was just desperate to find answers to the questions plaguing his mind.

He caught another flash of lightning and heard the distant rumble of thunder. He could see the pinpricks of lights on some of the ships moored up beyond the Bembridge lifeboat station. He thought of Freedman's body by the old houseboat and the fact that Gaye had said that Freedman with a bullet in him could still have walked or staggered some distance.

Climbing on his Harley, he made for the Eastney lifeboat station and walked around to the slipway to stand in front of the building. The lightning was getting more frequent and the thunder growing louder as the storm drew closer. It wasn't raining but it soon would be. He was facing the entrance to Langstone Harbour and beyond it the Solent. He couldn't see his Harley from here and neither could he see the road. More importantly, as he had considered the last time he'd visited here, no one could see him. Had the location been chosen specifically because of that, had it been a random choice or did it have some other meaning? Not that he knew this was where Freedman had met his killer but through his mind ran the thought that Dennis Lyster had been a sailor, and because of that he'd probably have been a member of the Royal National Lifeboat Institution. But that got Horton no further forward.

So which of them had killed Dennis? Evelyn because she wanted to be with Freedman and she was sick of Dennis under her feet? Or Freedman because he knew that Evelyn would inherit the house and get the insurance money? That, coupled with her own wealth, would be an attractive proposition; however, that wealth had been accumulated because there was still the matter of Evelyn's secretive nature, her purchase of the Isle of Wight property, her use of two names and her tendency to pay by cash – not in itself suspicious, but if he put that with her desire to travel one way to Guernsey and the fact that she was dead there had to be something. What had she been up to? Something that Freedman knew about or had managed to get out of her. Was it blackmail? Was there a criminal partner in Guernsey? Not if Freedman had thought he was on to a winner by killing her, and Horton didn't think a criminal living in Guernsey had arranged to meet Freedman and flown over here on Tuesday night specifically to kill him, although it was viable.

Perhaps Uckfield was right when he said

that Freedman targeted wealthy widows or widows-to-be with the aim of preying on them and conning them out of their money. Freedman thought he'd struck lucky with Constance Clements, only to discover her husband had spent most of her money and re-mortgaged the house, so he dropped her.

Lightning lit the night sky, illuminating the lifeboat station, and within a few seconds it was followed by a loud clap of thunder and a squall of lean, slanting rain. The wind suddenly rose and swirled violently around him. The waves crashed on to the shore. But Horton didn't move. His mind flew back to that first sight of Freedman's body under the houseboat and how he'd considered it an unusual place to find a vagrant on such a wild night, only he hadn't been a vagrant, and because he wasn't this was a fairly good location for a private meeting, especially for someone who had planned for it to end in murder. But there had always been the chance the lifeboat might have been called out, or that the lifeboat volunteers might have been meeting here that night. Elkins had spoken to Chris Howgate, one of the helmsmen, who said they hadn't. So had Freedman known he'd be safe here from interruptions on Tuesday night? He could have listened to the weather forecast and thought that no one would be foolish enough to be at sea in such a storm and taken advantage of that to arrange a meeting, but he would have gambled on the fact the lifeboat wouldn't be called out. Perhaps he knew the crew weren't going to be here for a meeting or a drill that night and, if that was the case then he, or his killer, had inside knowledge. No one had asked the lifeboat volunteers if they recognized or knew Peter Freedman or Vivian Clements. Horton thought it was about time he did.

Twenty

Saturday

Horton found Chris Howgate in his small office off the main factory floor of his sail-making business in the building adjoining the marina. His staff of four were busy cutting out sail cloth on a large table. Horton nodded to them as he went through. He knew Howgate well and, after a brief exchange of greeting, Horton explained why he was there. Howgate, a round-faced muscular man in his early forties, looked concerned.

'Dai Elkins asked me if I'd seen anyone hanging around the lifeboat station on Tuesday night and I told him I hadn't because I didn't go there and neither did anyone else. There was no training or meeting and it was a miracle we weren't called out in that storm or last night, but then anyone with an ounce of brain wouldn't have gone out in such atrocious weather. Point is that not everyone has an ounce of brain.'

Horton knew that.

'Only last week we had to rescue a man off the Bembridge Ledge who had bought a boat and a road atlas and was attempting to cross the Channel to France. Can you believe it?'

Sadly, Horton said he could.

He showed Howgate a photograph of Peter Freedman and asked if he recognized him. Howgate shook his head. He didn't know the name or recognize Vivian Clements either. Horton said he'd need the contact details of all the volunteers to ask them the same questions.

'You can ask Roger Stillmore now. He works for me and he's been on the lifeboat for years. He doesn't go out on shouts any more but he still helps out.' Howgate rose, crossed to his office door and hailed Stillmore, who appeared a minute later.

Howgate made the introductions. Stillmore, a sturdy man in his late fifties with fine silver-grey hair and a gap in his front teeth, examined the picture of Peter Freedman but after a few seconds he shook his head and did the same for Clements. 'I've never seen either man before.' He and Howgate also confirmed they knew no one called Constance Clements. Horton hadn't really expected them to but for thoroughness had thought he'd ask. He did the same for Dennis Lyster. At least he'd had a connection with the sea, according to his son, albeit a long time ago.

'It sounds familiar,' Stillmore said, frowning thoughtfully.

'He was a boat owner about eighteen or twenty years ago. He died last March. His body was found just off Ryde Pier. Ryde Inshore Lifeboat attended.'

'Yes, of course.' Stillmore's expression cleared.

268

'I read about the shout in our news bulletin. Terribly sad that.'

Horton should have considered that the news would have been circulated to all lifeboat crew and volunteers.

'I guess he never got over it.'

'Losing his job, you mean?' Horton said.

'Did he? I didn't know that. No, I meant what happened years ago. It never really goes away.'

'What doesn't?' Horton asked puzzled and deeply curious.

'The death of a child at sea. That is if it's the same Lyster.' Stillmore added hastily, seeing Horton's surprise, 'He had a son called Rowan. I remember that because it's the same name as the hospice and my dad was in the hospice at the time.'

'Yes, it's the same man,' Horton answered, keenly interested. No one had mentioned this and he was certain it hadn't come up at the inquest, otherwise Cantelli would have said. So why the silence? 'Tell me about it,' he said eagerly.

Howgate gestured Stillmore into the seat beside Horton.

'Dennis Lyster was sailing his yacht, a twenty-eight-foot Westerley, just off the Isle of Wight when he got into difficulty. He shouldn't have been out in the first place. The wind was force six and rising to near gale force, and the waves were like walls of water, eight feet and rising. Lyster had two young boys on board, aged ten. One wasn't clipped on.'

Horton raised his eyebrows.

'I know, bloody stupid,' Stillmore said with

sorrow. 'Lyster had reefed in and was running on his engine alone. The child was swept overboard. Lyster engaged man overboard manoeuvres but in that sea and wind it was near-on impossible. He sent out a mayday. The boy who entered the water was wearing a life jacket but this was February.'

And Horton knew what that meant. The sea temperature would have been about forty-one degrees Fahrenheit – bloody cold. Horton shuddered at the thought. He couldn't even bear to think how he'd feel if anything happened to Emma. Fear gripped his heart. He hoped to God that Catherine made sure Emma was safe when she was on board her boyfriend's floating gin palace and when she sailed on her grandfather's yacht.

'We got the child out of the water and he was airlifted to hospital by the coastguard helicopter but the poor little mite was already dead. Dennis Lyster was distraught, as you can imagine.'

'Can you remember the name of the child who died?'

'He was called Cary as in Cary Grant. I remember thinking at the time this poor little mite is never going to grow up like Cary Grant. I can't remember his surname. He was about ten – the same age as the other boy on the yacht, Rowan Lyster.'

'He wasn't related to Lyster then?'

'Not as far as I know. I couldn't attend the inquest because it was held on the day of my dad's funeral.'

Horton could get the name from the marine

270

accident investigation report and the coroner's office. He said, 'Have you seen or spoken to Dennis Lyster since then?'

'No. I read about him being fished out of the sea and it possibly being suicide and thought that it must have been haunting him for years.'

And what about Rowan? Had it haunted him? It certainly didn't seem that way because Rowan had pursued a career on the sea. Maybe he'd pushed it aside, or perhaps he'd been too young to realize the full horror of it.

'Do you remember Dennis Lyster's wife, Evelyn?'

'No. Like I said, I wasn't at the inquest so didn't get to meet her.'

'And she wasn't there when you got Dennis Lyster and his son safely back to the shore?'

'No. They were taken to Bembridge where an ambulance was waiting. The boy was suffering from hypothermia and both father and son were in a state of shock.'

And Evelyn Lyster would have been in Portsmouth and wouldn't have had time to get to the island before the ambulance. Maybe she had never got there but waited for her son and husband to return home. Perhaps she'd even been abroad, working. And what of Cary's parents? Who had broken the news to them? Where had they been at the time? Who were they? Did this have anything to do with the three deaths: Evelyn Lyster, Peter Freedman and Vivian Clements – four if you counted Dennis Lyster? But how could it?

Horton thanked them both warmly and returned

to his Harley, mulling over what Roger Stillmore had told him. What had happened to Cary's parents? Had Cary been their only child? How had the tragedy affected them? Maybe it had finally driven Dennis Lyster to suicide and his death wasn't suspicious. But why hadn't Evelyn Lyster mentioned it at the inquest? Perhaps she had just wanted to forget it and put it behind her. It explained why Dennis Lyster had worked overseas for so many years, though. Perhaps he'd been trying to put as much distance as he could between the place where the tragedy had occurred and himself. The marine accident investigation report would give him the details of Cary's parents and from there they would be able to trace them. He didn't want to disturb them though and bring back such harrowing memories unless he really had to. And the same might be said if they questioned Rowan about the tragedy. And he couldn't see why they should or how it could have any bearing on the murders.

He made for the station but didn't go inside. Instead he again headed for Gravity and found Ashmead in the shower room with a mop and bucket. 'We've got a leaky pipe – the plumber's on his way,' he explained.

Horton asked him if Freedman had brought a rucksack or bag into the café on Tuesdays when he worked as a volunteer.

'I never saw him with one.'

'Did you ever see him leave carrying a bag of any kind?'

'He might have done; I don't know. It wasn't the sort of thing I took notice of. Is it important?'

'Probably not.'

Ashmead was looking drawn. The lack of funding was clearly getting to him. Horton hoped the strain wouldn't prove too much and send him on a downward spiral to seek relief in alcohol. But soon Ashmead would get Freedman's legacy and although Horton didn't know how much that was he was certain it would help. A terrible thought flashed into his mind. He couldn't believe that Glyn Ashmead would kill for money. But surely he had to believe the unbelievable – that was his job.

He asked Ashmead if he recognized the name Constance Clements but Ashmead shook his head and neither did he recognize a description of her. He didn't seem to be lying, but nevertheless Horton considered the possibility that Constance might have donated some of her husband's clothes to the charity, including that Gieves and Hawkes coat. It seemed the sort of thing that Vivian Clements might have worn and it fitted his measurements. Maybe it was Ashmead she had met and fallen in love with. But would Vivian Clements have hung on to so shabby a coat? Possibly if Constance had packed it away and then decided to have a clear-out.

But perhaps Freedman had told Constance Clements he volunteered at Gravity on Tuesdays and Constance had come here to see Freedman and she'd met Glyn Ashmead. They'd begun a relationship. She wanted rid of her husband and Ashmead wanted Freedman's wealth. Maybe Freedman had told Ashmead that the centre was named in his will. Perhaps Glyn Ashmead was resentful of Freedman's success. Perhaps their relationship went way back to when they had both been on the road.

He thought of that coat Freedman had been wearing when he'd been shot. Perhaps it had been Glyn Ashmead's. He said he'd kept a belt as a reminder of his dark days on the streets in the hope that seeing it would ensure he'd never go down that route again but maybe it had been the coat he'd kept. Freedman had got hold of it and worn it and the other clothes as a taunt to Ashmead when they'd met by the lifeboat station. Ashmead had said that Freedman was contributing ten per cent of his income to the centre and the accountant had confirmed that but perhaps he hadn't been giving it voluntarily; he had been forced to do so as blackmail money. Ashmead had something on Freedman which he had threatened to expose but finally Freedman had said enough was enough. He'd threatened to stop paying. Ashmead was desperate for money, not for himself but for the centre. Ashmead could have acquired the gun from Constance and shot Freedman, then killed Vivian Clements. But where did that leave them with Evelyn Lyster's death? Neither Ashmead nor Constance could have done that, and why should either of them kill Dennis Lyster, *if* he had been killed.

'Did Freedman ever talk about his family?' Horton asked, postponing his line of thought for a moment.

'All I knew was that he had been married.'

'He still was when he died. No children. Did you meet him when you were both on the road?'

'If I did I don't remember him but then that's hardly surprising considering I was inebriated most of the time.'

'There's a kind of camaraderie on the streets. You meet up with the same people on the same circuit and look out for one another.'

Ashmead gave a hollow laugh. 'Only in the sense of what you can steal from them to fund that next drink or that next drug fix.'

'Did you do drugs?'

'Yes, and I didn't ask where they came from so I had no idea of the toxic stuff I was taking. That, and the drink, scrambles your brain cells as you well know. It leaves its mark no matter what you tell yourself.'

'What mark has it left on you?' Horton asked solemnly, wondering if he was going to hear a confession. He tensed.

'I get blinding headaches, sweats and memory loss.'

'Does that mean that if I was to ask you where you were on Tuesday and Wednesday night, you'll tell me you don't remember?'

'I was at home on Wednesday night alone, but I don't know where I was on Tuesday night. All I can remember was travelling home from Southampton on the train from that fundraising conference and the next thing I was waking up at three in the morning, thankfully in my own bed, in my flat. You think I could have killed Peter, don't you? Well, I didn't. I don't know how he died but there was no blood on my clothes, though they were damp.' Ashmead let the water from the leaky pipe swirl around his shoes while

275

Horton stood in the doorway. 'I had no reason to kill Peter. He was generous with his time and money. There was no resentment and no history between us.'

'He's left half his estate to the centre.'

Ashmead's surprise seemed genuine. He nodded knowingly. 'You think I killed him for the money?'

'You need it desperately,' Horton pressed.

'I'd rather have had him alive because he was more valuable for the work he did here helping others than the money.'

'But without it the centre might have to close. Was the overcoat he was wearing when he died yours, Glyn?'

'No.'

'Did it belong to Constance Clements' husband?'

'I don't know because I don't know Constance Clements or her husband. She might have brought it in. I'm sorry, Andy, but I can't help you. As far as I'm aware I didn't kill Peter but if you want to search my bedsit and take my clothes for forensic examination then please go ahead.'

Could Ashmead have killed Freedman while suffering from a blackout? It was possible. And they'd have to ask Constance Clements if she knew Glyn Ashmead and gauge her reaction. Horton left feeling uncomfortable that he'd had to doubt Ashmead and that it had soured their relationship. It was his job, he told himself, to suspect everybody. Sometimes the job stank.

Twenty-One

Horton made his way slowly back to the station. There were so many loose ends and it didn't look as though they were ever going to tie them up. Horton felt they were going round in circles getting nowhere fast. He bought a coffee from the vending machine outside CID and found Cantelli at his desk. There was no sign of Walters.

'He's phoned in sick, says he's caught Uckfield's cold,' Cantelli relayed with some scepticism.

Usually it was Walters' gut playing him up because of all the fast food crap he ate. He probably just had a few sniffles or hadn't relished the prospect of working on a Saturday. Cantelli, with his family and his sick mother, had much better reasons to spend his weekend at home, but Horton knew he'd never fabricate a story to do so. And he'd never duck out of an ongoing serious crime investigation unless it was absolutely vital. Horton asked how his mother was and was pleased to hear she was improving under Charlotte's nursing care and in her grandchildren's company.

'I think she was lonely and depressed after dad's death and too damn proud to admit it, even to her family,' Cantelli added. 'And, talking of families, I've got some interesting information from the head teacher of Rowan Lyster's school, Saint Levan's in Cornwall, a Mr Norman Fyning. He's been headmaster for twenty-two years and is retiring at the end of this school year. He rang back to check I was legit. The school is very expensive judging by what I could see on the website and what Mr Fyning told me about the fees. Way beyond my budget and even Uckfield's. It's probably beyond the ACC's. The Lysters' jobs must have paid very well. It's not Catholic and neither is Rowan Lyster. The school specializes in outdoor activities, as Rowan told us. It also has its own sailing ship, a fifty-six-foot gaff cutter, whatever that is.'

'Lucky them.' Horton didn't bother to explain that a gaff cutter or rather a gaff-rigged boat described the type of sails used – it would only have gone over Cantelli's head. 'It sounds like the type of school I'd have enjoyed instead of the failing inner city one I was forced to attend.'

'It sounds like hell on earth to me. The kids undertake ocean sailing, canoe racing, diving and triathlons, the poor little blighters.'

Horton smiled. He'd have lapped it up.

'There's mountaineering in the UK and abroad, cycling, running, swimming.'

'I take it they do also have lessons.'

'Must do but it's not what you would call an academic school. It specializes in educating children of the wealthy and professional classes who don't fit into mainstream education for some reason or another. Some are not academically bright and some have energy that needs to be channelled in certain directions, which was Fyning's rather tactful description. They're not necessarily problem children or kids who have got into trouble, he says, just strong-minded.'

'And which description fits Rowan Lyster – not academically bright or wilful?'

'Both, but he was very talented when it came to water sports, which was something Fyning said he would have liked to have discussed with Rowan's parents, but he never met Dennis Lyster.'

'Never!'

'Yep, and Fyning only saw Evelyn Lyster once a year when she showed up for parents' day. But he claims that isn't unusual in the school's case. Many of the parents are absent ones. Not that Fyning would say as much but it's a dumping ground for unwanted kids of the well-to-do. They even keep the kids for the school holidays, take them on outbound trips and holidays abroad so that the parents don't have to have them hanging round their neck for weeks on end, messing up their lives. I can't see the point of having kids if you're not going to be there to bring them up. Sorry, Andy, I didn't mean that about—'

'Forget it.' Horton didn't take offence. He knew what Cantelli meant and he would dearly have loved to have shared each and every day with his daughter. It made him think that maybe it was about time he did something to make sure he saw her more often despite Catherine's attempts to prevent him. Emma was a weekly boarder at her school which was only eighteen miles to the north of Portsmouth. He brought his mind back to what Cantelli was saying.

'Fyning said Evelyn Lyster was remarkably relaxed about her son's progress and obviously Dennis Lyster must have been the same. The school fees were always paid on time, from a joint bank account, and all additional expenses were met without a quibble. Rowan rarely spent the holidays with his parents. He'd stay at the school or occasionally with a friend, or he'd go off with the school party on outward-bound adventures. Rowan didn't seem bothered about his parents' lack of interest in him. He was happy just as long as he was engaged in some kind of sporting activity, preferably on the water, and preferably on his own.'

'Not a team player then.'

'No. He had friendships but they didn't last very long, not unless the boy or girl – it's a co-ed school – was submissive. Fyning's word, not mine. Rowan was extremely competitive. He excelled in sailing, especially when he was skipper, and in kayaking and windsurfing. Fyning said he wasn't surprised that Rowan had gone on to become a European windsurfing champion. He was very focused and not a good loser. I got the impression Fyning was being generous and cautious with what he was saying. When I pressed him he claimed that Rowan was a strong personality and extremely determined.'

Interesting as this was Horton couldn't see where it got them, but there were certain aspects in Cantelli's report that intrigued him. 'It's odd that after nearly losing their son at sea in that tragedy the Lysters, instead of being even more protective towards Rowan, distanced themselves from him.'

'What tragedy?'

Horton hadn't brought Cantelli up to speed with his interview with Roger Stillmore. He did now and swiftly. Cantelli's dark features looked sorrowful.

'Poor little mite. The parents must have been devastated. Maybe Dennis Lyster blamed himself for the accident and the very sight of his son being alive reminded him too painfully of the loss of the other little boy and how he had let it happen.'

'But you'd have thought Evelyn Lyster might have wanted to cling to her son even more given the death of the other child.'

'Perhaps she just wasn't the maternal type. Maybe her business meant more to her than her kid. It sounds like it judging by what Fyning said.'

Maybe but Horton thought it strange nonetheless. 'I wonder how Rowan took being shunted off to school after the accident. Stillmore said it occurred in February when Rowan was ten. When did he start at that school?'

'The beginning of April, just after Easter for the summer term. He was eleven the following August.'

'And Fyning said nothing about the accident at sea?' mused Horton. If he had Cantelli would have known about it.

'I can call him back and ask him if he knew about it.'

'And ask if Evelyn or Dennis Lyster told him about it, and if Rowan ever mentioned it. It was a pretty traumatic event for a child to have witnessed.'

'Maybe he had counselling or blocked it out.'

'Possibly. See what you can get on it from the marine accident investigation report. Details

281

should be on their website.' Horton asked if there had been any progress with the investigation from Trueman's end.

'Uckfield's had to let Constance Clements go. She decided she wanted a lawyer. She's been charged with intent to defraud the insurance company but we both know that won't stick. Her brief will say she had no choice but to participate because she was bullied into it by her husband. Uckfield held back on charging her with knowing about the gun being in her husband's possession.'

'Hoping to get more before he does,' Horton said.

Cantelli nodded. 'The house-to-house around Milton Common has drawn a blank. There have been a few responses to the media appeal about Freedman's coat and sightings of Clements in Milton. Trueman's team are checking them out but he says that most of them sound like the usual cranks.'

'Any news from ballistics on the gun that was used to kill Freedman?'

'Yes. It's the same gun that killed Clements. And Freedman's wife has confirmed Freedman's ID from the photograph she was shown.'

'Her reaction?'

'Surprise, relief, a touch of bitterness. Technically she's still married and she's been with her new partner for eight years. Freedman was drinking heavily after his garage business failed. She gave him an ultimatum: sober up or clear out. He chose the latter, or rather that's her story. She told the officer who broke the news to her that that was the last she heard from him. She moved away and got on with her life. And no, she didn't want to see his body.'

Horton relayed his interview with Glyn Ashmead, ending with the view that he didn't want to consider him in the frame but thought they should. 'It means we'll have to ask Constance Clements if she knows him but we'll wait on that for a while. Don't want to be accused of harassing her.'

Horton entered his office. He tried to concentrate on his paperwork and write up his interviews but that tragedy at sea nagged at him. The fact the Dennis Lyster, an experienced sailor, had taken out his yacht when the weather was bad and the forecast was for worse didn't make sense. And why take two small boys with him? It wasn't the act of an experienced skipper and neither did it fit with a cautious man, which Dennis Lyster must have been. After all, most engineers were.

He sat back and considered what Cantelli had just told him. Why had the Lysters despatched their only son to a school hundreds of miles away after the fatality and rarely seen him? Why had Dennis Lyster stayed out of the country for so long? Why hadn't Evelyn Lyster been anxious about her only child? It didn't add up. Why didn't Rowan seem affected by what had happened? Why had he taken up a career on the sea when his friend had died on it? Perhaps he'd faced his fears and overcome them, or as Cantelli had said, deliberately blocked it from his mind.

Then there were the dead boy's parents. Where were they? How had they coped with life after so tragically losing their son at sea? Had they also been sailors? Had they blamed Dennis Lyster for their child's death? Why had they allowed Cary to go sailing in such bad weather? Why had Evelyn Lyster permitted it? It could easily have been her child who'd died.

Ignoring the paperwork on his desk, Horton called up the coroner's report on Dennis Lyster's death. He was curious about a man who seemed to have been very elusive, especially after the tragedy at sea. Had he changed jobs so that he could escape the Solent and his wife and child who reminded him of it? Had it been a way of avoiding seeing the dead boy's parents?

He read the background that Cantelli had relayed to him earlier. There was no mention by anyone about the tragedy at sea and how it might have affected Dennis Lyster. Why hadn't Evelyn told the coroner that the incident might have returned to haunt him? Or that, having been involved in such an incident, perhaps he'd thought it only fitting he should take his own life by drowning as a form of punishment for a child's death at sea while the child had been under his care? Or was he just reading too much into it?

Horton read on. There was a fair bit of information on the fact that Dennis Lyster had been made redundant from a job that he had held with the same company, the Paitak Corporation, for twenty-three years, which meant he hadn't changed jobs after the tragedy. Maybe he had changed positions to encompass more travel. Horton read that Lyster had been a mining engineer. That wasn't what Gina Lyster had told them.

284

She'd said Dennis had been a civil engineer. Maybe Gina had thought they were the same thing. Possibly they were but Horton called up the company name on the Internet and soon found that they weren't.

An idea began to form in the back of his mind. He rang the company's UK office. It being Saturday, though, he got a security officer who told him the office was closed for the weekend and to ring back and speak to human resources on Monday. He then rang his former police colleague, Mike Danby, who now ran an impressive close protection and security company working for the famous, influential and rich, including Lord Eames, as well as some top corporations. A few minutes later he replaced the phone, his head spinning. He was about to call Cantelli in when he knocked and entered.

'Fyning had no idea about any tragedy at sea or fatality. The Lysters never told him and Rowan never mentioned it and neither, as far as he was aware, did Rowan suffer nightmares or show any reluctance to go to sea,' Cantelli announced, taking the seat across Horton's desk. 'Evelyn Lyster arrived with Rowan at the school on Friday the fourth of March, three weeks before Easter. She and Rowan were shown around the school and Rowan was told about the ethos and activities. Fyning knew that Rowan was already a fairly experienced sailor even at the age of ten but he didn't know how good. Rowan stayed for the long weekend to familiarize himself with the activities and meet the other pupils. He showed no reluctance to join the school – in fact, he was very keen when he saw that he was more experienced and had a greater aptitude for water sports than most of the other pupils in his year.'

The tragedy at sea had occurred four weeks before that on the fourth of February. Horton sat back thoughtfully as Cantelli continued.

'The boy who died was Cary Gamblin, parents Robin and Margaret. It occurred just off the Bembridge Ledge. Both the Bembridge and the Eastney lifeboats attended but Bembridge was already on a shout further round the island off Ventnor so the Eastney lifeboat reached there first, even then they were too late to save the boy. I've run a check on Robin and Margaret Gamblin; neither are registered as being dead or divorced. There's also no record with Her Majesty's Revenue and Customs for either of them so they're not working, or if they are they're certainly not paying taxes and neither are they claiming benefit. They could be living abroad. Perhaps they moved away to try and start a new life somewhere. They might have emigrated. The last record I can find for Robin Gamblin is seventeen years ago. His last known occupation was an insurance broker. He's got no previous and neither has Margaret Gamblin.'

Horton put this information with the ideas that had been swirling around his head, what he'd discovered on the Paitak Corporation website and what Mike Danby had told him. Eagerly, he sat forward. 'I've been asking myself why an experienced sailor like Dennis Lyster would go sailing in such atrocious weather and take two small children with him. I think it was because he was scheduled to meet someone and couldn't put it off.'

'At sea?' asked Cantelli dubiously.

'Yes. Or perhaps in Bembridge Marina on the Isle of Wight. He could have been coming out of the marina or heading there but got blown off course. Or he struggled to get into the marina – the harbour's quite tricky to navigate especially given that weather.'

'But why take the children?'

'For cover. A small yacht with children on board is much less likely to get stopped by the Border Agency.'

'Not drugs!' Cantelli cried, alarmed.

'No, diamonds.'

Cantelli's eyebrows shot up. Horton rapidly relayed what he'd discovered while a popular tune ran around his head, one his mother had sung before she had vanished – 'Diamonds are a Girl's Best Friend'. 'According to the coroner's report on Dennis Lyster, he wasn't a civil engineer but a mining engineer. He worked for the Paitak Corporation for twenty-three years and Paitak are involved in mineral operations worldwide. In one mine alone in Canada they've produced over six million carats of white, high-quality gem diamonds. Gina Lyster told us that Evelyn worked as a freelance translator for many different types of business people – consultants, brokers, accountants and dealers in jewellery and gems.' He watched Cantelli's eyes widen as he quickly caught on.

Cantelli said, 'Dennis was helping himself. What about security, though? Would Dennis have been able to get diamonds out?'

'Apparently so. I've just spoken to Mike Danby. He says it's not that difficult to steal diamonds if you're working at the place where they're being extracted. It happens all the time, apparently, although the advances in technology are making it more difficult – the introduction of intelligent security systems, thermal cameras, video analytics, fingerprint and facial recognition and the like – but theft still happens and he says will continue to happen. Jewels, gems and precious metals are a big temptation to the workers who are involved in mining them. As prices have risen, Danby said that gold, silver, platinum and diamonds have become more alluring. In a diamond mine it would be quite usual to have people stealing the diamonds from the process. The company can screen employees and put restrictions on them entering certain areas but they can't legislate for everyone. And if an employee has worked for the same company for some time and has an exemplary record then there's no reason not to trust him.'

'Until he got caught,' said Cantelli. 'And Dennis did.'

'My thoughts exactly. I'd like to know if he was really made redundant or got the sack. As he was a UK citizen his employment details would have been kept at the company's UK office but there's no one we can speak to until Monday. I think it's possible that Dennis Lyster was stealing diamonds from his employers – not huge amounts and probably not on a regular basis, he was very careful not to get noticed. And Evelyn Lyster, through her network of contacts, was selling them on. Not to the usual diamond merchants or to any

288

dodgy dealers but to her clients and those she met at the jewellery and gem trade fairs. Perhaps just a small quantity each time. And I think they'd been doing so for a number of years. Dennis was delivering to a client when the tragedy at sea struck. He had to go. The deal was lined up. Whoever was buying the diamonds was waiting for them.'

'But why did Cary Gamblin go? Why not just take Rowan?'

Horton shrugged. 'Perhaps the two boys were great mates and did everything together. After the tragedy, Dennis and Evelyn had to change the way they operated – they could no longer use Rowan as cover. They might have continued to use boats but not from Portsmouth. They didn't want to be tied down with Rowan at school in Portsmouth so he was sent away, leaving them free to continue stealing and dealing to pay for their son's expensive education and for Evelyn to buy expensive properties to clean the money and put some away in a Guernsey account. The Gamblins had no idea their son had been used to hide the Lysters' criminal activities. And they probably never discovered that. When Dennis lost his job the gravy train came to an end and he was no longer useful.'

'Evelyn killed him.'

'Maybe, or perhaps she got Freedman to do it for her. We're not sure how long they had known one another. She could have met him when he lived in Brighton or possibly she met him through a mutual client. Freedman was very skilled at eliciting confidences and perhaps

Evelyn fell for him big time. When love comes in the door—'

'Reason flies out of the window.'

'Freedman killed Evelyn after making sure he could access the Guernsey account. And then someone killed him. Someone who has no idea what the Lysters have been up to but killed Freedman because she too, like Evelyn Lyster, was besotted with him.'

'So we're back to Constance Clements.'

But even though he'd suggested it Horton still wasn't sure. Certain questions gnawed away at the back of his mind. He rapidly sifted through all the information he'd heard and seen over the last six days. Somewhere among it all was something that would make sense of these deaths.

Cantelli said, 'Perhaps that nervy exterior of Constance Clements is just an act and underneath she's clever and ruthless. She came up with the idea of an insurance fraud so that she could use the gun to kill Freedman and her husband. She could have used insurance scams before with some of her interior design clients. Or maybe she got the idea from Freedman. He probably knew all about car insurance scams having been a garage proprietor. He'd report a car had been stolen and then claim on the insurance when in reality he'd changed the registration numbers, arranged a re-spray and sold it off.'

Insurance. The gun theft had been an insurance scam. Why had Freedman dressed as a tramp to meet his killer? Was it possible? His brain scrambled to pull the threads together. Eagerly, he voiced one key thought that Cantelli had sparked.

290

'Didn't you say that Robin Gamblin had been an insurance broker?'

'Yes, but we have no idea where he is now.'

'Don't we?'

After a moment, Cantelli's expression registered astonishment as he quickly caught on. Excitedly, he said, 'You mean he's in the mortuary.'

'If he is then it changes everything, or rather it makes certain elements of the case slot into place. Evelyn Lyster knew Freedman from *before* he went on the streets. From when he was Robin Gamblin.'

'But his wife identified him.'

'Only from a photograph. Glyn Ashmead did the formal identification at the mortuary and he said it was Peter Freedman because that's who he knew him as. That's who Ashmead had been told he was.' Suddenly into Horton's mind crashed and exploded his conversation with Violet Ducale. When he'd shown her the photograph from 1967 and told her the fair man, the second on the left between Timothy Wilson and James Royston, was Richard Eames her head had shot up. He'd asked her if she knew him and she'd said, *Yes, and his brother, Gordon. Are you sure that's Richard?* He'd nodded. She'd accepted it but had she? Shortly after that she had been uneasy speaking to him. And when he'd confronted Richard Eames with the photograph in the exclusive Castle Hill Yacht Club in Cowes in August, Richard had neither confirmed nor denied it was him but had let him assume it. Gordon was dead. He died in 1973. But Jennifer *had* seen a ghost.

'Andy, are you OK?'

With half his mind still on the past, he said, 'Perhaps Mrs Freedman really did think it was her husband because she was told it was him and a life on the streets changes you and your appearance. Or perhaps Mrs Freedman lied because she was only too glad to have her husband formerly declared dead.' And Richard Eames, and those he worked for in British Intelligence, were more than keen to believe Gordon Eames was dead. Not without some difficulty, he forced his mind back on the case. 'We've had no confirmation from dental records that Freedman was Freedman but the dental records could match those of Robin Gamblin. The real Peter Freedman could be dead. Maybe Robin Gamblin killed him and took his identity. Perhaps he died on the streets, Gamblin helped himself to Freedman's belongings and when he was picked up by the police it was Freedman's ID he had on him so he became Freedman. That article you read about Peter Freedman in the local paper – were there photographs of him in it?'

'Yes. You think Evelyn Lyster could have read it and got in touch with him, knowing it was Robin Gamblin?'

'And someone else did. His killer. What else did that article say?'

Cantelli reached for his phone and quickly, calling up the Internet, found the article that had appeared in the local newspaper. 'It's dated the second of February last year. There's a lot of stuff about living on the streets, how his last term in prison transformed his life and how he is putting something back into the community by volunteering at Gravity.'

'Does it say when he volunteers there?'

'Yes. Tuesdays.'

'So Evelyn would have known where and when to find him. Why would she, though? To apologize for Cary's death? To tell him Dennis was dead? Or did Gamblin aka Freedman know exactly where Dennis and Evelyn were? Perhaps that's the real reason he returned to Portsmouth. He killed Dennis Lyster because he blamed Lyster for the death of his son and then he killed Evelyn Lyster after making certain she fell for him. Maybe she recognized him, maybe she didn't. But he managed to elicit from her details of her and her husband's illegal dealings and where her money was. And he believed that money should be his for sacrificing his son and for all the pain, torment and despair he'd suffered. Only he didn't expect to be killed by a woman who had become infatuated with him and who wanted her husband dead.' Horton paused. Then added, 'But that's not right because of the clothes.' That was critical to this case. And he had an idea why, especially if he put it with the location. The lifeboat station. Now he saw what must have happened. With conviction, he said, 'Freedman didn't go to the lifeboat station to meet either Constance or Vivian Clements. He went there dressed as a vagrant to convince his killer that he was still on the streets, that he had nothing and that he was still in the depths of despair. It was someone he couldn't refuse to see but who would ruin everything that he had planned. Someone who would become a millstone around his neck. Someone who had tracked him down or read that same article you did, Barney, and recognized him.'

293

'And whoever it is got in touch with him to tell him where to meet.'

'Yes, but how? Another tramp wouldn't use a mobile phone and if the killer called Freedman's mobile then Freedman had no need to go to the meeting dressed as a tramp because the killer would know he wasn't a vagrant. Freedman's phone number is public knowledge. It's on his website. But Freedman's killer knew where to get in touch with him – at Gravity. The killer got a message to Freedman when he was there and asked to meet him that night, Tuesday. Freedman assumed the killer thought he used Gravity because he was on the streets.'

'Glyn Ashmead took the call and passed the message on.'

'He says he was at a conference all day and didn't get back until late. We haven't checked if he really was at that conference. And he can't account for his movements that night but I can't see what connection he has with the Robin Gamblin of the past.' Horton paused, contemplating this and frowning.

'Gamblin might have been responsible for ruining him. Maybe Ashmead was a successful businessman and Gamblin advised him to invest his money in a fraudulent scheme. Ashmead lost everything and was declared bankrupt, and that led to him going on the streets.'

'If that's the case then it has nothing to do with Cary Gamblin's death or the Lysters.' Horton knew nothing of Ashmead's background. 'But that lifeboat station was chosen as the meeting point for a reason and not just for its privacy. It meant something to the killer.'

'Ashmead could have owned a boat or a marine-related business that went tits up because of Gamblin.'

Horton considered this. Then sprang up. 'OK, so let's go and ask him.'

Twenty-Two

Gravity was closed but Horton was convinced that Ashmead was still on the premises, mainly because he'd seen a van bearing the name of a plumber parked in the adjoining road as he and Cantelli had walked to the centre. Horton rapped loudly on the door and eventually saw Ashmead heading towards them.

'I take it this isn't a social call,' Ashmead said, letting them in, his tired eyes flicking between them.

Horton could hear banging in the rear, the plumber at work. 'Why did you end up on the road?' he asked without pre-amble.

Ashmead hesitated. His mouth hardened. Horton saw him draw himself up. Would he refuse to tell them? But after a moment, he began: 'I was working in the City. Long hours, high stress, lots of money but no time for anything other than work. I drank and then started to take cocaine, then I drank more and took more drugs. I lost my job, my flat, my girlfriend, my so-called friends. At first I was too ashamed to return to my family but, desperate, I eventually did. They didn't want anything to do with me, so I drank some more and took more drugs. I stole to pay for them. Thankfully I never got arrested. As I said to you before Andy, it doesn't take much to fall but it takes a huge effort to climb back up, sometimes aided by one small act of kindness and humanity.'

Horton could still see the pain in Ashmead's eyes. He knew it was the truth. Ashmead hadn't killed Freedman but he said, 'Did you know Freedman before he volunteered to work here?'

'No. I told you that earlier.'

'How sure are you that Peter Freedman was who he claimed to be?'

'As sure as I can be. That's who he said he was. I took him on trust.'

'Do you know or have you ever known a man called Robin Gamblin?'

'No.'

But there was something in Ashmead's expression, a slight hesitation, a flicker of doubt.

'What is it? You recognize the name,' Horton asked, also sensing Cantelli's interest.

'No, but . . .'

'Please. It's important, Glyn.'

'I don't like to betray anyone's trust.'

Horton remained silent, as did Cantelli.

After a moment, with a worried frown, Ashmead continued. 'Martha called Peter Robin once.'

'To his face?' Horton said, rapidly thinking.

'No. We were alone. She apologized and said Peter reminded her of someone she'd known called Robin.'

'What do you know of her background?'

Ashmead looked Horton in the eye and said, 'Nothing.'

Horton knew it was a lie but he also knew that Ashmead wouldn't betray a confidence. Firmly, he said, 'We need Martha's address.'

After a moment, Ashmead said, 'I'll give it to you but you won't find her at home. She's waitressing at a wedding this afternoon at Southsea Castle. She picks up casual work whenever she can.'

Ashmead relayed the address to Cantelli who jotted it down, making no comment that it was a street almost adjacent to Milton Common.

As they made to leave, Ashmead halted them. 'Andy, don't be too hard on her. She's a very fragile woman and she's had it tough.'

But they didn't get the chance to be hard or anything else because a harassed catering supervisor with one eye on her watch told them that Martha hadn't shown up. The wedding party would be arriving at any moment and she didn't want two policemen on the premises.

Horton quickly thanked her and with Cantelli hurried back to the car parked on the seafront. He jerked his head at the catering van as they went. 'Recognize the name?'

'Bellman Catering. Their van was outside Evelyn Lyster's apartment when we met Gina there.'

'Yes. And Bellman might also have been the caterers at Rowan Lyster's wedding.'

'Martha Wiley is Margaret Gamblin.' Cantelli started the engine and headed east along the seafront towards Milton.

'Yes, and she recognized her husband. But I

don't think he recognized her, which was why he agreed to meet her dressed as a vagrant. He hoped she'd see he had nothing to offer her.'

'She shot him. But how did she get the gun?'

'We'll ask her.'

'If she's there,' Cantelli said pointedly.

Horton was thinking the same. He rang Ashmead's number, praying he'd answer it. He did. Horton relayed the fact that Martha hadn't shown up for her waitress job and they were on their way to her flat.

'When did you last speak to her, Glyn? Don't try to fob me off and don't try to protect her. She needs help.'

Horton heard him sigh heavily before saying, 'It was two hours ago. I phoned her to see if she was OK.'

'Why wouldn't she be?'

'I've seen enough despair to know when to recognize it.'

'What did she say, Glyn?'

'That it was nearly over. I asked her what she meant but she hung up. She's got a pay-as-you-go mobile.' He relayed the number. Ashmead urged him to go easy.

Horton tried the number. There was no answer. He didn't leave a message.

Within ten minutes Cantelli was pulling up outside the modern block of flats. Horton felt Cantelli's tension beside him as they entered. He knew that, like him, Cantelli was preparing to steel himself to expect the worse. The fact that the flat was about half a mile from where

Clements' body had been found reinforced Horton's belief that Martha Wiley was connected with the murders and that she was in fact Margaret Gamblin. There was no hard evidence to prove that, which was what Uckfield and Bliss would have said if he had told them and he hadn't, but he knew it was her and that, as Ashmead had confirmed, she was a fragile woman in the pits of despair. Horton wanted to go carefully. She'd never spoken of a personal tragedy or her past and yet he'd seen great sorrow in her lined faced and sensed a pain that went so deep that it was almost beyond bearing.

There was no answer to Cantelli's knock. 'I'll ask a neighbour if they've seen her,' he said with a worried expression.

Horton saw him talking to a woman who poked her head out and scrutinized Horton. After a moment, Cantelli beckoned him over. 'This is Kathy Draycott. She wants proof that you're Andy Horton?'

Horton hid his surprise and showed his warrant card.

'Martha went out a couple of hours ago and said if you called I was to give you this.' Kathy Draycott handed over an envelope. Inside it was a key and nothing else.

Horton thanked her and when her door was closed he inserted the key in the lock of Martha Wiley's flat and, with a thudding heart, opened it. They entered a narrow hall and stepped into a sparsely furnished sitting room with a thread-bare carpet where Horton pulled up with a start and Cantelli drew in a sharp breath. Shaking his head sorrowfully, he said gently, 'The poor woman.'

Every conceivable surface was covered with photographs. They were of a baby, a toddler, a young boy: Cary Gamblin.

'It breaks your heart,' Cantelli said softly.

Horton heard the catch in Cantelli's voice and crossed to the window to gather his thoughts and emotions. His heart ached with grief for Martha. He stared across the common in the gathering dusk of the early winter evening, trying to put himself in Martha's shoes. Having killed the people she held responsible for her child's death, what was left for her? He shuddered and fear crept up his spine. Perhaps they were already too late. She'd had two hours to get away, to where, though?

He spoke as though to himself, 'Where would a tormented and bereaved mother go when there was nothing else left for her?'

Cantelli came to stand beside him. Horton knew he was thinking of his own five children in their small house a mile from here across the other side of the common. Horton had the answer to his question anyway. It was easy.

He turned to Cantelli. 'She'd go where any parent would wish to be – with their child.'

'She's killed herself.'

'Perhaps not yet. There might still be time. Call in and get the flat sealed off. I need your car, Barney.'

'Where are you going?' asked Cantelli, handing over the keys.

'To the Eastney lifeboat station where Elkins and Ripley can pick me up in the RIB and take me over to the Bembridge lifeboat station because that's as near as she can get to where Cary died. I just hope Elkins isn't too far away.' Horton was already stabbing a number in his mobile phone as he spoke.

'Shouldn't we alert the Bembridge lifeboat station?' Cantelli asked concerned.

'No. She'll be on the long pier that leads to it and if the crew turn up in a rush or she sees flashing blue lights or police officers she'll jump if she hasn't already done so. She might when she hears me approaching on the police RIB – it's a chance I have to take. But we'll be there and might be able to save her.' Into his phone, he said, 'Dai, where are you?'

'Just heading back along Hayling Bay from Sparkes Marina.'

Good, that wasn't far. It wouldn't take them long to reach the Eastney lifeboat station. He gave instructions for them to get there as quickly as possible and said he'd meet them there. Turning back to Cantelli, he said, 'Brief Uckfield. Tell him where I'm heading but whatever he does tell him to hold back on informing the island police until I can update him or you.'

Cantelli nodded and reached for his phone, saying, 'Good luck, Andy.'

Twenty-Three

Horton made it to the Eastney lifeboat station in eight minutes, which was something of a record. He hurried down to the waiting RIB and told PC Ripley at the helm to head for the Bembridge lifeboat. There was no time for explanations and the high-speed crossing would be too noisy for him to say much, but as he donned his life jacket he shouted, 'Possible suicide.'

Elkins nodded. It took all Ripley's concentration in the growing dark to navigate the Solent, guided by his prior knowledge, his GPS, the powerful light on the RIB and the pinpricks of lights on the shores of the island. The sea was deserted and thankfully relatively calm, although Horton knew from the forecast that this was the lull before the next front rolled in, due in a few hours' time. He sensed it would be sooner: already the wind speed was quickening and there was a heavy feel in the air that heralded rain. The forecasters often got it wrong. Perhaps that was what Dennis Lyster had been banking on the day he had taken Rowan and Cary out with him.

As they approached Bembridge, the sea grew choppier and the moon's appearance became more fleeting as the rapidly scudding clouds began to roll up into one. They were almost there. Horton could see the rounded structure of the lifeboat building on the end of the long pier. It had taken them less than ten minutes. With a tap on Ripley's shoulder and a wave of his hand, he indicated for him to ease down and make for the shore beyond the pier to the south. Eagerly he scanned the pier for a solitary figure and spotted her the same time as Elkins pointed towards her. Not that they could see her features but Horton knew it was Martha. She was close to the building, leaning on the railings. His heart leapt into his throat. His chest tightened. He felt her anguish and despair and, despite the fact she had killed he felt an overwhelming sorrow for her. His thoughts flicked to Emma. If anyone ever harmed her . . . His blood ran cold. His body stiffened. Roughly he pushed his personal feelings aside and tried to replace them with professional ones. It was far from easy.

As Ripley skilfully brought the RIB on to the sand and shingle shore, avoiding the outcrop of rocks some distance to the south, Horton watched the solitary figure on the pier. She must have seen and heard them but she gave no indication of it. Perhaps she was too deep in her memories and sorrow to hear, see and think about anything except her son. Horton understood that.

He leapt out of the RIB and asked Elkins to accompany him. The bulky sergeant fell into step beside him as they headed quickly along the shore. Horton didn't want to risk using a torch and alerting Martha but he had no choice. He requested Elkins to direct its beam downwards. Above them and to their left on the low cliff top, Horton could see the lights of the hotel and caught the sound of music in the wind. But soon they left that behind. No one was in the lifeboat car park or at the entrance to the pier as they climbed up on to it. He told Elkins to wait and call Cantelli. Cantelli would tell Uckfield they'd found Martha and to instruct Newport Police to arrive silently with no blue lights. He switched off his mobile phone, saying with urgency, 'Don't let anyone come on to the pier. Not until I say so.'

Elkins nodded. Horton took a deep breath and struck out along the pier thinking that his problems – his quest to discover what had happened to Jennifer and his loathing of Lord Richard Eames who he blamed for his bitter memories and experiences as a child – were nothing compared to this woman's pain. A pain that had driven her to murder.

He walked briskly and steadily towards the solitary figure. His gut tensed. She had climbed over the railings and was standing precariously poised on the very thin ledge on the seaward side, ready to jump into the swirling sea beneath her, her hands clinging to the railings. But she hadn't jumped. There was time to save her. His heart was hammering against his chest.

'This is where he died,' she said as he drew level. 'Alone, cold and afraid.'

His heart ached for her. Through his mind flashed an image of Emma, the same age as Cary had been when he'd died, struggling in the sea, terrified, fighting with desperation to stay alive, swallowing sea water, going under, her lungs filling up with water. He shuddered violently. Saying he was sorry was pointless. So he said

304

nothing. He just waited. Soon her arms would begin to ache. Could he seize her hands and prevent her from jumping?

After what seemed an age but was probably only a minute, she said, 'I'm not sorry I killed them, Andy, although it was wrong of me to kill Mr Clements. But he was going to tell you I had the gun.'

'Let's talk about this later, Martha. Let me help you climb back over.' He stretched out his hand but she shook her head.

'Don't touch me, Andy or I'll jump right now.'

He held up his hands and stepped back a fraction. 'I can get you help.'

'No, it's too late for that. There's no going back. It's time to be with my boy.'

'Martha, please.'

But with renewed urgency and finality, she said, 'No, Andy, there's nothing left for me. Cary needs me and I need him.' She lifted one hand from the railing. He had to stop her from jumping. He knew that Ripley in the RIB would be poised to rescue her from the sea but it was dark and the sea was blowing up rough. By the time Ripley reached her she could have swallowed enough sea water to drown. It didn't take long.

A drizzling, driving rain began to roll in from the south-west, making visibility poorer. She wiped a hand across her face and put it back on the railing. Horton breathed a silent sigh of temporary relief. Gently, he said, 'Tell me what happened, Martha.' If he could keep her talking . . . if he could reach out and guide her back over . . .

'Dennis said Cary had unclipped himself but he would never have done that; He was a very good sailor. Dennis taught him how to sail. He said that Cary was a natural. I don't think Rowan liked that; it put his nose out of joint. He was a spoiled, selfish child. Cary knew all about safety. He was only ten and yet he heard the forecast that morning and his last words to me were, "I don't think we should go sailing today, Mum".' A sob caught in her throat. 'I should have told him not to go then. To stay home with me. But I didn't. I said nothing.' Her voice hardened.

God knows how many times she must have gone over that, he thought. Endlessly, day after day, tormenting herself, and yet he'd seen her so many times – the smiling, welcoming face behind the counter, heard her gentle voice and witnessed her kindness to those at Gravity in unfortunate situations while all the time inside her gnawed the pain and heavy burden of her loss, the bitterness, guilt and self-loathing.

'Robin told him not to be such a scaredy-cat.'

And Robin's words had sent his child to his death. That had driven Robin to despair and drink and eventually to a life on the streets.

'What did Dennis say?'

'He said they should postpone it but Robin said they couldn't and Evelyn insisted they go. I tried to argue with her and Robin.' Martha turned her earnest expression on him. 'God knows I tried but I didn't try hard enough. I said what would a couple of days' delay make? Evelyn said a lost sale. The gems had to be offloaded that day to an overseas buyer who was waiting on his boat in Bembridge Marina. So they went. Money was far more important than my child's life.'

He'd been correct then except that he hadn't thought the Gamblins had known about the dealing. 'You knew what was going on?' he asked. He had to get her to climb back over to him.

'Yes. We were all in it, except the children, of course. They were cover. People are so greedy. Oh, I include myself in that. I'm also to blame for my boy's death.' She shifted. Horton held his breath. He thought she'd fall. He tensed, poised, ready to go over to save her. The lifebelt was some distance from them, but even if he threw it to her in the water, he knew she wouldn't take it.

He said, 'Dennis was stealing diamonds from his company and Evelyn was finding buyers for them.'

'Yes, and that wasn't all. Robin insured a lot of valuable possessions. He said there was always something dodgy in people's collections, something they didn't declare because it had probably been smuggled into the country or bought from a dubious source, or possibly stolen. He had a lot of wealthy clients and he suggested I start a small cleaning business, cleaning exclusively for certain wealthy people. He'd recommend me. I thought it would be a good chance for me to earn some money of my own. I liked cleaning. I didn't know then what he was planning but soon he asked me to nose around, especially if I was cleaning when the owners were out, which was usually the case. He gave me a list of their insured items and I was to see if there was anything else hidden away, or even on show, that they hadn't put on the insurance.'

Her arms must be aching. Her feet might easily slip on the now wet, small ledge. Horton eased forward a little. Could he grab her from here and hold her until assistance came? He was strong but he knew she would fight like a woman possessed to escape his grip. There was no one behind him but Elkins was waiting at the end of the pier and soon others would join him. If he grabbed her and shouted would they get here in time to help him? But how could he, or anyone else, make her climb back over on to the pier without using force? Then fear flooded through him. What would happen if the lifeboat had a shout? He prayed they wouldn't because she wouldn't hesitate to throw herself in if she heard the boom of the alert and saw the crew hurtling down here. The police officers wouldn't be able to stop the crew if there was an emergency at sea. He had to get her to want to climb back over to him. He'd keep her talking; she'd need to explain.

He said, 'You'd catalogue anything you found and tell Robin.'

'Yes. Robin had met Evelyn at a business function. I didn't know then that they were having an affair, not until after Cary died. Robin introduced me to her and Dennis. Evelyn was very clever and unscrupulous. And she was evil. Oh, not that you'd think that on the surface. She was glamorous and sophisticated but she was also very greedy. She travelled the world, attended trade fairs and meetings, acted as a translator for wealthy and influential business people. She picked up a lot of information about art, cultural objects and jewellery. Robin would tell her about his clients' collections and anything they had that wasn't insured. He asked me to take photographs and he showed her the pictures. Some of Robin's clients had financial problems, others had secrets they'd rather not be made public. Robin came up with a way to help them out of their problems.'

Just as he'd done with Vivian Clements.

'Often I'd hear telephone conversations or read correspondence that gave me information Robin could use to blackmail the owner. When you're a cleaner you become invisible. People talk and argue in front of you. You get the chance to poke around in cupboards and drawers. Robin would then approach the owner and say he'd keep quiet about their affair, their business fraud, their illegal possession of a gun or an antique, whatever they wanted to hide, if he was given something of value. If it was an illegally acquired antique, painting, piece of jewellery or weapon he told them he would sell it. He even offered to give them a small percentage of the sale, which was clever because it appealed to the greed of the owners and made them feel as though they weren't really being blackmailed. If it was a secret the client didn't want exposed then Robin would take something from their collection and sell it in return for his silence. Or if the client was in financial difficulty Robin would arrange a phoney robbery, the client would get the insurance money and Robin and Evelyn would sell the items to people who didn't ask questions about where they had come from.'

'And Dennis was the delivery man.'

'Yes.'

And after Cary's death Robin and Martha had disappeared and Evelyn and Dennis had continued with their illegal gem trading. The Gamblins could have revealed all but both were in too deeply and were too distressed and guilt-ridden over the death of their child. The public would have no sympathy with them when they discovered how they had used their son.

'It was very successful,' Martha continued.

Until Cary had died. And what had happened to the goods Dennis was supposed to have been delivering that day? Had they been thrown overboard or simply kept on the yacht until Evelyn could rearrange their delivery?

The rain was getting heavier. Martha's greying hair was plastered to her sharp, gaunt face. The rain was running off his own.

'I thought we'd be able to afford to send Cary to a private school and give him the education he deserved. He was so clever. After he died Robin blamed himself. He was right to. He took to drinking and eventually he lost everything. He walked out of my life but by that time I hardly noticed he'd gone. I suffered a nervous breakdown and went into hospital. I moved away but I couldn't move away from the pain. I returned to Portsmouth a year ago. I wanted to be closer to my son. I knew then that I would join him here when the time was right.'

'On the anniversary of his death?'

'Yes. That was what I planned. I took whatever casual work I could to pay the rent. I never heard from Robin. I didn't know where he was and he didn't make any effort to contact me. I never saw him until last February, two days before the anniversary of Cary's death, and there he was in the local newspaper. I postponed my plans. I went to Gravity and said I'd like to volunteer on Tuesdays. Robin was there, as I knew he'd be from the article. He didn't even recognize me.' She turned her anguished eyes on Horton and, despite what she had done, he felt an all-consuming pity for her. He was sure he could hear cars approaching. She didn't seem to notice.

'Glyn took me on as a volunteer. He knew things were tough for me. He'd help me out with money when he could. I ate at the centre and I got food from the food bank. I didn't want to sign on to claim benefit. I didn't want people to know I was here. Glyn gave me a reference for Bellman's Catering so that I could do some casual work for them, cash in hand, and I did the occasional cleaning job for people. I didn't tell anyone my real name. Not even Glyn. He didn't know anything about Cary or Robin. I said nothing. I waited for Robin to say something to me but in all the time he worked there he didn't recognize me. There he was picking up his life as though nothing had happened, as though our child hadn't died. He said his life on the streets had been caused by a business failure. It was as though Cary had never existed.'

Horton didn't venture to say that perhaps it had

311

been too painful for Robin to speak of. Martha could never have seen that.

'Then *she* walked in. She knew he was there. She must have seen the same article. It was the end of March but I had seen both her and Dennis before then.'

'At Rowan's wedding, where you were a waitress.'

'Yes. It was a very small wedding – only a few friends of Rowan's and Gina's but not her parents or any relatives. I don't know if she has any and Evelyn hadn't invited any of her family or Dennis's. The wedding breakfast was held in a hotel and they were short-staffed so they asked Bellman's to supply staff. Both Evelyn and Dennis looked right through me. Not surprising as my grief, which they caused, has ravaged me,' she said with bitterness and released a hand to brush her rain-soaked face. Horton eased forward.

'And there was Rowan Lyster all smiles, living his life as though Cary's meant nothing. It should have been Cary's wedding. I should have been celebrating my son's wedding, not dishing up food to his killers.' A sob caught in her throat. She shifted.

Quickly, Horton said, 'So you killed Dennis?'

She threw him a confused look. Her arms must be aching, the rail was wet and becoming slippery. She couldn't hold out much longer.

'No. He killed himself. I heard him and Evelyn rowing. I couldn't hear exactly what they were saying but he said something about Cary's death. I tried to get closer but I was called away to the tables. I was going to ask him about it but I didn't get the chance that day. Then I read about his body being found under Ryde Pier on the Isle of Wight. I thought good, that's one of them gone. He deserved to die.'

'And that's when you began to plan to kill Robin and Evelyn.'

'Yes, but I didn't know how. I thought about it endlessly. It helped me. It gave me focus and purpose. It kept me alive. I knew I only had to wait.'

'Martha, climb back over. Let me help you.'

But she ignored him. 'I shot Robin. It was the last thing he expected and it felt so good. He'd even come to the meeting with me dressed as a tramp hoping I would believe he was still down on his luck and that I'd leave him alone when I saw how low he'd sunk. He thought I wanted to resume our relationship. He thought I would ask him for money. He didn't want me messing up his oh-so-comfortable life. The look on his face when he saw me was priceless but he soon recovered and when I shot him he stared at me, amazed.'

'How did you get the gun?'

'He gave it to me.'

Horton stepped forward. He could reach out and grab her hands and hold on to them with all his strength and call for help.

'I didn't know that he had a gun until that Tuesday. I heard him on Glyn's phone. Glyn was in Southampton at a conference. Robin reminded Mr Clements that he expected payment in the form of what they'd agreed. He had someone who was very keen to get hold of the Robert

Adams gun and ammunition and that he'd take delivery of both that evening on the seafront opposite the beach huts on the corner of St Georges Road at six thirty.'

That fitted with what Constance had told them about her husband being out and his manner when he came home.

'It was the opportunity I'd been waiting for. I slipped out and phoned Gravity from a call box around the corner. I knew if I kept it ringing long enough he'd answer it. No one except me and Robin were authorized to use Glyn's office. He answered the call as Peter Freedman. I said that I'd heard that Robin Gamblin visited the centre. I said that I was desperate to see him. That I needed help, and that perhaps I could also help him. I was his wife. He took the bait. He said he could get a message to Robin. He usually came in on a Tuesday. I said I'd be at the Eastney lifeboat station at seven o'clock, knowing that he'd have to come immediately after getting the gun from Mr Clements. He was so shocked when he saw me and when I told him I knew about Mr Clements' gun. I told him that I hadn't asked him to meet me to blackmail him, or to resume our relationship, but to ask him for the gun to kill myself with. I wanted to end my pain. I asked if he had bullets for it. He said he did. He took out a small tin. There were three bullets inside it. He loaded one into the pistol. I watched him carefully.' Her voice caught.

Gamblin would have seen she meant it because she did.

She said, 'He handed over the gun and I fired it at him. He stared at me, aghast. He couldn't believe I'd shot him. I watched him stagger across the road in the vain attempt to get help. Then he collapsed. I followed him. He tried to get up. He shifted back so that he was slightly under the houseboat. Then he was dead. I straightened him up, went through the pockets of the coat and took his keys, wallet and mobile phone. You'll find them in the flat. I took the small tin containing the other two bullets. I thought I would use one to kill Evelyn but then I heard she was dead.'

'How?'

'I saw you arrive at Grand Parade with Gina Lyster and I wondered what you were doing there. I was waitressing in the club for Bellman. I discovered that Evelyn Lyster had an apartment there. I contacted Winner Watersports and asked to speak to Evelyn and Gina told me she was dead, so I didn't have to kill her. They're all dead now. I'm sorry I killed Mr Clements. I asked him to meet me on the Common where no one would see us. All I wanted to do was give the gun back to him only he kept going on about how he'd tell the police I'd killed Robin, or Peter, as he called him. That I was a thief and a murderer. I couldn't bear to listen to him any longer. I was tired. He was stupid and uncaring. He had no idea what Robin was like and what I'd been through. As I stepped forwards he fell back. I stood over him and shot him. I left the gun there. And now it's time to be with my lovely boy.'

'Martha, please. Cary wouldn't want you to do this.'

315

'Don't bother coming after me, Andy. I'll be fine. Cary's been alone for too long.'

And suddenly she was gone. Horton rushed forward. He bellowed for help and heard the RIB start up. Elkins must have relayed instructions to Ripley. Within an instant Horton had thrown off his jacket and shoes and leapt over the railings. He plunged into the dark, swirling sea. The cold stole the breath from him and his clothes pulled him down. Desperately, with a racing heart and trying to keep afloat, he scoured the black, swollen sea, searching for her as he heard the RIB growing closer. Its powerful beam lit up the surface of the water and picked him out. Then he caught sight of her. She was within three feet of him. He swam out, hampered by his heavy, sodden clothing and the rough sea. Within seconds he'd reached her and grasped her as the RIB drew closer. She spluttered and struggled against him. It took all his strength to hold on to her. The RIB was speeding towards them. It would be here in seconds. Then the rolling, giant wave hit them. It caught him off balance. Desperately, he held on to her as they went under. Then she was fighting him no longer. Her body went limp. She wasn't dead, he told himself, she was unconscious, but as Ripley drew alongside he knew that Martha had got her wish. She'd gone to join her boy.

Twenty-Four

Sunday

It was the early hours of the morning when Horton finally reached his yacht. He'd watched Martha's body being taken to the mortuary and then he'd been given dry, clean clothes at Newport police station before rejoining Elkins and Ripley and being taken back to Portsmouth on the RIB where Uckfield, Dennings, Bliss, Trueman and Cantelli were waiting in the incident suite.

Dennings confirmed that they had found evidence of blood spatter on Martha's coat in her flat and Robin Gamblin's wallet, keys and phone. Horton relayed what she'd said, although he'd already updated Uckfield earlier on the phone. Cantelli shook his head sadly. Horton knew he understood Martha's motivations. Cantelli had confirmed that Martha had suffered a nervous breakdown and had attempted suicide on two occasions following the death of her child. She'd spent years in and out of psychiatric hospitals in Portsmouth, Southampton and Basingstoke. She'd moved around, or been moved, restless and disturbed, and had gradually slipped through the system. It was easy now when there were so many demands and so many cutbacks. The vulnerable had become even more vulnerable.

'Do you believe she didn't kill Dennis and Evelyn Lyster?' Uckfield had asked.

Horton had said he did, and he was still certain of that now as he climbed on board his yacht. Suicide for Dennis Lyster was possible but not natural causes for Evelyn. Someone had put that beta blocker in Evelyn's flask and that someone could still possibly have been Robin Gamblin, aka Peter Freedman, the motive being that he intended to clean out Evelyn's Guernsey account which the States of Guernsey police still hadn't located. Evelyn Lyster had been clever and cunning and it would take time and resources to unravel the extent of her criminal activity, a task that neither he nor Uckfield would be involved in. It would be handed over to the fraud team who would liaise with Europol and Interpol, much to the relief of ACC Dean, who favoured Freedman or rather Gamblin as her killer because it tied up the case at their end and meant no further strain on their budget.

Horton removed the borrowed jacket and lay down on his bunk. He didn't expect to sleep. Every muscle in his body ached but it was the mental anguish that was the most painful to bear. The memory of Martha's smiling face in the Gravity café, her tormented expression on the pier, her despair and sorrow, the feel of her thin, struggling body in his arms and then her limp one as he failed to save her. She was at peace, he told himself as his eyes swivelled to the photograph of Emma pinned up beside him. Martha had died to be with her child. Would he do the same? Would he kill for Emma? He didn't even need to ask that question.

What would Rowan Lyster make of the real life of his parents? Had he known what they were doing? But how could a child of ten have known? Horton's mind turned to Jennifer. He'd been ten when she had left him. He'd known nothing of her involvement with the intelligence services. He still knew very little about her but slowly he was pulling together the pieces.

He must have fallen asleep because the next thing he knew it was seven o'clock and only just getting light. His body ached, his mouth felt like sawdust and his head was heavy and throbbing. He showered, changed and made himself a cooked breakfast, hoping it would pep up his sluggish brain and body. A strong injection of caffeine also helped. His mind cleared a little and his thoughts returned to what Martha had said about how Cary was cautious and a good sailor and that he would never have unclipped himself. Was that just a mother defending her son? Possibly but if it wasn't and Cary hadn't unclipped himself then that explained quite a lot, especially if he put it with what Cantelli had discovered from Norman Fyning, the head teacher of St Levan's.

He hesitated before ringing Cantelli because it was Sunday and he was reluctant to take him away from his family – he'd already been deprived of them yesterday – but he knew that Cantelli would want to see this through. He gave Barney the chance of opting out, which he didn't

319

take, and said he'd meet him at the Lyster's house but also asked him to call Norman Fyning at St Levan's and find out if Rowan had been at school with a girl called Gina. He wished they had her maiden name. Cantelli could get it from the General Register Office but they didn't have time.

Horton had another coffee then picked up his jacket, helmet and keys and locked up. Cantelli was waiting for him in his car, which was parked some houses down the road from the Lysters. He looked tired. Horton knew that it wasn't so much the lack of sleep but emotional fatigue over Martha's death.

'Norman Fyning says there was a girl at school with Rowan called Georgina Paignton. She was very athletic like Rowan and good at water sports. A quiet girl, never boastful, just did as she was told – certainly when she first came to them. She was not academically bright, rather plain, and the only thing she seemed to like was swimming and being in or on the water. Her parents, like Rowan's, were distant ones. She was their only child and he said a mistake and a disappointment to them. Also an encumbrance. Not that they expressed that but it was why she was sent to the school. They were top-class international lawyers. Tax exiles now, having made a fortune, which might explain why they didn't attend their daughter's wedding, if it is Gina. Fyning remembered she worshipped the ground Rowan walked on but Rowan never noticed her.'

'Looks as though he finally did and Gina got her man.'

The Lysters weren't at home but Horton knew where they'd find them – at Winner Watersports. He gave Cantelli directions, told him to request a patrol car and some officers and headed to the car park close to Fort Cumberland where he parked the Harley. A few minutes later Cantelli pulled up. There was only a small sports car in the car park. Gina Lyster's. It was still early and bitingly cold. There wouldn't be any windsurfing customers for the Lysters today. As they headed towards the hut that bore the company name Horton saw Rowan was there with Gina. Gina spotted them first. Her expression changed from surprise to wariness, while Rowan's became more sullen and antagonistic.

'Can't you leave us in peace?' he exclaimed grouchily.

Horton answered. 'We thought you'd like to know who killed Peter Freedman.'

'I can't see—'

'Or rather, I should say Robin Gamblin.' Horton watched Rowan carefully to see if the name got a reaction. It did but not much of one. His eyes narrowed slightly before he turned away, busying himself with some rope in a kayak.

Horton continued, 'Peter Freedman was really Robin Gamblin, the father of your friend, Cary, who drowned.' Rowan didn't look up. His hands were steady. 'Robin Gamblin was killed by his wife, Cary's mother, Margaret Gamblin.'

It was Gina who spoke. 'Why did she do that?'

'Because she never forgave her husband for letting their son go out on a yacht when a storm was forecast. And the reason why Dennis Lyster

321

– your father, Rowan – had to go was because your mother insisted.'

Rowan looked up. 'I was ten years old. Cary unclipped himself. He was stupid.'

'Was he? That's not what I heard.'

'Then you heard wrong.'

'Rowan,' Gina cautioned and flashed them an anxious look.

Rowan threw his wife a hostile stare but she didn't flinch under it as Constance Clements would have done. Horton could see both by her glance now and what he'd witnessed previously when they'd interviewed them together that Norman Fyning was right – she worshipped her husband but, unlike Constance, Gina was mentally strong. She'd got what she wanted and she was determined to hang on to it.

Horton continued to address Rowan. 'Your mother and father, along with Robin and Margaret Gamblin, were engaged in criminal activity. Your father was stealing diamonds from his employers and your mother was selling them. In addition, your parents and the Gamblins were involved in insurance fraud, theft and blackmail. Your father was delivering something to a buyer on the day Cary died.'

'Was he?' Rowan said dismissively while continuing to handle the thin rope.

'What evidence do you have?' Gina asked sharply.

'A confession from Margaret Gamblin before she drowned herself.' If he was hoping to shock them or shame Rowan he didn't succeed.

'I've no idea what you're talking about. I was a child.'

'You were and you couldn't have known about the theft and fraud, not then. But you overheard your parents rowing at your wedding.' Horton swivelled his gaze to Gina. 'What was the row about, Gina?'

'I've no idea. I don't know what you're talking about.'

Oh, but she did. He could see it in her eyes. Whether they'd get her to say though was a different matter.

Horton turned back to Rowan. 'Cary's death destroyed Margaret's life. She ended up suffering a nervous breakdown and severe depression. His father went on a downward spiral until he ended up on the streets and then in prison before starting a new life. Dennis couldn't bear to be in the same room, the same house, the same town as you, Rowan. Now why was that? And your mother rarely saw you, usually about once a year. Oh, yes, she was busy working, travelling, accumulating her wealth, making sure that Dennis continued to do as she bid but they both knew what you'd done. And they sent you away so that you couldn't tell anyone or let it slip. They hoped that water sports, the other activities and the ethos of the school, which specialized in dealing with children not suited to mainstream education for a variety of reasons, would keep you occupied, and it did.'

Horton persisted, 'Cary was a bright boy and a very talented and careful sailor. Maybe he unclipped himself as a dare. Is that what happened, Rowan? Did you cajole and challenge him to do it? Did you call him a coward? Did you provoke him into unclipping himself?'

'Of course not.'

'Rowan,' Gina urged.

'You didn't like Cary, did you, Rowan?' Horton interjected, seeing Martha's pain-ridden haunted eyes flash before him. 'But your parents insisted you play with him and insisted that he go out sailing with you. You hated the fact that he was cleverer than you but it was the fact that he was a better sailor which really goaded you, especially when you heard your father praising him and encouraging him. You were jealous. You didn't like anyone being better than you. Not then or at school where, I suspect, if we questioned the staff and previous pupils, we'd find other accidents. A boy getting injured or sick. Someone accidentally slipping or his rope fraying. You're fiercely competitive. So you unclipped Cary and pushed him overboard. And your father saw it.'

Gina quickly interjected. 'You've got no right—'

Horton turned his angry eyes on Gina. 'I have every right. A child died and his mother and father are also dead. What did you hear, Rowan, on your wedding day? What was the argument between your mother and father? Was it your father telling your mother that now he'd been sacked from his job he was no longer obliged to do what she wanted? Had six months of being unemployed developed in him a conscience or had he discovered that Evelyn had resumed her relationship with Robin Gamblin? That really stuck in your father's claw and he was going to tell Robin and the police what really happened. Is that why you killed your father, Rowan?'

'I got sick of hearing how brilliant Cary was.'

'Rowan, don't say anything.'

But he simply looked through his wife. 'Cary wheedled his way into Dad's affections. Dad was always going on about how good Cary was and what a delight he was to have along.'

'He liked Cary more than you,' said Horton.

'I didn't know he was going to drown.' Rowan didn't sound at all sorry. He said it as a matter of fact.

'And your parents knew, even before that, that you'd destroy anything that would stop you from doing what you wanted. When you overheard your parents at your wedding, you couldn't have your father ruining your career and your future, so you got your father on his own, probably here, on the beach, where you beat him over the head, probably with a paddle, and then you put his body in the safety dinghy and motored out into the Solent, where you tipped him over the edge and into the sea, to let his body wash up under the Ryde Pier.'

'I don't know what you're talking about,' Rowan said almost dismissively.

'I think you do.' Horton swivelled his gaze on Gina. 'And so do you. Maybe you even helped your husband. Knowing that Evelyn was worth a fair bit of money and resentful when she wouldn't give you more to buy equipment for the business, you put a beta blocker in her flask the Saturday you were in her apartment for dinner, knowing that she made her drinks up for the week on a

Saturday.' Horton remembered seeing the rows of flasks lined up in the cupboard in both the Portsmouth and the Isle of Wight apartments and recalled what Gina had previously told them about Evelyn's fear of being without a drink. 'You probably even offered to make her a couple of flasks of coffee. You didn't care which flask it was or when she drank it. It just so happened to be on Monday when she was on her way to Guernsey.'

'You've got no evidence. My parents are lawyers. I'll call them.'

And Horton wondered if they'd come running. He thought that perhaps not. But she was right. They couldn't prove it. They'd need a confession and Horton didn't think Gina was going to give them one. Rowan would be different, though. He would eventually tell. He was much weaker than his wife.

Cantelli summoned up the uniformed officers who were waiting in the car park. They were there within seconds. Two officers took Rowan and the third officer Gina, who studied them evenly and confidently before turning. Cantelli would drive her back to the station, but as Horton's phone rang he stilled Cantelli with a gesture and answered it, saying, 'It's Guilbert.' He listened for a moment then thanked him.

To Cantelli, he said, 'They've found Evelyn Lyster's Guernsey account under the name of Brookes. It's with Manley's Bank. There's also a safe deposit box and a property registered in her name, which must have been where she was heading, and where her belongings are, including possibly a laptop computer.' Horton didn't know how often she had travelled to Guernsey but it was fairly frequently, he thought, and always as a foot passenger and paying by cash, and possibly not always from Portsmouth. He suspected that sometimes she caught the train to Poole in the west and the ferry that sailed from there. The contents of the safe deposit box and the bank account might give them information on other properties she'd bought and sold and still owned as she cleaned her dirty money.

'I'll wait for SOCO to arrive. You'd better brief Bliss and Uckfield.'

Horton didn't think they'd be able to pick up any traces of flesh and blood from the paddle or from the RIB. The sea and rain would have washed away much of it and Gina and Rowan the rest, and it had been months since Dennis had died, but it was amazing how sometimes just a small speck survived.

He gazed out to sea, watching a motor launch head across the Solent towards the Bembridge lifeboat station, and thought of Martha's body, limp in his arms. If a spoilt and jealous child hadn't pushed a boy into the sea eighteen years ago six people would still be alive. But could he really lay all the deaths at Rowan's door? If the Lysters and the Gamblins hadn't been so greedy and engaged in criminal activity then all of them might still be alive. So much pain caused and there would be more to come, more lives ruined. But Horton knew the futility of going down the road of 'if onlys'. He'd played that game too many times in other investigations and in his own life. And now he thought of the latter.

He heard cars approaching but didn't turn to look; instead he stared along the coast of the Isle of Wight to where he could see the trees that bordered the shore by Lord Richard Eames' property, but it was the man Horton had met on Eames' private beach in October who came to mind. The beachcomber who had called himself Lomas. *His Lordship likes his privacy*, he'd said but claimed not to know him. Maybe that was the truth, maybe not. Because Horton was beginning to believe that Lomas was in fact one of two men, Zachary Benham, who had either never been in that psychiatric hospital or who had been but had escaped the fire, possibly after starting it, or Gordon Eames, who had died in Australia in 1973 and whose body was supposedly in the family vault in the small private chapel on his brother's Wiltshire estate.

His search to prove whichever one it was could wait because, as he heard footsteps crunching over the shingle beach, it was to Martha that his thoughts returned and to the little boy who had drowned. The vision of Emma swam before him. Nothing was going to bring back Jennifer and nothing would bring back Martha and Cary Gamblin. Emma was the present and very much alive. Emma was his daughter.

He gave instructions to the uniformed officers to seal off the area, and to Phil Taylor to examine the scene for traces of blood and flesh, then hurried to his Harley. Uckfield could wait too. Cantelli was there. He'd oversee things for him, and if Uckfield and Bliss didn't like it then tough.

He climbed on his Harley and headed north

out of Portsmouth to what had once been his marital home, hoping to find his daughter there. And if she wasn't then he would wait until she came, he didn't care for how long. All he knew was that he had to see Emma. He had to hold her in his arms. He had to tell her how much he loved her. And nothing or no one, especially not Catherine, was going to stop him.